I found myself i[...] [...]aller than people, an[...] and cloud-haunted sk[...] [...]en I thought: what can happen to me? I'm already dead. I went to sit on a tombstone, but it sucked me in; I became it.

"What is this?" I whispered.

"This is a dream," whispered the other tombstone. "Here we can talk, if we're kinda quiet about it. Now that you've chosen a form, you gotta stay in it till the dream ends, and do the dreamer's bidding. But when she looks away, we can talk."

A white wisp appeared above us: Mother. She flurried, confused, and then went to sit on a nearby tombstone, which swallowed her.

Howard, the ghost of the man who had built our house, taught us a lot in that first dream while baby Beth wandered weeping between gravestones, trapped in her own terrors.

He taught us more by vanishing for good in a later dream.

Somehow ghosts walk in dreams. Somehow they can move through dreams into something beyond, and leave the houses they haunt.

Mother and I entered every dream we could.

From "Night Stuff" by Nina Kiriki Hoffman

More Imagination-Expanding Anthologies
Brought to You by DAW:

BATTLE MAGIC *Edited by Martin H. Greenberg and Larry Segriff.* From kingdoms saved by the power of a spell, to magicked weapons that can steal the souls of countless enemies, to lands and peoples destroyed by workers of dark enchantment, here are adventures to capture your imagination and hold you spellbound till the final victory has been gained. Let such masterful conjurers of the fantastic as John DeChancie, Josepha Sherman, Rosemary Edghill, Jane Lindskold, Mickey Zucker Reichert, and Julie Czerneda carry you off to the distant battlegrounds where heroes face their greatest challenge.

MERLIN *Edited by Martin H. Greenberg.* Let Diana L. Paxson, Charles de Lint, Jane Yolen, Andre Norton, Lisanne Norman, Jean Rabe, Michelle West, and their fellow bards spin such tales for you as: a story that reveals the truth behind the fall of Camelot and Merlin's disappearance . . . a tradition transformed as the old Merlin passes on his knowledge to a new and far different Merlin . . . a wizardly confrontation with a foe defended by a power Merlin has never faced before.

CAMELOT FANTASTIC *Edited by Lawrence Schimel and Martin H. Greenberg.* Arthur and his Knights of the Round Table live again in these original and imaginative tales set in that place of true enchantment—Camelot! Let such heirs to the bard Taliesin as Brian Stableford, Mike Ashley, Nancy Springer, Rosemary Edghill, Gregory Maguire, Ian McDowell, and Fiona Patton carry you away to this magical realm. You'll find yourself spellbound by stories ranging from the tale of a young man caught up in the power struggle between Merlin and Morgan le Fay, to that of the knight appointed to defend Lancelot when he's accused of committing adultery with the queen.

PERCHANCE TO DREAM

Edited by Denise Little

DAW BOOKS, INC.
DONALD A. WOLLHEIM, FOUNDER
375 Hudson Street, New York, NY 10014
ELIZABETH R. WOLLHEIM
SHEILA F. GILBERT
PUBLISHERS
www.dawbooks.com

Copyright © 2000 by Denise Little and Tekno Books

All Rights Reserved

Cover art by Kinuko Craft

DAW Book Collectors No. 1149

All characters in this book are fictitious.
Any resemblance to persons living or dead is coincidental.

If you purchase this book without a cover you should be aware
that this book may have been stolen property and reported as
"unsold and destroyed" to the publisher. In such case neither
the author nor the publisher has received any payment for
this "stripped book."

First Printing, April 2000
1 2 3 4 5 6 7 8 9 10

DAW TRADEMARK REGISTERED
U.S. PAT. OFF. AND FOREIGN COUNTRIES
—MARCA REGISTRADA
HECHO EN U.S.A.

PRINTED IN THE U.S.A.

ACKNOWLEDGMENTS

Introduction © 2000 by Denise Little
1-900-NODREAM © 2000 by Diane Duane
Night Stuff © 2000 by Nina Kiriki Hoffman
Dream A Little Dream for Me © 2000 by Peter Crowther
The Piper © 2000 by Jody Lynn Nye
Rounded by a Sleep © 2000 by David Bischoff
Needle and Dream © 2000 by Andre Norton
Holy, Holy, Holy © 2000 by Jane Yolen and
     Heidi E.Y. Stemple
On the Edge of Sleep © 2000 by Jane Lindskold
Dreamfisher © 2000 by Nancy Springer
The Dreams that Stuff is Made Of © 2000 by
     Josepha Sherman
Consolation Prize © 2000 by Gary A. Braunbeck
A Butterfly Dreaming © 2000 by Susan Sizemore
Marty Plotz's Rules for Success © 2000 by
     Bruce Holland Rogers
Shelter © 2000 by Michelle West

CONTENTS

INTRODUCTION
by Denise Little

In a perfect world, would people dream? It's something that I've always wondered about. In our own all-too-imperfect world, the question never arises. Dreams are central to our existence, transcending all boundaries of culture, gender, time, and age. Everybody dreams, from the lowliest drudge to the most powerful head of state. While I'm not sure I want to know what Bill Clinton dreams about, I think it's clear from his actions that he's a world-class dreamer. My one-year-old niece has happy dreams about ice cream—we know this because she smiles and talks in her sleep. Dreams even transcend the boundaries of human experience. I'm not sure what my cats and dogs dream about, but all that twitching and sniffing in their sleep is clearly dream-induced.

Dreamers are rampant in the world of fiction. Think of King Arthur dreaming his days away until Britain's darkest hour of need, of Don Quixote tilting at windmills, of confused lovers wandering through the summer woods at the mercy of Titania and Oberon. Dreams have also been a recurring theme in fantastic fiction. Think of Stephen R. Donaldson's tales of The Land, of Frank Herbert's hero in *Dune*, of Ray Bradbury's *The Illustrated Man* and Phillip K. Dick's *Do Androids Dream of Electric Sheep?* The border between dreaming and waking is thinner, and the consequences of dreaming are generally more alarming in fantastic fiction than in literary fiction, but the jumping-off point is the same. From Shakespeare to Chalker, from Homer to Heinlein, dreams play a part in the stories we write. Clearly, we hold our dreams close. They matter to us. Whether we find prophecy or escape in them, whether they amuse us or frighten us silly, they impact our waking world.

This book is an exploration of power of dreams. In fourteen stories that run the gamut of the genre, some of today's finest writers look at where dreams come from, what they can do to us, and how they can leave us changed forever. So, dreamers everywhere, sit back and enjoy! This one is for you.

1-900-NODREAM
by Diane Duane

Diane Duane is the author of the popular young adult series that began with *So You Want to Be A Wizard*, and has since included three more volumes, the most recent being *A Wizard Abroad*. She has also written several *New York Times* bestselling *Star Trek* novels and television scripts for shows such as *Star Trek: The Next Generation* and the animated series *Batman*, *Transformers*, and *Scooby-Doo*. She lives with her husband, fellow author Peter Morwood, in a beautiful valley in rural Ireland.

"**D**ing dong dell," was the last thing he heard before he woke up. "Pussy's in the well—"

Jim started awake, the sweat running off him in trickles, as always, and stared around at the bedroom: then closed his eyes again, sighed, and rubbed his face. He ached all over. He was still able to feel the weight of the rubble that had been piled over him, and the thud of every chunk of it on his body as it came down—for though her body had mercifully been dead by then, her soul had not yet come to believe that the affiliation of twenty-six years had been severed, and had experienced everything that happened to her slowly cooling corpse as if it *hadn't* been. First the horrible and protracted rape. Then being dragged wrapped in the bloodstained blanket to the old unused well at the back of the farm, her head bumping loosely on the uneven waste ground all covered with boulders and weeds. Then the drop to the bottom of the well, long bones splintering and shattering as she came plunging down onto the rubble already there. After that, the rain of boulders and broken concrete blocks, one after another, thudding down onto the increasingly wet and pulpy mass that had been Shayna's body. And always over it all the inane, amused voice of the killer, singing the old poem as he mixed the concrete to pour over the remains of the woman he had killed.

And since Shayna had felt it all, naturally Jim did, too. He would ache for days. Even after the pain faded, he would still hear that high thin wailing in all his unguarded moments, every time he sat back and relaxed. *I was murdered. I can't rest. Do something! Tell them! I want to be properly buried! I want to rest!*

He would hear it now if he didn't get up and get busy.

Jim got up and rooted around in the little bedroom's closet for his bathrobe, then made his way to the shower. It was a small apartment, but he couldn't afford anything bigger. He could only afford to work part time up at the computer store, which suited the company that owned it, and it was just as well it did. For the sake of his own sanity, he had to spend about half his waking hours on the business of finding out where the bodies were of the people whose souls came to him by night. Some he never found, no matter how he looked; all he could do in those cases was wait until the wailing died away . . . which routinely took months.

He got out of the shower, dried himself off perfunctorily, and sat his long thin frame down at the computer. Fortunately he had a flat-rate agreement with his Internet provider, but he still spent too much on phone bills . . . and he couldn't help that either. Unfortunately the dead were not usually terribly complete in the information they gave him. He might feel every crash of a boulder down onto his smashed skull, in one of the dreams, or every exploding impact of a bullet in his guts, but mostly the dead would say to him, "I've been shot!" and only very rarely, "I've been shot in Gascon, North Dakota!" Before he could get in touch with anyone who could locate and bury these people, he had to *find* them . . . which meant endless trolling of news services and the web pages and newsgroups which catered to people searching for others who had disappeared. Some of the murdered, though, had no one looking for them, and so Jim had no help at all in their cases; and through every night, the thin miserable wailing would continue in his dreams, and the murders would be relived, again and again. . . .

He spent an hour and a half looking through the Internet and the Web for anything that would seem to have any bearing on Shayna's murder. Finally it got to be eight thirty, the time he would have to leave for work . . . and he got offline long enough to get up and call in sick. "Jim," his supervisor said, "you know what Rory's going to say."

He'd say you've had too much sick time as it is this year, and if you do it once more . . . But Jim couldn't help it. Rory did not have to hear the wailing in the middle of the night. "I know," Jim said. "Look, I'm sorry." He hung up, turned off the ringer on the phone, and went back to the Web.

Four hours later he had still found nothing that threw any light on where Shayna's body might have been hidden. Jim was desperately tired, but he didn't want to go to sleep. He knew what he would hear if he did. And who knows, it might be too soon for anyone to have missed her. . . . Assuming there *was* anyone else to miss her. Those were the worst cases: the lonely ones, without family or friends, who had no one to wail to but Jim. They took the longest to go away. . . .

He had little appetite, but around twelve Jim got up and made himself a box of macaroni and cheese for lunch anyway, and ate it sitting on the couch in front of the TV. Eating, somehow, blocked the voices. Jim had already noticed that he was starting to put on weight. He didn't like it, but there was nothing he could do. He surfed idly through the channels between bites, with little result. This time of day, about the most intelligent thing on was Cartoon Network. All the other channels, local or cable, seemed to be full of either news (which he watched eagerly, but with no useful results today) or confessional talk shows featuring people looking for an excuse to beat each other up.

He sighed and groped for the remote again, ready to watch the Weather Channel if he had to. At least no one there seemed about to start a fight. Then he paused, for after a Federal Express commercial the screen went black and filled with a series of hazy-focus images blurring into and out of one another: women in drifting white, green fields starred with bright flowers, trees blowing in the wind against an implausibly blue sky.

"Do your dreams rule your life?" the announcer said. "Do they fill you with foreboding, or excitement? Want to know what they *really* mean? Or do you simply want to control the content of your dreams, have them take you where *you* want to go?" The soft-focus images continued, but a toll-free number now emblazoned itself across the screen: 1-900-DREAM4U. "Take command of your inner life! Learn what the future holds for you! Or set yourself a new direction and make your way toward greater fulfillment and self-actualization! Call 1-900-DREAM4U!"

Jim blinked. He couldn't recall ever having seen an ad like that one before, though God knew he had seen enough for fortunetellers, "reputable psychics" (though why would anyone call a *dis*reputable psychic?), Tarot readers, and every other kind of New Age and old-age scam. *Well, it had to happen eventually. Nine-hundred-number dream analysis . . .*

The TV was now showing the beginning of an infomercial starring an annoying man in a sweater who was apparently preparing to set the hood of a car on fire. Jim poked the remote, and the channel changed; shortly he was watching Daffy Duck, in a bellhop's hat, carrying suitcases down some hotel hallway. But he could not concentrate on the cartoon, even with the fear of hearing "Ding dong dell . . ." again in the back of his mind.

That commercial . . .

No. Jim rejected the idea. He had tried often enough to stop this, in the past, and had failed every time. Psychiatry had been as frustrating and useless as the quacks and crystal-mongers and psychics had been. It was no use trying to get rid of the dreams. He had to live with them.

Jim finished his macaroni and cheese, sighed heavily, and got up to go back to the computer. Behind him the TV talked and laughed and played music for hours and hours as he websurfed, sifting through one search engine after another, without result. He did not hear the commercial on the TV again.

But he heard it in his head. And it was nearly midnight when he stopped work, finally, and stared at the TV.

No, he thought. *Useless.*

But Jim still caught himself trying to remember which channel he had seen the commercial on. *CNN?* He got up from the chair in front of the computer and went to sit down on the couch again. *But why bother? I remember the number. 1-900DREAM4U....*

Jim reached over beside the sofa and picking up the phone, dialed. And waited while it rang, and cursed himself for being too weak to handle the difficulty life had sent him, too stupid to know that nothing was going to make any difference—

"Thank you for calling 1-900-DREAM4U," said one of those too-hearty voices that populate value-added phone services. "If you have a question about a dream, please dial 1 now. If you have a chronic or routine problem which you dream about repeatedly and for which you are seeking help, please dial 2 now. If you have—"

He punched 2 and waited, still cursing himself inwardly, but feeling oddly curious. He had not yet been asked for a credit card number, which surprised him somewhat. *God knows what they're charging per minute for this, then....*

"Thank you," said the too-hearty voicemail voice over. "Please wait for one of our expert advisers to come on the line. You are not being charged for this waiting period. Charges begin at one dollar fifty cents per minute when our adviser begins to speak to you. For quality control purposes, your call may be monitored or recorded. California, Massachusetts, New York, and New Jersey residents will be charged six percent sales tax. Iowa and Illinois residents are advised as required by law that this service is for entertainment purposes only and Dream 4 U will not be responsible for any consequences which ensue from either acting on or failing to act on statements made by our advisors. Louisiana—"

He never found out what a Louisianan was intended to make of all this, since there was a click on the other end of the line and a new voice said, "Dream 4 U, this is Bernice. How can I help you?"

Jim swallowed, feeling stupider than ever, and said, "I have very bad dreams, and I want them to stop."

There was a pause. "I am required to inform you that this is not a psychiatric or counseling service and that we do not warrant to make any improvement in your condition or accept responsibility for any deterioration in it."

"Yeah, sure," Jim said, reflecting that his psychiatrist hadn't claimed that she would do so, either.

"Very well. What are your dreams about, please?"

He told her, and heard nothing at the other end but an occasional faint scratching noise, as of a pencil on a pad, and another occasional explosive sound as Bernice popped her chewing gum approximately once every three minutes. Finally Jim ran out of steam, and sat there silent, feeling more foolish than ever.

"Caller ID shows this as your number. Is this correct?" Bernice said, and read out his number aloud.

"Uh, yeah," Jim said.

"An adviser with a specialty in your area will call you shortly," Bernice said. "Thank you for calling Dream 4 U." *Click.*

Jim sighed and put down the phone. *The brushoff*, he

thought. They had him tagged already as some kind of looney. He very much doubted that he would—

The phone shrilled.

Jim jumped with the suddenness of it, and snatched the receiver up. "Hello?"

"My name is Cumaya," said a soft whispery little voice with an accent Jim couldn't quite place, "Mrs. Cumaya, from Dream 4 U. You just called one of my screening people and told her a very interesting story, Mr. . . . "

"Sthenopolos," Jim said. "James Sthenopolos." *How did she find out about this so fast? Was she monitoring the call, or—*

"Very interesting," Mrs. Cumaya said. "I think you were giving Bernice the short version. Would you give me the long one?"

He did. It took him nearly an hour, and though the back of his mind was shrieking about the cost of the phone bill, the front of it was busy being astonished at the fact that someone seemed genuinely interested in his story without seeming even slightly surprised by it. *Who is this woman, what does she do. . . . ?* he thought, as Mrs. Cumaya asked him questions about himself and prompted him for details about the dreams. Her manner was little like that of a counselor, all "ifs" and uncertainties and disclaimers, more like that of a plumber or repairman asking where the leak was or how long the TV had been making that particular kind of "snow."

Finally Mrs. Cumaya stopped him. "All right," she said, and paused. "Mr. Sthenopolos, would you be willing to come and see me? I think your problem can be solved."

He swallowed. *"What?"*

"It will naturally be partly up to you," said the little soft voice at the other end of the line. "But you seem like a good candidate for the kind of intervention I specialize in."

Oh, God, what have I gotten myself into! "What is this going to cost?" he said.

"To start with," Mrs. Cumaya said, "airfare to Los Angeles, since I don't do this kind of work at a distance. Outside of that—if it works, you pay me what you think the work was worth. Yes, the contract you sign when you get here'll say that. Don't worry about it, this isn't a scam." She laughed, a little rusty sound like a starling sitting on a phone line. "When can you come?"

Jim gulped. "Uh, tomorrow? But I'll have to check the flight schedules."

"Any time in the afternoon's fine," Mrs. Cumaya said. "My schedule's clear. Here's the address." She read it off. "Anything else?"

Jim was trembling. He would go, though he was already deriding himself as a dupe. He was also going to have to explain another day's absence from work. And then he remembered, and his mouth fell open. "Wait a minute!" Jim said. *"How did you get my phone to ring?"*

"Dialed it," said the creaky little voice on the other end. "See you tomorrow." And Mrs. Cumaya chuckled, and hung up.

The next afternoon Jim got out of the rental car into the breathless, baking air in front of a nondescript apartment building on a long straight street in the San Fernando Valley, a beige building standing back from a beige sidewalk and an unwatered lawn that, this time of the summer, was understandably beige. Jim made his way through the front door into the courtyard at the center of the building, and up a flight of stairs to number 23.

A little nameplate above a doorbell button in the middle of the door said S CUMAYA. Jim pushed the button, producing a tinny-sounding ding-dong. A moment later the door swung open. Jim looked in, and then down.

She was about four foot eight: tiny, thin-boned, and frail-looking, dressed in a white short-sleeved blouse, blue sweat pants, and white sneakers. Her hair stood out like a slightly frizzy halo around her head, very fine and very white. Big pale green eyes looked at him sharply, like the eyes of some small, acute bird. She was old, her interested-looking face completely covered in fine wrinkles. "Mrs. Cumaya?"

"Yes. And you're Jim Sthenopolos. Come on in. Want some iced tea?"

"Uh, thank you, yes."

She led him briskly down a hallway, past a couple of open doors into which he glanced. One of them was full of phone equipment and what at first glance Jim mistook for VCRs, then realized were tape cassette players, about twenty of them. "That's the mechanized part of the 900 operation," she said, as she led him down into the kitchen of the apartment, "the parts of it that don't need a live adviser. You'd be surprised how alike most people's dreams are to one another. Forgive me for not taking you into the living room, but it catches the sun full on this time of day. Turns into an oven. . . . "

It was a surprisingly big kitchen, bright and shiny in the stainless-steel style, with an uninspired view down into the apartment building's parking lot. Mrs. Cumaya pulled out a chair for him at an incongruous scrubbed-oak table on which lay legal pads, pens, a couple of tea mugs. Jim sat down and watched her in bemusement as she got glasses, rooted around in her freezer for ice cubes, and produced a pitcher of iced tea.

"Now then," she said, putting a filled glass down in front of him, and taking a drink of her own. "You have a hotel room around here somewhere?"

"The Holiday Inn in Woodland Hills."

"That's all right," Mrs. Cumaya said. "Within fifty miles is close enough to get the job done. I won't have to sit at your bedside tonight, if you were wondering."

Jim drank, mostly to hide how his hands were beginning to shake again. "Tonight? Do you really think you can—"

"It depends," Mrs. Cumaya said, sitting down and pulling one of the legal pads close. "You've already answered about half the question just by coming here. You're obviously serious. And the shrinks haven't done you any good . . . so you're desperate enough to gamble. That makes a difference, too."

She doodled on the pad for a moment. "A lot of people," Mrs. Cumaya said, "might think that your—talent—would be interesting to have."

"'They'd be sick in the head," Jim said forcefully.

"Well, that's what we need to be sure of," Mrs. Cumaya said. "That you really want to be rid of it."

"That I *want* to be—!"

"Some people," she said, looking at him carefully, "would think it was a gift. Maybe a gift from God. Anyway, a way to do good."

"Maybe I've done some good over time," Jim said.

"But if it *is* a gift, I'd return it and never ask for a refund, if I just knew *where*. . . . "

Mrs. Cumaya looked at him for a few moments more, then nodded slowly. "Well," she said. "The only thing we didn't get around to covering yesterday was the family history. Where are your parents these days?"

"My father's dead," he said. "My mother's in a nursing home in Duluth."

"Incapacitated?"

"No, just old," he said, somewhat surprised.

"Why doesn't she stay with you?"

The thought made the hairs on the back of Jim's neck stand right up on end. To have that endless, cloying regard trained on him night and day from close quarters? The phone calls were bad enough. His mother never seemed to have understood that he was a grown man, for God's sake, that he got enough to eat, had a life, had work to do. And the endless inquiries about what he was *doing* at work . . . why he wasn't running the store, instead of just working in it . . . Jim sighed. "It wouldn't work out."

"How did your folks sleep?"

After I came along, in separate bedrooms, he thought, uneasy: but he wasn't going to tell her *that*. "My father? Like the proverbial log."

"But your mother was a lighter sleeper?"

"Yeah."

"And now?"

"Uh . . . " Jim had no idea how she slept lately. While he was growing up there had been a lot of sleepless nights for her. Back then, the excuse had been that she was "high-strung," that Jim's birth had done something to her . . . something unspecified. It didn't get any better for a long time. All through his early childhood, as he got ready for school, Jim would see his mother looked haggard and wretched in the morning as she made his and his father's breakfasts. Then later the nights had become sleepless for Jim, too, as he awakened again and again to find her sitting over him, watching him, as if afraid he would stop breathing. "My boy," she would say, "I just love watching him sleep . . . so peacefully . . . " But it had always been creepy. That shape, in the darkness, leaning dark over him . . . Jim had started having nightmares about it. Finally she had stopped, realizing that she was creating some kind of problem, and her own problem eventually seemed to go away. A while later, the nature of his own dreams changed, and put her old trouble out of Jim's mind. But sometimes he still thought of that dark shape, bending over him. . . .

"The wrong question?"

"Uh, no," he said. "She sleeps okay, as far as I know."

"Good," Mrs. Cumaya said. "Normal hours?"

"Yeah, but— Look, it's my dreams, *my* sleep we're supposed to be fixing here!"

Mrs. Cumaya gave him a very sharp look. "What kind of doctor, if you went to one," she said, "wouldn't ask whether you had a family history of a disease? Heart trouble? Mental illness?"

"Well, since you put it that way—"

"I do. Now, hush a moment."

She sat looking out the window for a moment, tapping with her pencil on the legal pad while she watched someone in a blue Chevy parking, and doing it badly. "Okay," she said. She turned another of those sharp looks on him, held it, so that he had trouble keeping still in the chair. "Are you still sure you want to get rid of this?"

"Sure I'm sure!"

"Be very clear," Mrs Cumaya said. "Some people in your position wouldn't want to. They would want to keep the ability, but have it become tolerable. If I intervene, it's to end this situation completely, and forever. Just be real certain that you're not simply looking for improvement, because you're not going to get it."

Jim thought for a moment of what satisfaction there was from his constant attempts to help the murdered find peace. Except for the eventual quiet, there was precious little. Certainly no slightest amount of fame or praise rewarded his efforts. There were reporters who tracked him down intending to freelance his story yet again to the *National Enquirer* . . . a story for which he would as usual get not a penny. And there were endless encounters with the embarrassed cops who needed his "services," but would never admit that in daylight for fear of their careers being over as a result. From the cops, sometimes Jim might get a payment, always under the table . . . never anything approaching what the job was worth. And then came the nights . . . the flat, wet smell of blood in his dreams, and the thin, bodiless wailing in his ears, voices miserable or furious or desperate beyond the comprehension of the living, whining or moaning for justice, for the revelation that would set them free. And never a night off . . . for there was no hour in the Earth's turning during which some human being did not kill another in hate. "No," Jim said. "I want it *gone*. I want my life for myself! *I want to sleep and not to be afraid to wake up thinking I'm dead! Dead again!*"

Mrs. Cumaya actually started back a little when he shouted at her, and then smiled in surprise. "Yes," she said softly then, "you do. At the moment, anyway. . . . "

She took a drink of her iced tea. "All right," Mrs. Cumaya said. "I have some paperwork for you to sign. Let me get it sorted out for you. Then we'll get to work, late tonight."

"How late?"

"Oh, I think you know when these dreams come," she said. "The clear ones, with real detail. Always just before dawn, aren't they? Around four A.M . . . or up to an hour or so later in the wintertime."

Jim raised his eyebrows. "Now that you mention it . . . "

"Late-cycle REM sleep," Mrs. Cumaya said. "The daily low in the biorhythm pattern. The bottom of the dopamine 'neurochemical swing' in the brain. There are about fifty reasons for it, depending on which paradigm you're working in . . . medical, psychiatric, philosophical. It's the 'Horn Gate' phenomenon . . . that being the gate which true dreams pass through before dawn, as opposed to the Ivory Gate, for false ones that happen in the middle of the night . . . at the beginning of the dreaming cycle. 'The elephant's tooth is full of untruth, but the Gate of Horn is ne'er forsworn.' " She leaned back in the pine kitchen chair. It creaked. "I don't waste my time with early-cycle dreams. Too often they're just lactic acid byproducts on their way through the brain and out of the body. The corpus has to discharge a lot of useless energy and chemistry in the sleep cycle before it gets to the important stuff."

"You know a lot about this," Jim said.

"I must," Mrs. Cumaya said. "I have a 900 number, don't I?" The look she gave him was so ironic that it bent her face somewhat out of shape, and for a moment the glint in her eyes looked just slightly malicious. But then Mrs. Cumaya smiled. "Sorry," she said.

"So what do I do?"

"Go have a nice dinner at your hotel," she said. "A glass of wine or so wouldn't hurt. Don't overdo it. Then go to bed."

"That's *all?* Go to bed?"

"Believe me," Mrs. Cumaya said, and pushed her chair back, "after that, it gets interesting. Make sure you throw the bolt on that door when you turn in." She stood up. "And one other thing. When you go to bed . . . take a knife."

Jim blinked. "A *knife?*"

"Go down to the mall," Mrs. Cumaya said as she walked him to the door "There's a nice cutlery shop down there. Make sure the knife is steel."

He swallowed and paused at the door. Her expression was still just slightly wicked. "Why would I need a knife in bed?" Jim said.

She waggled her silvery-white eyebrows at him, smiled, and closed the door.

Jim drove to the mall near his hotel. At the cutlery shop there, he contemplated everything from a foot-and-a-half-long machete to a curly-hilted knife associated with an extremely butch alien species in a TV series, and finally, in embarrassment, bought a Swiss Army Knife with every possible attachment, on the grounds that it would be useful for something after tonight. He then went to dinner and had a large steak and a salad, and a glass of red wine. And after that, he went to bed in his underwear, and put the Swiss Army

Knife, open, under the pillow with great care. Then he lay between the cool sheets, in the darkness, and could not sleep. Jim tossed and rolled back and forth until one-thirty in the morning, and finally could think of nothing more helpful than to put CNN Headline News on and bore himself to sleep with endless repetitions of the world's woes.

"—the Dow closed at—"

"—after Dell Computer filed second-quarter earnings of—"

"Ding dong dell—"

He sat straight up in the bed in horror.

Except he was not in the bed. He was sitting on the ground in a dark place, somewhere out in the open, and cold mist rolled all around him, lit faintly as if by moonlight, but there was no moon. Jim looked around him in sudden fear, feeling a cool wind breathing on him—actually breathing, the huge matter-of-fact breath of something listening to him, watching.

"Don't let it bother you," said a voice from behind him, "it's just the ether." Jim launched himself to his feet, clutching the thing that had been under his hand, and whipped around to face the source of the voice.

Mrs. Cumaya was standing there, looking at him in amusement. She had exchanged her sweats and short-sleeved top for a sort of poncho or kaftan, all white, and belted up high. Behind her, towering above her, was a great doorway without a door—two lintels and a crossbeam, a huge beige-brown-and-cream structure translucent in places and shadowy in others, all intricately carved with images of men and beasts, and with other symbology he could not understand. "It's beautiful," Jim said.

"There speaks the innocent," Mrs. Cumaya said. "You plainly don't have anything to fear at the moment."

"Except more of the dreams," he said.

She gave him a thoughtful look that Jim found hard to decipher. Over one arm, like a bouquet of flowers, she was carrying a smooth dark stick . . . and Jim gulped as he realized that the stick was looking back at him. Twice. Little tongues flickered, tasting the air—little black beady eyes gazed at him, unblinking, and the dark smooth shining bodies of the snakes twined and slipped over one another and around the stick as they watched him. "Uh, are you medical?" Jim said.

She laughed. "Not at all. These two are part of the access package . . . and a way to get people's attention. Got the knife?"

He showed it to her. She laughed. "Hey," she asked, "has it got the thing you take stones out of a horse's hoof with?"

"Probably." He turned it over in his hands, trying to work out where the thing might be or, for that matter, what it looked like.

"Never mind that," she said. "Dawn is coming. Is that the longest blade? Good. Let's go."

He went after her, through the Horn Gate, and as he passed under the lintel, Jim felt a chill pass over his skin as if he were diving into cold water. "Truth," Mrs. Cumaya said over her shoulder. "It's cold. Don't let it bother you."

"Where are we?" he asked. Near them there were no features, no landmarks. Away at the edge of things, he thought he saw jagged peaks, barely visible in the sourceless light against the utter black of the sky.

"Where everything said is true," she said, "or becomes that way in a hurry. Watch what you say, or it can be used against you."

He swallowed as he followed her through the mist. Ahead of them, he thought he could see a flat area where it thinned a little, or more of the darkness beneath it showed. "Didn't take long for us to get here . . . "

"Oh, getting down here is easy," Mrs. Cumaya. said. "Getting *out* again . . . that's a little tougher. But you're here in a good cause. I think They'll let you go."

" 'They'?"

"Unwise to mention their names at this point," she said. "Especially since Sleep has a brother, and sometimes they get confused and answer to each other's names. . . . "

She stopped, and Jim paused beside her and looked ahead of them. The mist writhed and curled over the surface of what seemed a great wide pool of black water. There was no other motion, and no sound but that low, slow breathing, all cold. "What now?" he said.

"Sacrifice," said Mrs. Cumaya.

Jim gave her a look. "We're a little short on virgins."

She laughed again, a scornful sound this time. "Thank you . . . I think. You've been watching too many movies, son. Look there." She pointed off to his left with the snake-entwined staff.

Jim glanced that way and saw a blot of darkness standing there in the pale curling mist. A pallid gleam of eyes caught the light that was not there, and the eyes rested on Jim, considering him.

It was a ram, a black one, and surprisingly big. "Sacrifice it *how*?" Jim said.

"A smart question," Mrs. Cumaya said. "It's not complicated, fortunately. Cut its throat. Spill its blood out on the ground here."

Jim swallowed. The ram's eyes were on him, and the expression it presently wore suggested that it might not take kindly to this prospect.

"This is some kind of symbolic thing, isn't it?" Jim asked.

Mrs. Cumaya shrugged. "Maybe it's just a sheep," she said. "Maybe it's your innocence, your inability to take responsibility for dream . . . which you gave up when you came to me. But, either way, it's blood, and the dreams and the souls that dream them will not answer your desire without blood."

He looked at the Swiss Army knife, which seemed unequal to the task. Then he looked at the ram, which looked back at him. Its expression was a shade more nervous now.

It's just me, Jim thought suddenly. *And it's no kindness to keep it waiting. . . .*

He strode over to the ram and took it by one horn. It did not fight him. Jim wrapped his fist around the handle of the knife, braced it with a forefinger over the end of the pommel, and put it straight down into the ram's eye. He felt the pain in his own eye, and cried out. Under his hands, there was a moment's struggle, no more.

As the ram started to fall, Jim leaned down and cut its throat. Because of the thick curly wool, it took two tries. The second time, the black blood poured out onto the ground and pooled there.

The pool grew fast as he let the ram fall, too fast. There was no way the ram had that much blood in it. Jim stepped back as this smaller pool ran down the slight slope into the greater one before which he and his guide stood, and he put a hand to his eye, half expecting to feel the blood running from it as well. There was none, but the pain in it was white-hot. In the waking world, he would have screamed with it. Here, it seemed strangely unimportant, almost secondary.

Mrs. Cumaya nodded, satisfied, and raised the staff, and the two snakes wrapped around it reared up and looked out across the water, over which the mist had thinned to almost nothing. "Now let the powers of this place hear Jim's desire," said Mrs. Cumaya, standing very straight, seeming taller than her height would allow, "for he has come the long journey to shake off his burden at last. Let all those who have had a claim on this man's dreams now come and renounce those claims, leaving him forever free."

She stood quiet, then, and waited. For long moments nothing happened. "This is going to be bad," Mrs. Cumaya said softly. "Don't lose it."

Jim gulped. The knife felt hot in his hand, and the pain in his eye was dying, like an ember losing its glow. In the water, something stirred, a ripple, spreading . . .

That was when he began to hear the voices. Not just one at a time, but a slowly growing chorus: the moans, the wails, sound of despair or rage adding to sound. In the water, the ripples grew, and the shapes causing them began, slowly, to break the surface. The heads of men, of women, of children, came rising through the dark water, lank-haired, empty-eyed, arms hanging power-lessly down by their sides as they made their way up into the air, slowly, as if coming up stair-steps out of the depths. Their mouths hung open, as if incapable of speech, like mere instruments of grief being played in a hollow consort of pain.

Out of the black water they ascended, up onto the misty shore, surrounding Jim and Mrs. Cumaya. They crowded around the two of them and the pool of ram's blood in a tightening circle—the lank dark dripping forms, the thin wailing voices wordlessly crying for justice, crying for vengeance. Jim held the knife and shook with terror. But Mrs. Cumaya held out the staff and said, "Keep your distance, lost ones! One at a time you may advance and drink, and having drunk life again for a moment, speak your truths clearly. Having so spoken, justice shall be done you. But do not drink all. One is awaited. . . ."

The figures closing in around them stopped still and did not move.

Jim tried to swallow, but his mouth was too dry. "I am here," said the pained voice. "Let me drink and speak my truth. I am buried in the cellar."

"Come and drink."

A woman came forward, dressed in jeans and a T-shirt. She bent and drank from the dark pool, then straightened. "I'm sorry," she said, her mouth black with the blood, and the stain black against her hand as she wiped her mouth. "There wasn't anybody else to help me, you were the only one. The cellar is in Westchester County. A town called Chappaqua. Fourteen Oak Garden Road. Thank you for helping. . . . "

Jim could only nod. She stepped down into the water again and was gone.

One after another they stepped up onto the land out of the dark water, bent over the darker, thicker pool running down into it, drank a brief swallow's worth of life, and spoke in sorrowful, whispery voices, but the sorrow for the first time seemed about to be lifted, and some of the murdered even smiled at Jim—a little girl with a beat-up teddy bear who had been sexually assaulted and then drowned by her rapist, a man whose wife had had her lover shoot him and bury him in the woods, a woman whose husband had slowly poisoned her with arsenic and then abandoned her in the middle of a wildlife preserve, assuming bears would eat her corpse and destroy the evidence. They recited names and dates and addresses and endless other details to Jim, and he felt them burning into his brain in that great dark silence. Slowly the moans and the wails faded as only a few of the murdered remained, until only one was left, a sad-faced man whose best friend had killed him at the height of a drunken argument. This man, tall and thin, stepped down last into the water, and the ripples from his passage quieted, and Jim stood there, shaking his head in wonder and sorrow for them all. But there was still something niggling at him. He turned to Mrs. Cumaya.

"There's one more," Mrs. Cumaya said. "Pull yourself together, now."

"I was wondering," Jim said. "There was still one that I hadn't. . . . "

He fell silent. The shape slowly rose out of the dark water as all the others had, as if coming up a flight of stairs. It was a woman in a bathrobe, with a nightdress under it, a short, stocky, corpulent woman, with her thin gray hair pulled back tight. She came up out of the water with a vague expression—not a dead person, but a live one dreaming. . . .

"Mother?"

Knee-deep in the black water, she made straight for the dark pool. Mrs. Cumaya stepped quickly between her and the ram's blood. "Not for you, "she said, holding out the staff, and Jim's mother stopped there in the water, stock still, as if she had hit a glass wall. Her hands came up as she pressed against some barrier which Jim could not see.

"Let me," said Jim's mother.

"No. Say why you came," said Mrs. Cumaya.

"*They* came," his mother said, eyes still unfocused and vague. She didn't believe in all this, she thought she was "only dreaming." "I haven't heard them in so long. . . . "

"Because you stuck *him* with them," Mrs. Cumaya said. "With the 'gift.' "

Jim stared at her.

"You couldn't cope with it yourself," Mrs. Cumaya said. "But someone in your own family whispered to you that if you wished it onto someone else, someone too confused to know what was happening and too weak to refuse it, it would lodge in *them*. You did what you had to do to find out. . . . "

"What are you talking about?" Jim whispered, suddenly thinking of all those nights, the dark shape bending over him, listening to his breathing. . . .

"One shrink I knew called it the 'hot potato syndrome,' " Mrs. Cumaya said. "Lots of families choose one of their members as a scapegoat, to manifest some trait the rest of them don't want to be stuck with."

Jim swallowed. His mother looked toward him, unbelieving, empty-eyed. "It's easier to do than you might think," Mrs. Cumaya said. "Peer pressure, emotional blackmail, the little things families have the time and privacy to do to each other . . . they all make it possible. And other things can be shoved off onto the innocent, the ignorant, as well. Potentials . . . powers. Fortunately, when talents or gifts like *this* are involved, there's a loophole. You can successfully throw the potato back. Assuming you realize you're holding it in the first place."

Jim opened his mouth, shut it again. *"Mom—?"*

His mother's slack face began working through one expression after another, every one of them familiar: surprise, patient understanding, concern, affection. But for the first time, in this place where nothing but the truth could be understood, every one of them looked false. "Honey, you have to understand. I wasn't ready for it. I was too young. I—" She broke off, and Jim heard her changing stories, as clearly as one can hear a train switch clicking over so the train can change tracks. "I wasn't strong enough. You have to be strong for this kind of gift. You're so good at it, look at all the good you've done—"

Lies.

She stuck me with this!

Yes. Now all you have to do is throw the "potato" back.

But it's my mother.

"You have to understand, honey," said the soft, familiar, pleading, controlling voice. "I couldn't possibly be a good mother to you if I had to be doing *that* all the time. . . ."

He looked at Mrs. Cumaya. She spoke no word aloud, but her expression said very clearly, *Are you really going to buy into this crap?* And the snakes looked at the woman standing in the black water, and their tongues flickered quick with contempt.

Jim's mother's face had an expression of gentle concern applied all over it. "I always wanted the best for my boy. . . . "

And so she handed me this pain. This endless unease, never a night's sleep untroubled, never a day without the night shadowing it . . . .

"Always wanted you to be something special. . . . "

And so she let me take the strain, while taking it easy herself. It's okay if I wind up being "special" in an institution somewhere. . . .

" . . . and this way I can go on being a good mother for you. . . ."

Until one day I kill myself in despair.

Jim swallowed hard.

"Take it back," he said, hardly to be heard, hardly believing himself.

"But, honey, if I have to do that, I'll—"

Jim gulped again. He could feel her spirit pressing against him, trying to make him change his mind, trying to make him leave things the way they were so that everyone would be happy, it would all be for the best, he was so much stronger than she was, and he wouldn't want her to *suffer,* now, would he—

"Take it back," Jim said, louder. The pressure was building up all around him, squeezing his chest, tightening around his throat, blinding his eyes. He had no business talking back to her, *she* knew best, Jim should do what he was told, he should make himself useful to people and be grateful for God's gifts and—

"Take—it—*back!*" Jim cried, shocking the depth of the silence all around him with the cry.

His mother stood still there in the dark water. Jim stood gasping with effort. Mrs. Cumaya lifted the snake-entwined staff and said, "The law here is as it has been since the Gate was raised. Three times a lawful wish has been spoken with intention, and so it becomes truth, on this side of dream and on the far side. Go and make truth manifest."

Jim's mother just stood there in the water. Then slowly she turned and made her way back down into the depths, step by step, vanishing. Finally the water closed over her head, and only ripples remained, smoothing themselves to nothing.

Jim was still having trouble breathing. When it eased off a little, he looked over at Mrs. Cumaya. For the moment she was looking out over the water, as if watching for any sign of a reappearance.

Jim sighed and looked sadly down at the body of the ram.

To his complete shock, the ram winked at him. Then it got up, shook itself, and walked away into the dark.

"Uh," Jim said.

Mrs. Cumaya chuckled softly and turned back to him. Beyond her, away across the water, Jim thought he could see a faint light, as if somewhere, in another world maybe, dawn was coming.

"All those poor people," she said. "You'll be taking care of them when you get home."

"Absolutely." Jim was ready to smile at the prospect now. "But that wasn't all of them. One was missing."

She looked at him with a very dry expression. "Indeed," Mrs. Cumaya said. "Doubtless the Powers on that side of the Gate intended it that way. Don't worry yourself about it, she's not your problem anymore. Someone else's."

"Oh," Jim said, and felt disinclined to argue with her, for the snakes were looking at him with what for the moment seemed like an amused expression. "So what now?"

"Now you go home," Ms. Cumaya said. "You don't need to see me tomorrow, and I won't be home anyway. Call me the day after tomorrow."

And he opened his eyes, and found himself staring at the hotel ceiling, on which the faint light of dawn was painting itself in a beautiful smog-born shade of orange-rose.

Jim did as he was told and went straight home. He fell asleep once on the plane, and had a dream, a perfectly normal and irrational dream about one of the flight attendants, and woke up from it laughing. He rejoiced all the way back, sat laughing in the traffic jam he got caught in on the way back from the airport, and when he got back to his apartment and picked up his phone messages, discovering that he had been fired, he danced around the place in joy. He had never been so glad to be fired from a job in his life, for now he *had* a life again, one in which jobs and such other ordinary things would be worth caring about.

The next night, he called Mrs. Cumaya. "I have to write you a check," Jim said.

"How have your dreams been?"

"Inconsequential," Jim said. "Stupid. I love it!"

"All right," Mrs. Cumaya said then. "You want to pay me: fine. Whatever you think is fair. You can fax me the check. My bank can handle that."

"Uh, how do I spell your first name?"

"Sybil."

"Call you right back."

Jim wrote the check out, and put it in the fax machine. Five minutes later he called her back. "Is that okay?" he said.

"It's fine. And thank you very much. But are you sure you can afford that much?"

"Leave that to me," Jim said. "I just want to thank you again. . . ."

"Well, you're welcome." Then, after a moment, Mrs. Cumaya chuckled. "Whoops," she said, "you misspelled it."

"What? Your last name?"

"No, the first one. You swapped the vowels. But never mind."

Jim blinked at that . . . and then thought again about how *very* old she looked.

"I don't think you'll be needing to talk to me again," Mrs. Cumaya said. "It might be better if you forget having met me at all. I don't want to see any of those *National Enquirer* people on my doorstep . . . and if I did, I would come looking for you. *You* know where."

"Yes, ma'am," he said, "I do. Be unpleasant, I imagine."

"It would. So farewell, Jim," she said. "Sleep well . . . and use your dreams for what they were meant for."

And that night, a woman in the Springfield Greens Retirement Care Facility in Duluth, Illinois, awakened screaming at dawn. The night-shift nurse, then in her office doing the last notations on meds and the last few patient notes before she went offshift, came running down the hall and into Mrs. Sthenopolos's room to find her sitting upright in bed, clutching her thinning gray hair in handfuls, and screaming a children's rhyme. The nurse did her best to quiet the woman, but she wouldn't be quieted. The whole place rang to her screams, and finally the duty nurse hurried back down to the nursing station to call the on-call doctor and get a sedation order from him, and then to make an appointment with the local hospital's psychiatric resident to see if the poor woman had had some kind of psychotic break. *You just can't tell*, the nurse thought as she dialed the on-call's pager number and waited for the beep. *These people go along as quiet as you please for ten, fifteen, twenty years, and then all of a sudden . . . bang! Senile dementia time.*

The beep went off. The nurse left her message, having to raise her voice over the increasingly horrified-sounding shrieks from down the hall, and then hung up and made her way back down there to see about some restraints. "Ding dong dell, pussy's in the well! *Ding dong dell—*"

NIGHT STUFF
by Nina Kiriki Hoffman

Nina Kiriki Hoffman has been pursuing a writing career for seventeen years and has sold more than 150 stories, two short story collections, and one novella, *Unmasking,* one collaborative young adult novel with Tad Williams, *Child of an Ancient City,* and four novels: *The Thread that Binds the Bones,* winner of the Bram Stoker award for best first novel, *The Silent Strength of Stones, A Red Heart of Memories* and *Past the Size of Dreaming.*

The six-foot-long snake looped around a bowl of fruit on the kitchen table in Ryan's dream, so I figured it would be safe to possess. It seemed out of the way.

The central drama in this dream involved Ryan arguing with a woman. Anger twisted both their faces. I didn't want to possess either of them. I wanted to feel, but not to feel mad.

I had never been a snake before. As I settled into its shape, I felt marvelous things: how all of me was armored, though none of me was armed. I lifted the tip of the tail. Such a flex and mesh of muscles, the shift of scales, slither of my surface against the tabletop, unlike anything I'd felt before. I flicked out my tongue and tasted a wilderness of new.

I fell in love with Ryan all over again. He dreamed with such clarity!

The dream took place in a room that resembled our house's kitchen. Mother seeped into the dishwasher.

Perhaps she was in an inanimate mood. I had no affinity for furniture, though it was often safe to be.

We had learned it was better not to possess a major character in Ryan's dreams. We had no control over what the central characters did or said; we could feel what they felt, touch what they touched, taste what they tasted, but we couldn't choose their words or actions. Things Ryan and his dream characters did and said made me feel, well, very uncomfortable.

Even uncomfortable was better than normal ghost existence. When Mother and I were embedded in Ryan's dreams, we didn't have to play out our own pattern, the one we had been repeating since I had killed her and then myself fifty-six years earlier. If we were sufficiently peripheral, we could even whisper to each other without having to repeat our awful final fight. Perhaps, if we found the right words to say, we could move past our final moments and stop haunting our house.

When I entered the dream, I didn't realize how angry Ryan was with this woman. Or that it was one of Those Dreams, where a snake wasn't exactly a snake.

I suspected that the dream woman represented a real person who in waking life had rejected Ryan. Most of them did. Ryan was pale and thin and still believed in long sideburns. One got the impression that his hands sweated easily. He had a pathological difficulty with conversation when faced with a real person, though he managed some wonderful exchanges when he was practicing with himself. Ryan had been living in our house for two years, and we had never seen him get a woman past the living room on the rare occasions when he managed to bring a woman home at all.

Perhaps the fact that Mother and I haunted at night had something to do with his failure rate.

Ryan's idea of intercourse wasn't very realistic, but it was interesting. I hoped the waking-life woman would never know what Ryan imagined doing to her with a snake in his dream. It would embarrass all three of them dreadfully.

As for me, I knew I should have been horrified about the uses to which I was put; I was sure that Mother was appalled. And yet, I had some new feelings to consider, and many new sensations. I was hungry for anything new.

It was possible, I supposed, that during the time Mother and I have been trapped in our house, I had lost all moral sense.

It was possible I was never strong in that area to begin with.

Mother and I didn't haunt in the morning. We haunted whenever a realtor showed the house, and at night, which was when we had had our big fight. Since Ryan bought the house two years ago, Mother and I had stopped putting much energy into our haunting. Sometimes Ryan was out in the evenings, maybe on dates that ended happily elsewhere, or perhaps he went to bars with friends, or to movies alone.

What was the point in haunting if there was nobody around to appreciate it?

When Ryan was home and we haunted, he ignored us.

The morning after the snake dream, I watched Ryan punch the coffeemaker in the kitchen into making him some coffee. He looked bleary but satisfied. I supposed he enjoyed what he had done in that dream.

Ryan was the ninth person to live in our house since I

murdered Mother. There was an exquisite clarity in his dreams, the clarity of a world well-observed through the gray lenses of discontent.

I didn't like the content of Ryan's dreams as much as I had liked the dreams of Euphemia Wilson, the woman who had died in our house in her sleep two years ago at the age of eighty-seven. She lived with us almost twenty-five years. Our haunting hadn't bothered her; she kept her hearing aids turned down when she was alone in the house, so she almost invariably missed it. She had some rowdy dreams, some bawdy dreams, and many sweet dreams; they all had an innocent exuberance that Ryan's dreams lacked, and we had been safe possessing anything we saw in them. She hadn't dreamed with Ryan's intensity, though.

We didn't know what Ryan did during the day. Presumably he worked. He dressed in rather formal clothes and left the house at eight-thirty every morning, and he returned, wrinkled and tired, around five-thirty in the evening. He had enough money to pay most of the bills and to keep himself in rum and Coke. He didn't bring friends home from work, and his telephone rarely rang. When he was home, he sat in the living room and watched a lot of television, which suited Mother and me. We watched and learned, and sometimes, in the corners of Ryan's dreams, we talked about what we had learned. He also brought home stacks of videos. Mother and I loved movies.

That morning, as on almost every morning, Ryan went out on the front porch and got the paper. He read it and drank coffee and ate PopTarts. Mother and I hovered behind him, reading over his shoulders. I wished he weren't so interested in sports, that he liked the news parts of the paper more. He always changed channels away from news, too.

It wasn't that news would do *us* any good. I wanted Ryan to connect to his own world, to know what was happening to other people.

He just didn't care.

I glanced at Mother as Ryan flipped to the comics and Ann Landers page, one of our favorites, and one on which Ryan never spent enough time. Mother, a floating wisp of white with black pits for eyes, looked back at me. I wanted to talk to her about Ryan: how I worried about how little he knew, how little he did, how little he cared; how I wished he could actually find that special girl, the one who would mean the world to him, so they could start a beautiful life together. I wanted to talk to Mother. But if I tried, all I would be able to say were the words I'd said that last night.

"Doris," Mother said in her distant voice, "where have you been?"

No, Mother. Not the pattern. Not now. Not in the morning!

"That's none of your business, Mother." The words jerked out of me. Pattern initiated, haunting to follow.

"You better believe it's my business," she said. "You live under my roof. Everything you do is my business."

Ryan crackled his newspaper in annoyance. He had reason. We weren't supposed to haunt the kitchen, or in the morning. Our fight had taken place near midnight in the master bedroom, and that was where our tired fight always repeated itself, up until now, except when realtors and their clients came to the house.

"When will you treat me with the respect I deserve?" Mother said, hurt bleeding into her voice. "I gave up bone and blood to make you. I suffered for hours to bring you into this world. I gave up my youth and beauty to perfect you. I created beautiful art! And look what you've done to my creation. Night after night, you shame and lower yourself with those filthy beast boys. You let them touch you. You let them paw you. You slash my beautiful canvas!"

Ryan set down his paper and sighed. He glanced in my direction.

"Did I ever ask to be born?" I wailed. "I wish I were dead."

Ryan sighed again.

"When will you stop running around at night? What kind of bad blood is in you to make you so wild? Who taught you to be such a wicked girl? How can you do this to me?"

"When are you going to tell me the truth?" I screamed. All those ridiculous overblown feelings, rage and hurt, shame and confusion, flooded through me again, the way they did every time we had this argument. The feelings were so large I scarcely had room for them. I had never known how to step out of them, how to sort through the things Mother said and discard them.

All I knew was that she had hurt me, and I wanted to hurt her worse.

"The truth?" Mother said.

"About the telegram!"

"The telegram," she whispered. "The telegram, Doris?"

" 'We regret to inform you!' " I cried. "How long were you going to wait before you told me Daddy's dead?"

"Don't say that!" she screamed.

Ryan took his paper and his coffee and his PopTarts and moved to the living room, leaving us to rage at each other for another six and a half minutes. I had timed this fight. It only took my mother ten minutes to enflame me into a murderous rage.

I had lived with my mother for twenty-one years. During the last of those years, when contact with her turned poisonous, I twisted and shriveled up inside and searched endlessly for someone to take me away from our house; but all the fine young men had gone overseas to war. The Company B boys, "Be here when you leave, be here when you get back," did not impress me favorably. In my last days I went out with some of them, though, as many as I could find. None of them ever called me again. I could not even engage secondary men.

Why was that last night different from all other nights? It was not as though Mother had never said these things to me before, nor were my remarks to her different. I guess throwing Daddy's death into the mix intensified everything. Mother had known he was dead for a year, and she had not told me. I had found the telegram crumpled in the bottom of her sock drawer. After the staggering shock of that discovery, I had hugged the secret as tightly as Mother did, keeping it inside more than five months.

What made us both go crazy?

I don't remember wanting to kill her. I only remember picking up that ashtray and flinging it with all my might. I was horrified when it hit her head and she collapsed with terrible snorting sounds, more terrible when they stopped.

It took Mother ten minutes to make me mad enough to throw the ashtray. It took me two hours afterward to figure out that I couldn't live with myself and what I had done. I spent another half hour trying to figure out how to die. Eventually I climbed up on the roof and threw myself down, jumping toward the concrete parking spot behind the house. I didn't want my dead body to be visible from the street. People would have to come into the house and look out the back window to find me. They'd be right by the breakfast nook and could easily collapse onto a chair after they discovered me.

We used to think, in the forties, that the mere sight of something horrifying could make people faint.

I was fortunate: for me, jumping off the roof achieved the desired result, death. The eleven-year-old who moved into our house during the fifties did a copycat jump off the roof, but she only broke her arm.

After Mother's final scream, the ashtray crash, and the thump as she hit the floor, we had finished our haunt. I went to find Ryan.

He had toppled sideways on the couch, the newspaper still clutched in his hand, though the bulk of it had slipped to the floor. He snored.

I stared at him, overcome with warm and helpless affection. He was so silly, but he was all we had. I stroked my hand over his forehead and he snorted and sat up. "Wha—?" He glanced at his watch, then struggled to his feet. "Gotta go," he muttered. He grabbed the pre-tied tie hanging by the back door and slipped it over his head, nodded, waved his hand as though to us, and left for the day.

That night, Ryan dreamed of the margins of the world. Turquoise water, hemmed with white lace, rolled to a white sand beach below a turquoise sky. The Ryan who strolled by the water under that white sun was strong, tan, and muscular, and his hair did not thin on top of his head. I recognized him because I had seen him look like this before, and he retained his trademark sideburns. Other than the sideburns, he looked rather a lot like one of *People*'s most beautiful people in the world.

For a little while he walked on the beach, leaving a single line of footprints near the water's edge, and Mother and I drifted, trying to see something safe to possess. Nothing swam in this cosmetic ocean. The beach stretched away from the water to sketchy, watercolor underbrush. I was thinking one of us could be the beach and the other the sea when the bunny-girls ran up.

Ryan spent a lot of time in his room studying bunny-girls and manipulating himself. Mother, horrified, never watched him while he was thus employed, but I had. Before I died, I hadn't understood much about men. Ryan was an education to me.

"Ryan. Ryan!" the bunny-girls cried in their breathless little voices, oozing admiration. I counted fifteen of them, and headed for a redhead in the back. We'd seen dreams like this before. Ryan thought he wanted all of the bunny-girls, but after two or three he would fall out of this dream, I knew.

"Hey, girls," he said.

I was inside the redhead enough to squeal with delight at the sound of his voice, like all the others. "Ooh, ooh!" one of them shrieked, and "Oh, Ryan!" said another.

White sand burned against the soles of my feet with delicious heat. My legs prickled with the feel of water drying on them. I could smell wet salt on the warm summer air, and strange unknown tropical fruits, and hints of oil and sweat and the musky earth of the others, perhaps of myself. Oh, Ryan, I thought, not caring that this was just another in his legion of wish dreams.

The blonde beside me whispered, "Doris?"

"Mother?"

"Oh, good."

The girls in front of us were stroking Ryan's muscles, murmuring things to him. One of them handed him a drink. It came in a hairy coconut shell and sported three paper parasols and a crazy straw. Two girls held up tubes of suntan lotion, and one laid a giant multicolored beach-towel on the sand. Four others pushed Ryan down onto it. "Hey, girls! Hey! What are you doing to me?" he asked, laughing, as they held him down.

"We've got to make sure you're safe!" several of them cooed, squirting suntan lotion onto their hands and smoothing it onto him.

"Nobody wants Ryan to get hurt!"

"We want you to live forever!"

"And we want you to have a perfect tan."

"What was it you tried to tell me today?" I murmured to the blonde beside me. The only reason she would have started our haunting at the wrong time that morning was because she strongly wanted to tell me something.

"I—" A huge bowl of pistachio ice cream popped into her hand. "Oh dear," she murmured as her feet walked her away from me. "I seem to have a speaking role." She dropped to her knees beside Ryan and said, "What is your wish, Master?"

"Oh, that looks so good," Ryan said. She fed it to him, and knelt to kiss some of it off his lips. He groaned and grabbed her.

I could have told her not to possess a blonde. Ryan liked them best.

We didn't have time to talk any more during that dream.

Mother and I learned to ride dreams from a ghost who was already in our house when we died.

We didn't notice him right away. After our deaths, we were so strongly clutched in the grip of our own haunting that we knew nothing except the awful energy of our rage. Each night we poured it out, horrid heat and fury, to the limits of our last argument, and then we disappeared, unsatisfied, but unable to do anything else until the next midnight approached and called us up again.

Mother's younger sister Beth moved into the house some time after we died. I didn't notice her until she screamed during our haunting. What a syrup-flavored scream that was, smooth and sweet and lovely. Mother and I stopped mid-haunt to taste it.

For the first time we realized that we could do something other than play out our pattern.

Then Beth stopped screaming, and we picked up where we had left off.

Each time she screamed, we supped. She screamed loudest at the tunk of the ashtray, Mother's collapse, and fall. Then she ran.

Mother and I lingered, charged with unknown energy.

We saw the strange flickering white of another ghost.

He dove through the master bedroom wall, and we followed. For the first time we realized we could move away from our haunting ground.

He led us down to the living room, where Beth huddled on the couch, wrapped in a quilt, and talked on the telephone.

"It was just like they were still alive," she said. "I swear I heard them. They said such horrible things to each other. I heard Margaret die!"

A voice on the phone clacked in her ear.

"No. I don't want to stay here alone," Beth said.

More clacking.

Tears ran down Beth's face. "I am *not* a baby," she said. "Why are you so mean to me? I know it's late. I know you've worked hard all day and you have a husband and four children to take care of and I don't." For a long while she cried silently and listened to the voice on the phone, which I figured must be Aunt Millicent. Aunt Millicent never suffered anybody's weaknesses gladly.

"You can have the house," Beth said finally in a tiny voice. "I don't want it. I never did."

More listening.

"All right. I *am* an idiot. Please don't leave me here alone, Millie. Please send Hubert to come get me. Please."

A few more words, and Beth hung up the phone. She pulled the quilt tighter around herself, total hopelessness in her face.

She didn't sleep until several hours had passed. The strange ghost watched and waited, so Mother and I did, too. At last Beth's puffy eyes closed. Her body relaxed. More time passed.

I had never watched a person sleep before, and it made me feel strange, as though I were invading Beth's privacy. I treasured privacy. It was something I had had even less of than I knew. I discovered only a week before my death that Mother had been going through my drawers, sifting my trash, searching out my diary and reading it while I was away at college during the day working toward my teaching certificate so I could get a job and move out.

Every detail of every date that I thought I was confiding only to my future self, Mother stole.

But then, I was watching her trash and searching her drawers, too.

Beth's eyes moved beneath her eyelids.

The strange ghost floated above her, a frozen patch of white smoke.

A thin ribbon of color twisted up out of Beth's forehead, danced in the still night air. The other ghost flickered forward and touched it. He vanished!

Was that all it took to truly die? I wondered. Grasp a colored ribbon and be gone? I flew to the ribbon and touched it, and then I found myself in a graveyard full of tombstones taller than people, and ominous angels under a dark and cloud-haunted sky. For a moment fear froze me. Then I thought: what can happen to me? I'm already dead. I went to sit on a tombstone, but, like the ribbon, it sucked me in; I became it. I could read it because I could feel the letters from the inside. "Here Lies Doris Chandler," it said, "1923–1944. Leave Her to Heaven."

My own gravestone! I'd never seen it. This was what it said?

"Hello," whispered the tombstone to my right.

"Huh?" I said. My first unscripted word since I died.

"Not so loud. Don't let her notice you."

Somehow I could see. I saw a little girl in a pale

nightdress and a huge blue hair bow wandering among the stones, wailing.

"What is this?" I whispered.

"This is a dream," whispered the other tombstone. "Here we can talk, if we're kinda quiet about it. Now that you've chosen a form, you gotta stay in it till the dream ends, and do the dreamer's bidding. But when she looks away, we can talk."

A white wisp appeared above us: Mother. She flurried, confused, and then went to sit on a nearby tombstone, which swallowed her.

Howard, the ghost of the man who had built our house, taught us a lot in that first dream while baby Beth wandered weeping between gravestones, trapped in her own terrors.

He taught us more by vanishing for good in a later dream.

Somehow ghosts walk in dreams. Somehow they can move through dreams into something beyond, and leave the houses they haunt.

Mother and I entered every dream we could.

Ryan's dream the next night began in our house's kitchen again. Mother and I hovered, watching the table and the stove and the cabinets and the sink form from drifting dream stuff. I wondered if Mother and I could be plates and bowls inside a cabinet, something Ryan wouldn't even think about, and thus converse; but when I peeked through a glass-paned cabinet door, there was nothing inside the cabinet to be.

Mother glanced here and there. She wrote a question mark in the air. In our own forms, we couldn't make verbal sounds without falling into our pattern, but we could gesture. I understood Mother's question: where were the players in this dream?

Not that furniture couldn't be a player. Some of the dreams we'd been in, especially the dreams of Mr. Spencer, who lived here with his three daughters before Euphemia Wilson moved in, had featured wild furniture, angry, barking, sometimes shrieking furniture. In some of Mr. Spencer's dreams, furniture shot drawers at people, or stuck out legs to trip or batter them. Everything in Mr. Spencer's world seemed inclined to attack him through his dreams. While the Spencers lived in our house, Mother and I spent most of our dream life in the daughters' dreams.

Furniture in Ryan's dreams rarely moved.

I had questions of my own. Was this going to be a working-out dream or a wish dream? Bunny-girls on the beach last night, that was a wish dream. The argument in the kitchen the night before had been a working-out dream, where Ryan's mind wrestled with some waking life problem and tried to resolve it. Most of Ryan's dreams fell into those two categories; he didn't have many drift-alongs or deep art dreams, and none of the empathic or clairvoyant dreams that came from an outside source.

I pointed to the dishwasher, wondered if Mother would like to embed there. It had kept her safe last time we were here.

She shook her head.

A dark-haired, older woman walked into the kitchen. Lines bracketed her mouth, and her eyebrows pinched together into a frown above her nose. One white streak of hair rose from her forehead to thread through her waved coiffure. She wore an ugly lime-green polyester pantsuit.

Mother and I mimed question marks again. Neither of us had seen this woman in Ryan's dreams before. Both of us shrugged.

A skinny girl in a skimpy silver skirt and a black leather jacket jangling with chains marched into the kitchen. She had magenta-dyed short hair and wore lots of makeup, and she stood with her arms crossed over her chest, staring with angry eyes at the woman.

I glanced around. Where was Ryan? Unlike some people, he was almost always present in his dreams as some form of himself.

"Doris," said Mother, "where have you been?"

No. Not here! Not in a dream, where we could be free of our pattern! What was Mother thinking?

I waited for the pattern to pull me in.

"That's none of your business, Mother," said my voice.

I whirled and saw that the leather-and-miniskirt girl was speaking my lines.

"You better believe it's my business," said the dark-haired woman in Mother's exact voice. "You live under my roof. . . . "

I glanced at Mother's ghost self. She looked at me. We both dived for a cabinet at the same time, and then—

I felt it. Her fear, her frustration. How she had been trying so hard to hold our lives together after the government told her that her beloved Seth was dead, how she loved me with all her heart, even when I defied her. She felt helpless in the face of my defiance: where was

I going? How could she stop me? How could she save me? Couldn't I see that I was heading for disaster?

How could she love me as much as she did and still hate me?

How could she release me when I was running toward a cliff?

Flesh of her flesh, bone of her bone, body of her body. Life, gift of all gifts, she had given me. When would I ever be worthy of such a gift?

(And somewhere in the background, a voice said these same things to her when she was young, and to her mother when she was young, a thousand thousand off-center echoes speaking down the generations, a thousand thousand rebellions.)

"Oh, Doris," Mother whispered through my thoughts. "You're like a little trapped bird. I'm like a huge awful cat! I never knew."

Above us, our last argument raged, in our voices. Here inside the cabinet, we huddled together and felt all sorts of things we had never known before.

"When are you both going to shut up?" Ryan asked from somewhere outside us.

The cabinet didn't have anything we could use for eyes, but we could hear.

"Who are you?" asked my voice.

"I live here now, and I'm tired of you guys always yelling. Would you for chrissakes get over it?"

A working-out dream, I thought. Ryan's mind wrestling with the problem of . . . us.

"Young man, watch your language," said Mother's voice.

"Watch my language? How can I see language? Language is something you hear," said Ryan.

"Don't try to distract me with stupid word tricks," Mother's voice said, only there was a sharp, unfamiliar tone to it. "That's all you men ever do, twist me around with words, words, words. You *know* what I mean." With each syllable it spoke, the voice shifted away from Mother's tones. "You better know what I mean, because you know what I'll do to you if you don't do what I say." The slap of supple leather against the palm of a hand.

"Hey," said Ryan, "this wasn't—hey, Mama—"

"Did I hear you telling me to shut up, Ryan?" said this stranger's voice, slicing bright. "Did you speak to your mama in that tone? Did you tell me you're tired of listening to me?"

"No, Mama," Ryan whispered.

"I swear I heard those words come out of your mouth, boy. Are you calling me a liar?"

"No, Mama."

"Is that how I sound to you?" Mother whispered to me.

"No," I whispered. Ryan's mother was worse than mine, and I'd killed mine. Killed her. Why hadn't I just run away? Sure, Mother was hard to live with, but she'd had the same experience with her mother, and she hadn't killed *her*. Ryan had had hard times with his mother, and—well, we didn't actually know how that had ended. . . . "Mother? I'm sorry about the ashtray."

"You should be," she told me.

"I didn't mean to hit you." I didn't even remember aiming. I just was so full of feelings I had had to throw something.

For a minute Mother didn't say anything. We listened to the strange woman say more terrible things to Ryan. "I know you didn't, honey," Mother said to me at last. "I didn't realize how upset you were." She paused, then said, "I forgive you."

I felt strange and light-headed, wobbly and loose. For the first time in a dream I pulled up out of something I was embedded in. "Oh. Oh! Mother?"

"Doris!" the cabinet called as I rose toward the ceiling of the dream kitchen.

"Mother! Come on!"

I was floating up out of the dream. Ryan, below me, looked like a terrified six-year-old boy, and the polyester pantsuit woman had grown into a fire-spitting demon with six-inch-long claws polished bright red. Both of them stared up at me. "Ryan! Mother!"

At me. Not a white cloud with black pits. I could see my own body again, a trifle stout, but pleasant, in my favorite dress.

"Doris?" said Ryan. His voice was high and small.

I had no anchors anymore. I was ready to let go of the house and Mother and everything that held me here, and move on. To where? Heaven? Hell? Some other place? Wherever it was, it tugged at me. I felt so light, as if I didn't care about anything. Silver sparks fizzed around my edges.

I reached back down into the cabinet. "Mother," I said, my voice already fading. I found her hand. I pulled.

She came up out of the cabinet. She looked younger than I had ever seen her, and sparks flew from her, too, golden ones.

"You look at me when I'm talking to you, young man," Ryan's mama said. "Don't you look away. Don't you dare blink!"

"Ryan," said Mother, "It's all right. You can grow up now."

Or did she say, "You can wake up now"?

I only remember that he smiled at us. I loved him utterly in the moment I lost him.

That was the last thing I needed.

DREAM A LITTLE DREAM
FOR ME …
by Peter Crowther

Peter Crowther is the editor or co-editor of twelve anthologies and the co-author (with James Lovegrove) of the novel
Escardy Gap. Since the early 1990s, he has sold some
eighty short stories and poems to a wide variety of maga-
zines and anthologies on both sides of the Atlantic, and two
collections of his work, *Lonesome Roads* and *The Longest
Single Note*, were published in 1999. His review columns
and critical essays on the fields of fantasy, horror, and science fiction appear regularly in *Interzone* and the *Hellnotes*
Internet magazine. He lives in Harrogate, England, with his
wife and two sons.

> We are such stuff
> As dreams are made on; and our little life
> Is rounded with a sleep.
> —William Shakespeare, *The Tempest*

> Behold, this dreamer cometh.
> —*The Book of Genesis, 37:19*

Everybody has a dream; everybody dreams.
The man who told me that—the same man who
spent his time showing an old dog-eared piece of card
around in Vinzenz Richter's Wine Tavern, in the long
shadow of Meissen's Albrecht Castle—was a long way
from home … always assuming, of course, that the
dead have someplace to hang their hat at the end of a

busy working day. And something to do when they get there.

When I was in full time employment, for a big financial organization, all I ever wanted to do when *I* got home from work was write.

Every evening I would finish dinner as fast as I could reasonably chew it, and then hightail it into my small booklined office and boot up the trusty computer. Seems I had more energy for writing then, though that seems ridiculous when all I have to do now is write.

Back then, when I was in and out of meetings filled with corporate types who felt they needed permission to break wind, I made silent (and sometimes not so silent) promises to whatever deities ruled the world that if I could ever get out of the mindless slog of listening to minutes being read out day in, day out, and into a silent world of my own thoughts and words I would never ever complain again. And, when it happened, I didn't. I was true to my word. For a while. Well, why not? After all, I had nurtured a dream—as the woman by the statue of the pissing boy in Hamburg had known . . . among many things, as it turned out—and my dream had become a reality.

But it was the dead man with the old card that was to enable me to recognize that my dream was not the only one. Nor was it the most important.

But first things first.

My first novel, a minor espionage epic set in Britain, Holland, and the United States and over which I had pondered and sweated and agonized for almost three years, sold to the third publisher who read it. And it sold well, made a second printing in hardcover and a couple of nice book club sales and then went into a paperback edition which hovered around the lower edges of the bestsellers listing for almost two months. The all-important second book was eagerly awaited. Mostly by my publisher.

"So how's the book coming along?" James Farraday asked me a couple of weeks before events were set in motion to change my life forever. He posed the question as nonchalantly as the mouthful of tossed salad would allow.

We were in a small restaurant off Columbus Circle, sitting in the smoking section—there's not many of those around these days—and I was pulling on a Salem Light and pushing olives around on my plate like toy soldiers on a military campaign map. He waited a few seconds, washing most of the salad from his teeth with a mouthful of Shiraz, before grunting, "Well?"

The truth was, the book hadn't been coming along too well at all. In fact, the book wasn't actually started as such. After four months, since the day I had proudly announced in Farraday's office that I would be starting that very afternoon, typing in those mystical and terrifying words *Chapter One*, I still had nothing. Worse still, since the advent of computers and word processors, I couldn't even take him back to my apartment and show off a full wastepaper basket brimming with scrunched-up starts. With the exception of a loose-leaf notebook containing a few pages of scribbled notes, I had zilch. Nada.

"Well," I started, pacing the lie so that it tumbled out easy and sounded more like the Artist's reluctance to say too much about his next project until the final period was typed in and pored over a while, "it's coming along.

It's coming along a little slower than I'd like but, you know, it's coming along."

James nodded and splashed more wine into our glasses. "Yeah?"

"Yeah."

We were as close as most authors and their editor could reasonably hope to be, and closer than many. We had shared other bottles of wine and other meal-table chats, some even when there was no real need for him to be there. But I think he saw something in me that struck a chord. Just as I think there were few people he could call real friends. His real friends, I believe, were the books he worked on.

"But it is coming along," he said, returning to the promised novel.

I nodded. "But like I say, slow."

"Mmm." He forked a piece of pasta into a mound of lettuce and transferred it to his waiting mouth. "Is it started?"

His expression told me that he knew the answer already but I decided to persevere. "Let's just say it's not going as well as I'd hoped."

For a long minute, he said nothing. Then, "You know," he said, chewing, "maybe you need to take a break. You thought about doing that? Taking a break?"

I stubbed out my cigarette and thought about lighting another, but it was difficult enough making him out through the haze I had already created. I pushed the ashtray away from me and thanked whatever god looked after diners that most good restaurants train their staff to empty ashtrays after each butt. Sure enough, a young man with a smile that looked like it had come from a catalog appeared as if by magic and replaced the offending item with a clean version.

Before I could say anything, James leaned forward and, with a sly wink, said, "You could put it down as research." He straightened up again and forked the last of the salad onto the final few strands of linguini. "Think about it. Somewhere you've always wanted to go. Shoehorn it into the book someplace and write it off." He laid his fork on the cleared plate and snapped his fingers. "Just like that. Say four weeks. Six maybe. Then we can see how things are coming along when you get back." He lifted his glass, swirling the wine around as he studied me. "Can you think of anywhere?"

I could.

The air in Europe smells of confectionery, my father had told me. *Even in the bars where it mixes in with the smell of alcohol, cologne, perfume, and the pungent aroma of French and German tobacco, you can smell candy. Makes you feel like a kid all over again.*

He had been right, as I was to find out. But my first week had failed to ignite the same enthusiasm in me as it had in him and already I was showing signs of being homesick.

At night, in the sumptuous hotel rooms, you could look out of the open window and have to strain to hear anything. No planes flying overhead, no stilted rap music from passing cars, and not even the distant wail of police sirens prowling the concrete corridors of Manhattan looking for transgressors. Or the perfect cup of coffee.

The fact was, the coffee tasted too bitter and there probably weren't any transgressors here. And believe me, when a New Yorker starts to get misty-eyed about the prospect of not being mugged, then you know something's wrong. I'd known it pretty well since the second day. But it hadn't really hit home until a chance meeting with a middle-aged but very attractive woman with a hauntingly soothing purple hair coloring.

It was my eighth day in Europe.

We happened to be standing next to each other in Neugartenstrasse, an otherwise empty street, staring at a cherubic statue of a naked young boy. In fact, I had been so engrossed in the statue that I had not even seen the woman approaching: one minute I had considered myself alone and the next she was there.

The boy had his hands held aloft behind his head and his pelvis thrust forward, an abundant and constant stream of water fountaining from his little delicately sculptured penis and rattling noisily into the small lake around his feet. Presumably the water was circulated by means of a system of tubes and pumps, though no evidence was visible. I didn't know and was beginning to care even less. This lack of interest had undoubtedly been heightened—if not caused entirely—by the fact that, somewhat foolishly, I had bought a German–French phrasebook and so was having a hard time making sense of anything. But the pictures were vaguely interesting.

The woman glanced up the street and produced from her coat pocket a small tin cup which she then held beneath the stream until it filled. Turning to me, the cup already lifted to her lips, she said, *"On ne sait jamais, paraît qu'en buvant de cette eau, on trouve un bon mari."* Then, with a throaty laugh, she drained the cup and turned to me, smiling proudly. "Ah," she said, dabbing at her lips with a gloved hand, *"c'est magnifique, non?"*

I frowned, smiled, and shook my head. "I'm sorry, I don't understand." The words came out as a rattling stammer, and I made a mental note to spend some time studying foreign languages before I next ventured behind Europe's lace underskirts.

"You are not French, *monsieur?*" She looked shocked.

I shook my head. "American. New York," I added, as though the first admission were not a sufficiently heinous crime.

She frowned and pointed to the guide book in my hand. "Then why do you have a French translation book?"

I waved the book and gave a small laugh, feeling my ears turning bright red. "Ah, yes," I began. "A. Mistake. I. Bought. It. In. Error," I explained, separating the words as though teaching rudimentary English to a visiting Martian . . . one of those saucer-eyed, spindly-legged figures that habitually stop cars on Nevada highways in order to engage in a little anal exploration with passing hayseeds driving pickups, called Duane or Clyde—the hayseeds, not the pickups. "What was it that you were saying?"

"I said, legend has it that by drinking this water one will find a good husband."

"Ah." Her English was perfect which meant that any further utterances from me could be effected in a fraction of the time I might otherwise have taken. But no further utterances seemed to be forthcoming.

"You are here on holiday, yes?"

"Vacation, yes." I waved a hand at the urinating statue. "Seeing the sights."

She frowned again and smiled a little slyly as she returned the tin cup to her ample coat pocket. "But you are looking for something, yes? You are not simply on holiday."

I shrugged and shook my head. "No . . . I mean, yes. I'm just taking a break."

She took hold of my arm at the elbow and leaned close. I could smell peppermint and perfume, a heady and intoxicating mixture, and, just for a second, I felt my pulse quicken. "I know," she confided, confirming this revelation with a series of sharp nods. "You are looking for something. You are chasing a dream.

"We are all chasing dreams, Mons— I am sorry, Sir. But it is only when one learns not to look that one can truly find. When you have mastered that, perhaps you will have success. You must go to Meissen."

"Meissen?" It sounded like something Dick Dastardly's dog, Muttley, might have said, his teeth clamped on some unfortunate's pant seat.

She lifted her shoulders and made a sad shape with her mouth. "Perhaps, perhaps not," she said, answering some unspoken question as she looked me up and down. "But most everyone finds what they are looking for in Meissen. There is a magic there that . . . oh, I don't know." She laughed. Then I laughed.

We could have been sitting in a bar off Fifth Avenue, drinking margaritas and discussing a new Neil Simon play. But we weren't, and suddenly that fact hit me: I was a long way from home.

Her face became serious. "You must find the dream," she said. "But take care, for there are those who would take it from you." The light in her eyes gave them a momentarily fearful glint, and then it was gone.

I smiled respectfully and considered several responses, none of which seemed appropriate. Instead, I decided to stonewall it out and wait for her to say something else.

She removed her hand from my elbow and patted the bulge in her pocket. "Ah, well, perhaps you will wish me luck in finding my own dream, eh? And I wish you luck with yours, whatever and wherever you eventually find it to be." Then she was on her way, her high-heeled shoes clacking on the paving slabs, sashaying up the street like a would-be movie star. But in truth, she was already fading and still looking for her leading man.

I left the phrase book beside the statue. Maybe it would turn out to be somebody else's dream.

That night I tried to figure out just what my own dream was.

By three o'clock in the morning, an empty bottle of hoc and a full ashtray on the table beside me, I had decided, in that wonderfully light-headed and euphoric way that comes only after too much alcohol, that the woman had probably been right. I had to go to Meissen. Why not?

I'd done the galleries and sidewalk cafes of Paris and Brussels, and now Hamburg, until I was cultured out, and I'd seen and marveled at enough gargoyle-festooned architecture to make even Frank Lloyd Wright yawn and ask what was on at the movies. My mind was made up and it felt good. A decision had been made. I pulled off my trousers and stretched out on the bed.

Sleep came immediately.

Beneath its sheet of oblivion my father came into my

hotel room and sat beside me. It was a very clear dream . . . so clear that I saw the light shining briefly into the room from the corridor outside. Then the darkness returned and I saw only my father's shape until he reached the bed. Then, in the glow of the moon through the windows, I saw him in his entirety.

He was wearing an army uniform and though he was much younger than when I had last seen him—lying in a hospital bed surrounded by drips and blinking machines that were busy stealing him from me—I recognized him right away.

When you see this, he whispered to me, *you must look at it*.

I could see something in his hand but couldn't make out what it was. But whatever it was, it wasn't very big. *What is it?* I asked.

A dream, he said. *It's only a dream. But it is not yours alone. It belongs to everyone. And you must show it to them.*

If he said anything more, I don't remember it.

Feeling groggy, even after breakfast and several cups of black coffee plus half a pack of Salems, I caught a train later than I had planned, packing my suitcase in a haphazard fashion that I was sure I would regret when it came time to remove the clothes so casually thrown inside. Then, with the memory of my late father's nocturnal visit still as fresh in my mind as though it had really happened, I arrived in Dresden where I boarded the *Theodor Fontaine*, one of only two cruisers built to negotiate Germany's second-longest river, and set off along the Elbe to Meissen.

It was like sailing into a children's storybook.

My guidebook—this time an English language edition—told me that the city of Meissen had escaped the Second World War with barely a cup and saucer being rattled. It showed.

On either side of the river, wildflowers grew in such abundance that it was hard to imagine humans living there at all. Ubiquitous herons and buzzards and kites seemed to support such a conclusion and the occasional Hansel-and-Gretel riverside houses, and the barely glimpsed spired churches and turreted castles nestled as though forgotten deep in the lush woodland, heightened the feeling of being deliciously trapped inside a fairy tale. I sat transfixed watching it all float by, daring myself time after time to jump ship. Like the man in the old *Twilight Zone* episode, I felt I had found my very own Willoughby—a magical domain that waited for anyone brave enough to relinquish all that had gone before and take a chance on finding true happiness.

We stepped off the boat and into this fairyland grotto speaking in the hushed and reverent tones of acolytes seeking an audience with their god. And well might it have been so.

If God had decided to spend his time making pottery instead of people, he would first have had to create somewhere like Meissen. The city is home to the oldest china factory in Europe, where some six hundred artists are employed to hand paint each item. But with price tags that range from $100 for a thimble to around $8,000 for a six-piece floral coffee set, it's a hobby that's affordable to only a few. Gods included.

Following a brief check-in at my guest house and the welcome putting down of my bags, I washed and hit the streets. There was a stillness and calm about the place, drifting up the narrow house-lined streets and down cobbled alleyways in which the very air itself seemed to have lain undisturbed since the dawn of time. Fragmented footsteps echoed desultorily, hunched rooftop gargoyles stared with wide and unmoving eyes, beveled storefront windows reflected our passing images like funhouse mirrors, making the resulting elongations and distortions somehow more in keeping. And so it was, road-weary but mentally alive and even strangely rested with the onset of twilight, I came across the welcome glow and muted hum that characterizes a bar in any country in the world.

Vinzenz Richter established his notorious wine tavern on Am der Frauenkirche in 1873, notorious because of the array of weapons and instruments of torture housed in its cellar . . . the function of every item explained in gory detail (though thankfully not demonstrated) nightly by the current owner, one Gottfried Herrlich.

It was here, drinking my third stein of Muller Thurgau, that I saw Dennis Dannerman.

The last time I had seen Dennis was maybe five years earlier, in Salsa Posada, a small Mexican eatery on Thompson Street, right across from El Rincon de Espana—what a delight: the best Mexican or Spanish food in town and right across from each other.

Dennis tended bar at Salsa's, seeing to folks while they waited for a table, feeding them Gold and Silver Label tequila, copious amounts of Dos Equus or Tecate beers, and mixing cocktails for the folks who like to go to Mexican restaurants to drink them (and who, presumably, like to go to cocktail bars to listen to Los Lobos on the PA system). And all the time, he could carry on a conversation—a real conversation, not one of those cheesy streams of polite but vacuous niceties you get from some bartenders—and he'd laugh and take drink orders for the tables already eating and not miss a single beat or get a single order wrong. And best of all, he didn't throw the bottles around, though I always believed he could have done if he'd wanted to because I believed he was a special person, one of those people you come across maybe only two or three times in a lifetime.

But there were two more things that made Dennis special, at least as far as I was concerned: the first was that, like me, he loved jazz music, particularly anything by Horace Silver or Chet Baker; and the second was that we both shared the same birthdate—the Fourth of July. I didn't find the second one out until, when I had been going into Salsa Posada for several years, Nick Hassam and I had called in there just for a few slammers to celebrate my birthday—the fortieth—before continuing around a few well-chosen dives in the Village to get completely blitzed. When I asked where Dennis was, the girl behind the bar explained that he'd taken the night off to celebrate his own special event, the Big Three-Oh. I couldn't wait to call in again when he was on duty, just to compare notes . . . in that strangely metaphysical way that many Cancerians seem to do. But I never did get the chance.

It was maybe a month later, six weeks at the most, that I finally got back to Salsa Posada, again with Nick. Still no Dennis. This time, when I asked about him, the girl behind the counter gave me a strange smile and sidled off to the woman by the payments desk. A brief hushed conversation resulted in the woman coming up to me and telling me, in a tone of muted respect, that Dennis was dead. He'd piled his Corvette into a road sign on the Brooklyn-Queens Expressway on his birthday.

And now here he was shuffling around a tavern in Meissen, Germany.

At first, I figured it must be Dennis' double.

But, as I watched him going up to different people— not everyone, just one or two, seemingly picked out after careful consideration—and showing them something, talking to them quietly, holding onto their coat sleeves, I decided that, no matter what we're taught about dead people being considerably immobile—not to mention silent—this one was the exception.

There was no question that it was Dennis so, obviously, the announcement of his death was somewhat exaggerated. Clearly, a mistake must have been made. Maybe he'd lent his car to someone and they'd totaled it, destroying any evidence to the contrary in the resulting conflagration. Maybe it suited him to be dead. After all, here he was several thousand miles away from New York apparently immersed in another life. Lots of maybes. But I decided to bite the bullet and speak to him.

When he finished talking to an elderly couple over by the bar, the man nodded and placed his drink on the counter. Then the man took his wife's drink—I assumed the woman was his wife—and, even though neither glass was empty, the two of them just turned around and walked out. I recorded all this at the time, but it didn't seem particularly significant. At least, not then.

I picked up my own glass and wandered across to Dennis, approaching him from his right side as he surveyed the other people. He was just standing there, not doing anything, no drink, nothing. Just as I was reaching out, I saw that he was holding a piece of old card in his right hand. Then I made contact.

He didn't turn to me but simply glanced in my direction and then his eyes faced front again.

"Er fragt, wo man am besten isst," he said without looking around. He laughed and shook his head. *"Und was kann ich fur* Sie *tun?"*

"Dennis?"

Still he didn't turn, but when he spoke his voice was almost a whisper. "Is it *really* you?"

I moved around so that I was facing him. "That's what I thought about *you.* How are you?"

He stepped back a little so that he could get a good look at me, which also enabled me to get a good look at *him.* "I'm fine. How about you? How's New York?"

"Same as ever. It's just New York."

"New York is never only 'just' *any*thing."

"No, I guess you're right there."

He nodded, gave a small smile and started to look some more at the people around us.

"They told me you were dead," I said. His expression didn't alter, and he continued to scan the room. "The woman in Salsa Posada."

"Cheryl."

"Cheryl," I echoed. "She said you'd crashed the car."

Still nothing. I followed his gaze and scanned the faces. They were just people having a good time, drinking the beer, talking, making out. Pretty much like any bar I'd ever been to. Without turning, I said, "You waiting for someone?"

"Kind of," he said.

I turned back to face him. "Do you live here now?"

His eyes shifted back to look at me. "Look," he said, "I'm really busy right now. Can we do this some other time?"

I shook my head in a mixture of annoyance and amazement. "I don't get it. They tell me you're dead and then I find you in a bar in . . . "

"Meissen," he offered.

"In Meissen, and you won't even pass the time of day." I pulled out my pack of Salems and lit one. "I had something to tell you that I thought you mi—"

"We both have the same birthdate. Fourth of July."

"How did you know that?"

"I know everything." He waited a minute or so and then went on. "I knew you were here, for example . . . here in Germany."

"How?"

He sighed. "Siglinde Erhard told me." Then he said, "And I knew she had told you to come to Meissen."

Siglinde Erhard had wanted a man to care for and to care for her more than anything else in the world. This was what Dennis Dannerman told me as we walked along the bank of the River Elbe, the moonlight playing amidst the ripples in the water.

Although she had been forsaken—Dennis's word—by many men in her life, she had never lost the hope that she might find someone worthy of her affections. But eventually every abstinence, whether forced or voluntary, must have a respite, and without that respite things just go from bad to worse. So it was, on an evening when she was feeling particularly desperate, Siglinde Erhard hanged herself in her apartment with a pair of her own nylon stockings. She thought it would be a release. But she was wrong.

The bitterness and resentment and desperation that had so fueled her life continued to run thick and strong even when she was dead. And so she still walked the streets of her beloved Hamburg, looking for someone in whom she recognized a basic goodness. One of her favorite visiting spots when she was alive was the statue of the pissing boy in Neugartenstrasse. The statue still held an attraction for her in death, perhaps even more so.

"Jesus Christ," I said, "isn't there *any*one here who's alive?"

"The percentages are the same wherever you are, whatever country you're in," Dennis said. "It's just—" He seemed to search for the appropriate words. "It's just that we usually don't get sent back to the place we left. Too many people might recognize us."

Over on the opposite bank, a heron flapped its wings wildly.

If Dennis Dannerman thought this was supposed to explain things to me, he was wrong. But he would not give any further explanations. "Don't ask me to say any more," he said.

We walked in silence for a while, and then Dennis said, "Siglinde is not like me. She's just a ghost."

"And what are you? Can you tell me that, at least?"

He shrugged. "How about an angel?"

"An *angel?*"

"It's as good a description as anything. I know I don't

have any wings, but they went out with the Ark. I'm just—" He paused, again searching for some meaningful word or phrase. "I'm just doing a job. That's what Heaven should be all about, doing jobs. A big company, run like any other big company." There was something in the way he spoke that made me feel a little uneasy. Or maybe it was just that *I* had worked for a big company, and I didn't like it. Office politics, backstabbing, lying and cheating . . . surely the Elysian Fields were above all that.

"And what job are you doing?"

"What angels have always done: teaching people how to live for others and not be selfish." He seemed to consider this for a few seconds and then added, "But it's not always a popular occupation."

As we kept walking, I tried to reconcile such altruism with the grubby self-serving reality of Big Business. I failed miserably. The two concepts seemed mutually contradictory.

Perhaps sensing my confusion, Dennis stopped and turned to me. Producing from his jacket pocket the piece of card I had seen him showing in the tavern, he held it out to me. "Take a look, tell me what you see." I frowned and took an involuntary step backward. "Go ahead," he said, thrusting the card toward me. "But you may not keep it."

I took the card and turned it over.

It was either some kind of out-of-focus photograph or a painting, dog-eared and stained with use, the image creased and faded. "What is it?"

"What it is isn't important. It's what you can see . . . that's the important thing."

I shifted around so that the moon's glow was directly behind me. "It looks like . . . it looks like some kind of blur." That was the best way I could describe it. The card was a haze of swirling shapes and shades and tones . . . maybe in color, although I had no way of knowing that in the moonlight. In fact, maybe it was the moonlight that made the thing seem to move on the card, like billowing dry ice smoke or graveyard mist . . . and was it my own shadow cast on the card or was there something behind the mist? Something big and . . . old, though I wondered what it was that made me think that; something which seemed as eager to see me as I was to see it. "I don't know," I said, handing the card back. "I have no idea what I can see."

Dennis took the card and slipped it back into his pocket. "It'll come to you, but when it does, you must look with your heart, not with your eyes."

"And how do I do that?"

He smiled. "Like I say, it'll come to you."

I started walking, suddenly aware that the night had turned cold. Pulling my coat tightly around me and speaking over my shoulder, I asked Dennis what he had meant when he said that what it was wasn't important.

But it was my father's voice that answered. *A dream*, it whispered. *It's only a dream.*

When I turned around, the path was empty. Dennis Dannerman had gone.

I walked around for half an hour or so looking for him, smoking cigarettes and wondering, each time I passed someone, whether they were truly alive or simply shadows of themselves.

I considered returning to the tavern but decided I had had enough of crowds for one day, and so I went back to my hotel.

In truth, it was more a guest-house: cozy, pleasant, and warm, a spice-smelling reassuring bolt-hole of sheets, frilly tablecovers, and flocked wallpaper, and, in Frau Maier, a bustling, somewhat burly woman who smelled of mothballs and had a habit of making tiny humming sounds when she was listening to me. Her English was every bit as perfect as anyone else's, and this further emphasized my need to learn at least the basic fundamentals before making such a trip again.

She welcomed me in personally, as though I were a long-lost relative returning from some fabled war fought on horseback and with oversized cutlery. Her hands clasped at her stomach, her back ramrod-straight, and her smile tight but genuine, she asked if I would like any refreshment before retiring to bed—so much more eloquent and image-conjuring than simply "hitting the sack." But I declined. Already the beer I had consumed was making me feel a little woozy . . . but maybe the conversation I had had with Dennis Dannerman on the banks of the river had contributed to that. I bade her good night and went up to my room. Within minutes, I was tucked up in bed. Sleep seemed to come almost immediately.

Colors were everywhere, swirling around me, so deep and dense they were taking my breath away. The shapes billowed and withdrew, wafting suddenly one way and then the other, and all the time there were other shapes—real shapes, shapes of people—just behind the haze, standing there watching me.

When I opened my eyes again, the room was dark. But not so dark that I couldn't make out the shape sitting in the chair by the window. I knew right away who it was.

I wanted to ask how he had got into my room but such questions seemed a little redundant when asked of an angel. And anyway, maybe I was still asleep. I reached for the pack of cigarettes. "Forget something, Dennis?"

He sighed. "We've stopped dreaming for others," he said. "All I wanted to do was put things right . . . or, at least, make them a little better."

"Dennis," I said, blowing smoke and hiking myself up in bed, "you're going to have to bear with me a little here. What do you mean about our stopping dreaming for others?"

He got to his feet and walked across to the window. "It's a cyclical thing, Charles," he said. "Most of the time, people care for each other pretty well, but things tend to get run down." I could see his head turn around to look at me, but I couldn't see his face. "And it starts when they're asleep.

"People don't know it's happening most of the time," he said, "they're just reacting to the way things are around them. Times get tough, and the people get tougher. It's a fact of life. They dream for themselves . . . they dream of success and wealth . . . about winning the lottery or being promoted; they dream of nice clothes and great vacations; about making out with people they've always wanted to make out with. They stop dreaming about the other poor schmuck who's maybe got even less than they have because they want it for themselves . . . and they want it all. Then, when the dreaming gets selfish enough, they stop even *thinking* about other folks." He looked back out of the window. "And that's where things are right about now. The collective dreaming for others stopped a long, long time ago. Collective thinking will follow soon."

I didn't say anything for a moment. "If you think that explains things, then you've been away too long," I said at last.

"I'm not through," he said.

He walked back to the chair, and I switched on the lamp by the side of the bed. The dim light gave the room a slightly surreal tone, as though everything that could be trusted was here within the parameter of its glow . . . and everything beyond it was hard and cold and dangerous. I shivered involuntarily, even though I was still fully clothed, and hoisted the sheet up to my chin.

He settled deeper into the chair. "Got a cigarette?"

"But you're an angel."

"So?"

I tossed the pack across and followed it with the matchbook.

Dennis lit up and blew out smoke, sighing dreamily. "Good," he said. "Okay, let's say I've been a little economical with the truth. I'll take it from the top. Two things: first, the Dream."

He waved a hand. "Oh, I'm going back hundreds—thousands—of years. Back to the beginning, almost. In the beginning, there wasn't The Word . . . or even *a* word. There was only a dream, a dream for mankind. It was God's dream. He felt that men should bond amongst themselves, look after and out for each other. But what works in theory doesn't always work in practice. Where individuality exists—and individuality is the essence of existence—there will always be strife, struggle, and envy.

"Of course," he went on, "there was no way he could

give a collective intelligence to men—that stuff only works in science fiction and not always even then—because there were too many distractions. But only too many distractions while they were fully aware of them."

"I don't follow."

"He figured that if he could stop those distractions, just for a while, he could get them to bond . . . become almost a sentient multi-multi-headed creature. And so he hit on an idea—two ideas, actually. The first was to remove the diversions and the distractions, and the second was to place something—one thing—in their stead.

"And so," Dennis Dannerman said as he stubbed out his cigarette, "God invented sleep, and he created something to fill that void of existence . . . a dream of togetherness to bond people together."

"Jesus Christ, Dennis, what are you telling me here? I feel like Spencer Tracy in *Inherit the Wind*. What happened to Darwin in all this?"

"Oh, evolution happened just the way that Darwin said it did. But God gave us sleep, and the ability to dream. What we've lost over the millennia, is *The* Dream . . . the one that God gave us to bond us all together."

Dennis explained that God had overstretched the dream idea. What had worked when the entire world population was but a few hundred thousand didn't work so well when it numbered into the billions. There were now too many people for the collective dream to be effective.

"So God decided that the original concept of the

dream had to be recorded somewhere as a physical entity, and that it must then be shown to people, unlocking the seed and the ability he had planted in the first of mankind at the beginning, and which had been passed down—'genetically,' if you will . . . albeit in an increasingly diluted fashion—as a kind of race memory. After a lot of work, he finally did it. In other words, he managed to give substance to the insubstantial."

Dennis produced the piece of card from out of his pocket and held it up. "And here it is."

I stared at the card and made my single biggest mistake of the evening: I said . . .

"You said there were two things. What's the second?"

He looked at me, smiled tiredly and said, "The second thing I wanted to tell you about is that the Devil wants the Dream."

I was probably expected to say something there, but I couldn't bring myself to do it.

Dennis Dannerman stood up and walked across to the window, leaning on the sill like a man who had run a marathon. "When Lucifer was expelled from . . . from the other side, he took something with him. Just one thing."

"Why do I think I know what that was?"

"Right. He took the Dream. And he's kept it all these thousands of years. Kept it 'down below' to use the theatrical term for Hell." Dennis turned around.

I was frowning. "But you've— So how did you get hold of the Dream?"

"It's like nothing you could imagine, Charles," he said. "Down there. Nothing in your wildest nightmare can prepare you for that place. Just . . . just a void, an empty space filled with crags and rocks and tunnels, hot . . . hotter than—and I know I'm repeating myself—hotter than you could think hot could be. No sky, no ground, just rock everywhere, dark tunnels which glow with some kind of half-light, and all we do is crawl through them, minute after minute, hour after hour, day after day, looking for a way out."

"*You* crawled through them? But I thought—"

"That's where I went. When I died. I wanted to keep it from you, but there's no way to do that."

"Why did you want to keep it from me?"

He looked down at his tightly-clenched hands. "Because I was ashamed."

"Is that why you gave me all that other stuff . . . the 'angel' stuff? Because you were ashamed?"

He nodded "Partly."

"And what was the other part?"

"I want you to do something for me, and I didn't think you'd want to do it if you thought I was bad."

"Do what?"

He waved a hand. "When I died, all the things I'd done caught up with me. I won't bore you with the details, but suffice to say the scales were weighted against me. I accepted my lot with some reluctance, but I did accept it. When you hear the list of charges, it's difficult not to be contrite." He shook his head and let out a small laugh, though it was entirely without humor. "Some of those things I didn't even remember. But there was no arguing against them. And anyway, most of them I did remember. So . . .

"The rumor of a way out of Hell has been circulating down there for as long as Hell has existed. As has the rumor of the Great First Dream, the blueprint for humanity's goodness, lost to the gods since the time Lucifer was sent packing. It was held, the stories went, in some inner sanctum looked over by the Devil itself." He waited for that to sink in for a few minutes and then added, "And I found it."

He took a deep breath. "There were three of us, a mercenary from eighth-century Antigua called Paul Theolomides and a heroin dealer from 1960s Madrid— Salvatore something-or-other.

"We came across the small cave separately, dropping into it from three different holes in the wall pretty much at the same time. There's no sleep down there—although you're tired all the time . . . I mean dog-tired, falling down dead tired. And there are no meals, no coffee breaks, even though you're always thirsty and always hungry—thirsty like a man crawling the desert for days, hungry like someone who hasn't eaten for weeks. But not sleeping and not drinking or eating doesn't harm you in any way. You just go on . . . tired and thirsty and hungry.

"Anyway, we dropped into the cavern and there it was, sitting on an outcrop of rock."

"The Dream? That piece of card you carry?"

He nodded. "It was glowing like fairy lights, casting shimmering shadows around the walls, throwing hues of color across the ground like light ripples on a still lake. And the whole cave was hissing, a permanent state of anger and mistrust, and maybe even fear.

"Paul recognized it pretty much straight away. Sal didn't know shit about anything, even though he'd been there years longer than me."

"And where was—" I hesitated: what the hell was I talking about? "Where was the Devil?"

Dennis shrugged. "Taking a dump? Checking the furnaces? Who knows. All I know is that when each of us took this thing in our hands we could feel it, you know? We could feel the power of it, feel the light and the warmth, feel . . . feel the goodness.

"They—Paul and Sal—wanted to use it as a bargaining chip . . . strike up a deal with 'the authorities.' But I wanted to take it away from that hateful cave, wanted to take it away from Hell forever, maybe restore it to its rightful owners. There was a scuffle—we all have bodies there, bodies which cannot be inflicted with pain from each other, but which are in pain every minute of every day . . . bullet-wound pain, back pain, chest pain, headache, gut ache, nausea, pancreatic cancer, gout, hangnails, and tequila hangovers . . . all rolled into one. All the time. God, you wouldn't believe.

"Anyway, there was this scuffle and I got the Dream. I scurried back up one of the tunnels and, though they followed me in, I soon lost them, turning first this way and then that, then another, keeping going all the time, the card jammed into my mouth. Pretty soon I was alone, or as alone as you ever get down there . . . occasionally coming up on some other guy's bare backside swaying to and fro in front until you take a different path.

"Then, without any warning—I have no idea how long I was crawling that way, crawling with the card— there was a light up ahead, and the crawlspace was getting wider." He raised his arms in the air. "And I was out, bare-ass naked, but out. In a cave in Rheinisches Schiefergebirge—the Rhenish Slate Mountains: I didn't know that at the time, of course, only later.

"I made my way down the highlands into Hunsruck,

through Taunus, Eifel, and Westerwald, down through the wine-growing region, until at last I came upon houses. Under cover of darkness I stole clothes—still don't need food, still don't need sleep . . . but the pains have stopped, and the tiredness and the hunger and thirst—and then I made my way to Hamburg and, eventually, here to Meissen. By the time I found out what day and year it was, I'd been out for four days, sleeping out in the fields and the woods. It was the fourteenth of July in 1995—ten days after my death. Which meant I had been in Hell for five or six days." He gave an involuntary shudder. "And I thought I had been there for years . . . years and years.

"My mother found me in Hamburg, only she wasn't my mother. 'She' was the Devil itself, come to retrieve the Dream . . . and me."

"He was wearing a disguise?"

"Not 'he,' 'it.' When Lucifer went down, he was simply pissed off. The ensuing time spent forging a domain out of hard rock and reflecting on how badly he felt he had been treated turned the pissed off into pure madness. The Devil probably doesn't even recall its life as a god. Doesn't recognize the name Lucifer."

"So how did you manage to—"

"It was your father that saved me."

"My father? How?"

"The word had gotten out. The Dream had been rescued from Hell and the gods knew all about it. After he had introduced himself, in a silvery spidery voice that whispered in my head, your father told me that the woman was not who she pretended to be. And that I must not give the card to her. I must not give the card to anyone. Instead, I must use it . . . must carry the message forward to all who would listen."

"But why didn't she—I mean, 'it'—why didn't the Devil just take it? And how did you get away?"

"The Devil may only take what is offered to him voluntarily. When I told this *thing* that I had been informed that she was not my mother, there were some tears—how could I say that of her and all that—but eventually, she showed her true form." He shuddered again, and I had no wish for further explanation.

"I left late at night, running down the streets of Hamburg carrying only what I wore on my back . . . plus the card containing the Dream. And that is where I met Siglinde Erhard. She told me that she had been waiting for a man in whom she could trust and that voices had told her that I was that man. I must leave Hamburg that night, she explained, and forever do good work. She said that it was only through good work that I may be redeemed. And she told me to go to Meissen."

He paused for breath and sat down in the chair once more. "Since then, I have passed the card around to all who would listen . . . letting them touch it, feel the power, but each time telling them that they could not keep it. You see, I could trust no one . . . and yet the very nature of my task was such that I had to trust everyone. Your father told me that the end to my work was near. Someone was coming, he said. Someone who could take my burden from me."

I didn't say anything, just raised my eyebrows questioningly.

He pointed a finger. "That someone is you."

"*Me?* Jesus Christ, what's going on *here?*" I jumped up off the bed and walked to the bureau where my spare

cigarette packs were stacked up like reassuring bricks of
normality. "Why doesn't someone from Heaven come
down and just take the damned card back?"

"Because nothing that has ever been in Hell may
enter Heaven. It's tainted . . . but it can still be used here
on Earth."

"But you said . . . I mean, your redemption? Doesn't
that mean *you're* going to go there? And *you've* been in
Hell." I waited for a few seconds, watching Dennis
Dannerman's vacant expression, and then something
began to gnaw at me. "And if I take the card—which I
have no intention of doing, let me add—what happens
to you?"

"I can't answer any of those questions. What is it
they say about 'faith'? I only know this: you are to
take the card—of your own free will—and . . . you are
to release me."

I lit a cigarette. "And what will happen to you?"

He held the card out to me. "No idea."

Then the door opened, and my father came into the
room.

"Take it, son," my father said. "Let him go. He has
earned his rest."

In the years since my father's death I had forgotten
what he looked like. Forgotten the sound of his voice.

I had photographs, of course, and, occasionally, when
I was feeling in the mood or when I stumbled across an
old photo album while looking for something else, I
would flick through the images of him—photographs
taken sometimes with me, sometimes with my mother,
and sometimes just by himself. But those static re-
minders can serve against memory and not for it. You

forget the movement of the mouth the adjustment of hair, the turning of the head. A million tiny movements and affectations that make the person who he or she really is. No amount of photographs can reproduce that.

In the small room in the Meissen guest house the memories of my life with this man came flooding back to me. How I wished, in that instant, for my mother to be magically whisked from the rest home in Wells on the Maine coastline, and carried halfway across the world to my room. But then, in that same instant, I wondered how she would feel . . . her a frail but still beautiful woman in her eighties and him a relatively young man not quite sixty years old. Just the way he had been when he had been taken from her—from *us*—all that time ago.

"Oh—" I began, not quite knowing what to say, placing my cigarette on the ashtray and preparing myself to lunge across at him and take him in my arms.

He shook his head as though sensing my thoughts. "Accept the Dream, Charles," he said, pointing to the card. "Accept your destiny."

Without further hesitation, I stepped across to where Dennis sat, still holding the dog-eared piece of card that contained God's first dream for mankind, and I took it between my fingers, feeling, with a momentary puzzlement, some reluctance on Dennis Dannerman's part to let it go. Perhaps, I thought, when the chips were down, his faith had deserted him . . . just for a second. Perhaps he was wondering where he would be transported to, wondering whether he would open his eyes onto pastoral fields or would suddenly find himself crouching once more in the labyrinthine stone tunnels of eternal damnation.

As I pulled, I saw his lips begin a word, a 'Ch—' word . . . and then he was gone. The chair was empty.

I looked down at the card and watched the shapes swirl and eddy, felt the shifting of sound and the movement of light, heard the unmistakable serenity of silence and smelled the depth of hope. It made me want to cry . . . but to cry with joy.

"Let me see it," my father said. "Let me look upon it, son."

And, may God have mercy on me, I handed the First Dream to my father.

Only it wasn't him at all.

Most of the rest of it is a blur now.

But, sometimes in an unguarded moment, particularly in the warmth of my bed where I lay, another deadline missed, waiting for sleep but praying that no dreams will come to haunt me, I replay those final seconds. I still hear, in my memory, the sharp intake of breath of the man who accepted the card I had voluntarily passed to him, a sound not like any sound I had ever heard from any human being . . . let alone from my father. And whatever tricks the memory might play, that is something of which I am certain.

And the deep voice that said, in a sarcastic tone, "Thank you," and then added, with a hint of gleeful humor, "I look forward to meeting you again," was no voice I had ever heard around my childhood home, not even when my father was telling me scary stories of shambling monsters made from piles of rain-soaked fall leaves and a chance bolt of lightning, while I lay beside him tucked in my bed, eyes as wide as saucers.

I suppose the immediate vanishment of my 'father'—

and the card—should have been accompanied by a maniacal laugh, a puff of reddish smoke and the unmistakable odor of brimstone, but there were none of these vaudevillian staples and Hollywood CGI effects.

There was only a stark emptiness. And the imagined silent tears of the gods raining on a beautiful and endless plain somewhere far, far away. . . . Somewhere I may never see.

THE PIPER
by Jody Lynn Nye

Jody Lynn Nye lists her main career activity as "spoiling cats." She lives near Chicago with two of the above and her husband, science fiction author and editor Bill Fawcett. Among Jody's novels are the *Mythology 101* series, *Taylor's Ark, Medicine Show*, and four collaborations with Anne McCaffrey: *Crisis on Doona, The Death of Sleep, The Ship Who Won*, and *Treaty at Doona*. Recent works include *The Magic Touch, The Ship Errant,* and an anthology, *Don't Forget Your Spacesuit, Dear!*

Callia watched the small beryl sphere twirl between Don Renglass' fingers. The light of it enveloped her mind, endeavoring to draw her into the honey-colored veil, to lose her contact with the conscious world and set her adrift.

"Wait," she said, putting out a hand and covering the sphere. She sat up, disconnecting the metal disks glued to her forehead and temples. "I can't go under. I can't go in there again."

Don frowned at the blonde woman on the couch. "Of course you can, Callia. Just sit back." He plucked at her fingers, but she didn't let go. She didn't want even a glimpse of the ball to cloud her mind. "Stop that. The client is waiting."

"I can't go into a trance, Don! Those things will kill me. There are more of them than before. It's getting worse."

"You told me," Don said, imagining he sounded patient, but Callia knew every nuance of his voice and understood how upset he was. A less-civilized man might have taken a swing at her. Callia's physical appearance also belied the unusual. The natural-hued makeup on her heart-shaped face, the neat suit, and salon-curled hair suggested her occupation might be real estate agent, not professional dreamer, but there wasn't a voyiste on the planet Earth who wouldn't recognize her picture as the guide of choice. Don ran a hand through his wavy, dark hair and focused those dark, deep-set eyes on her, compelling her to believe him. He smiled, the wide mouth spreading appealingly over his narrow, tan face. "They're only dreams, sugar. Brainwave patterns. Your own brain. They can't harm you physically."

Callia turned her back on him and hugged her thin arms to herself. She felt the sharp bones in her elbows like knives. "Maybe they can."

She wasn't accustomed to feeling fear, any more than she had had experience with weakness, but that was before the devastating accident that had left her in a light coma for two years. Funny how things worked out. If she hadn't been a daredevil, a tomboy, and a spoiled rich kid, she would never be sitting in a mahogany-paneled office on a leather couch, waiting to escort another spoiled rich kid through her dreams.

Like most of her overprivileged friends, when she was not away at her expensive boarding school, Callia Nelson had spent her early life traveling from one fabulous international destination to another, first with and then without her parents. She had good reflexes and no fear of hard work, so she soon became enamored of what the travel agents called "adventure travel." There was always an element of danger in what she did. The accident that struck her down came while she was spelunking in a southern Missouri cave with friends. The doctors all said that if it had happened in a more remote country she would never have survived. Sometimes Callia wished she'd been in the back of beyond, where her broken body never would have been found and revived. Her legs were still in braces, and might be for years.

People of her economic status talked about visiting the farthest corners of Earth the way others discussed seeing the latest movie blockbuster. To the wealthy, the exotic had become ho-hum. Bored with their own lives, they were always striving to find somewhere new to go, new sights to see. Having conquered their own world, and in between waiting for space travel to take them to new planets, they had turned their attention inward. They began to take an interest in mystical pursuits: ritual magic, meditation, Earth religions, ancient philosophies. Supposed sightings of angels and demons had increased a millionfold. Entertainment had gone over almost exclusively to the metaphysical. The next obvious frontier was dreams.

The dream-walking fad had started as the result of an experiment some years before with coma patients. Some researchers decided to see if monitoring their deep-sleep brainwaves for meaningful or communicable images could help seriously ill people to heal themselves. If there was a way to use them to guide the patients back to consciousness, it would be a boon to modem medicine. The researchers were surprised at what they found. When they hooked themselves up to the comatose patients, they found themselves thrust into vivid dreams that were as compelling as any they had dreamed themselves, with the important difference that they, the researchers, were awake and aware inside them.

The guidance technology turned quickly from a diagnostic and healing tool to an entertainment device. As soon as possible, someone got a hold of a used machine, and started selling dreams. Destitute junkies, their heads full of wild images, were in demand for a while; then writers and artists, then the criminally insane; but the best images came from coma survivors. As when a person loses one normal sense the other senses sharpen in compensation, when all senses are blunted and turned inward, the brain kicks into high gear, as though humans can't stand to be confined inside their own heads. During the two years Callia had spent unconscious in a hospital bed, dream-walking had developed into a widespread craze. At the St. Louis hospital where Callia had been taken after the rock-slide, the underground buzz quickly spread of her superior brain function that produced incredibly intense alpha and delta waves. Attempts by would-be "voy-istes" to hook the dream monitor up with her while she was in long-term care were foiled by her family and the supervising physician, but when she awoke, Don Renglass was by her side with a deal it was difficult to refuse.

A brash New Jerseyite who had come to Washington University on a full scholarship, Don Renglass was a researcher who had had trouble finding funding for his own neurological studies. He saw in Callia a meal ticket and a focus group of one. He explained to her what had evolved while she was unconscious. Callia felt vulnerable and helpless, having discovered the extent of her injuries and the muscular atrophy of two years. Don offered to pay for and oversee her recovery if she signed an exclusive contract with him to train as a dream guide. This was something she could do, even from an invalid's bed. Callia thought it sounded exciting. She was never one to refuse a challenge, and Don would be there to hold her hand when she needed him.

Learning to guide herself in stages down into a state of near coma was terrifying at first, but Don's smooth, deep voice was always there to bring her out again. Once Callia realized that she would maintain her awareness in trance, she started enjoying herself. She had been a vivid dreamer even as a child, but she would awaken with only scattered memories. Now she could experience the whole process with her mind's eye wide open. Things that seemed weird at first, like the ever-changing landscape, got to be familiar, even dear to her. In dreams, her broken body was strong and fit again. The image of it didn't necessarily always look like the person she remembered, but she could feel the vitality of her muscles and the confident strength of her bones just the way they used to be.

It wasn't all easy. Dangers lurked even in this nebulous state. She experienced devastating falls from precipices, was chased by monsters, and was haunted by nightmares that wore the faces of childhood terrors like her neighbor's bulldog that had once savaged her arm. In time she learned what to look for to protect herself. The dreamscape wasn't controllable, but she took the changes in her stride. Her confidence grew with each new success.

Soon, she started guiding people into the dream state with her. Word spread of the quality of her dreams, like news of a rising rock star. Her wealth of life experience and her natural fearlessness made her the most sought-after dream guide in the business. Everyone wanted to go dream-walking with her. She guaranteed them dreams better than any they had themselves, and no one had contradicted her yet. Callia got a lot of attention, good from fans and friends, and bad from the cranks, media, and jealous outsiders. She'd been scoped out by fraud-hunters, and found to be a genuine talent, so they left her alone. She didn't promise psychic healing or time travel or whatever it is those people were looking for. Her business card said "directed dreaming." This office was simply the entrance to an infinite fantasy world, no more, no less. People came for all sorts of reasons, but officially, as Don said, these trips were purely for entertainment purposes.

She knew he'd figured out a way to make her dreaming pay for him, but he did provide the support she needed. Over two years had passed since she had come out of the coma, and she still could not walk more than a short distance without tiring. She'd climbed mountains in the Andes, scaled rocks in Australia, skied across Swiss glaciers, but now could not go grocery shopping by herself. Moreover, honesty compelled her to admit that without Don, she might not have progressed as far as she had, emotionally or physically. She couldn't do *anything* that she used to. Darn it, she hadn't had sex for four years!

Exercise was bringing her back slowly, but she feared she would never return to normal. Don was always encouraging, always urging her to take the next step in her recovery. He was the one who brought her breakfast in bed every day, then made her get up for stretching exercises. Rain or shine, they did tai chi together on the sheltered balcony of her apartment. He was so good to her. She was grateful, but hated that anyone *had* to make her get out of bed. She wasn't used to feeling weak or helpless. Don made it sound like a natural stage, nothing to be ashamed of, but he was adamant that she should use her talents to bring her confidence back to normal. He was an attractive, charming man, genuinely interested and concerned for her, and he had those compelling eyes. When he gazed at her, he could convince her of anything. She wanted to please him. Gratitude and a growing mutual affection kept her going through the arduous training until she became interested in the work on her own.

A couple of years passed before she noticed that blobs of formless darkness were following her back to her starting point. Callia dismissed them at first, but the dark images persisted, trailing her like shadows. Occasionally, she glimpsed something out of the corner of her eye but ignored it. Lately she had seen them every time she went into the dream world. She had never seen such nightmarish beings in her dreams before her accident. Maybe her intensified brain waves, amplified by the electronic gizmos to which she was attached, created an energy trail that dangerous things could follow.

But why were they following her? Callia spent a lot of time thinking about it. It occurred to her that there might be a price to be paid for all these exciting, wonderful fantasies she had been experiencing, and no one had paid it yet. She was afraid it would have to be her. There might exist in the dream world some balance that had to be maintained. For every good dream her clients took away with them, they could be leaving a bad one behind. She had said as much to Don, who assured her her fears were without merit, but *he* hadn't seen the shadows. She had. He didn't want her to quit. She didn't want to quit, either. She needed the money and she really did enjoy the work, but she didn't want to die of dreaming.

Don was still looking at her, waiting. Sighing, Callia clipped the electrodes onto her scalp again and leaned back on the creaking leather couch to switch on the biofeedback unit by her side. She didn't really need it or the crystal ball anymore, but she held on to them the way she held on to Don, as crutches. How she despised crutches. She lay back and started her relaxation technique. She heard Don get up.

"I'll be right back, sugar. Start counting."

She heard him go out the door to tell the client they were beginning. Callia put her fears to one side and, in her mind, created the doorway into her inner consciousness. It looked like the doors in the office, high mahogany lintels with frosted glass panels and brass doorknobs. She made it swing open, and walked through into the dream world.

She felt the presence of the new client almost immediately. He was tentative; most of the new ones were. The dream landscape was purple and orange today. The books said those colors indicated unrest in her mental state. She glanced around for the shadows. There were none to be seen, for which she was grateful. Then she went looking for her client.

She knew her companion was a grown man because she had heard his voice in the outer office, but the mind-state of voyistes rarely looked like their earthly bodies. It took her a while to find him. In the midst of a clump of thornbushes, a lonely waif clad in rags was huddled with his arms around his knees. His wrists were so thin she could wrap a finger and thumb around them. Inside the confident, grown man was a poor, neglected boy, his belly swollen with starvation. As soon as she touched him, he grew up into a fierce, steel-cased giant, but the eyes were empty. Callia felt sorry for him. He was hollow. Inside, he was still the waif.

"Come with me," she said. She pulled at his hand, but he didn't move. He was trapped in some quagmire of personal misery. Callia planted her heels into the ground and leaned back, straining with all her might. He popped loose and staggered a couple of clumsy paces. "Come this way. You'll like it."

He plodded along beside her, not looking up. She concentrated on finding her way to a place of joy, drawing on the energy he was giving off for clues as to what he felt represented joy. She had a talent for "hooking in" to the dreaming state of others. Researchers had told her it was a kind of psychic connection that few people were capable of making. Don always tried not to make it sound special, no doubt fretting that she'd leave him and strike out on her own. Callia, for all that she resented the situation that had left her dependent on him, was clearheaded and grateful to Don for taking care of her. She'd only leave if he gave her too good a reason, but not otherwise.

As they walked together, the giant shell broke away in pieces, like a knight shedding armor. When he emerged, he was a small, thin boy in shorts and a striped shirt. Callia felt her own form swaying with unaccustomed weight. She looked down at herself. She was buxom and hippy, dressed in an expensive jade-green pantsuit about twenty years out of date. His mother, she assumed. He was imposing her shape on Callia. How sad, Callia thought. He wanted his mother. Didn't she ever have time for him when he was little?

They walked over farmland drenched with golden sunshine. All of the buildings were oversized. This must be a memory from his childhood. Bulls filled one pen near the barn, and bears hulked in another.

A few children were gathered in a dirt yard near the back door of the farmhouse. They looked kind and happy, and they held out their arms to the scrawny little boy with accepting smiles. He shied away from them at first, but when Callia behaved as though all this was normal, he began to relax. Someone held out a yo-yo. Another had a wooden train car. A small girl offered her doll in exchange for the engine. The children began to trade toys back and forth, milling about and shouting at one another. Callia's boy had nothing to trade, but someone gave him a toy out of kindness. He traded it for a bigger one, then a bigger one. Soon, he was in the center of a whirlwind of toys, touching one after another. Amused, Callia guessed he worked on the stock exchange in his daily life. It must be hard to break the habit, even in his leisure time. When a woman in an apron rang the dinner bell for close of trade above their heads, the others melted away. Callia's client-child had had in his hands the best of all the toys, a huge, colorful, beautifully-made teddy bear. He was staring at it.

"Well," Callia asked, squatting down to his level, "what are you going to do with it?" He just stared at her, puzzled. No wonder his waif-self felt like it was starving. His whole life was work. He didn't know what to do with success when he achieved it.

She thought it would be good if the teddy tapped him on the shoulder. As things often did in the dream world when she thought they ought to happen, it did. After that, the man's own desires and strangely, those of the teddy bear, took hold. The boy spun around to see who'd touched him. The bear's eyes twinkled, and its mouth looked like it was smiling. The boy gave a glad cry and leaped to hug it. The bear wrapped its arms around him, and they wrestled on the floor like toddlers.

They played games in that yard for hours, whooping and calling to one another with the uninhibited bliss of children. At last, the boy stood up and brushed himself off. The teddy on the ground, no longer needed, faded away in the air. When the child turned back to Callia, he had the face of a man. Callia put out her hand to him, and he came over to her smiling. He walked back to their starting point with his back straight and eyes clear, refreshed, vital, and confident. One good dream was like a month of psychoanalysis, so one of Callia's medical clients had told her.

Before they slipped out the portal, Callia glanced back at the dream world to thank it for helping make this child-man happy. To her alarm, she saw shadows creeping across the land toward her like huge, ominous spiders. She hustled the boy through the door and slammed it on the gathering darkness.

When Callia came out of her dream state, she was looking up toward the ceiling, panting with fear. Don's face appeared in her field of view momentarily, tracked her eyes with a fingertip, then disappeared.

"The fee for today is three thousand," she heard him say.

"I want to meet her," said the client's voice. As Callia struggled to sit up and take the electrodes off her temples, the man pushed his way into the inner office with Don trailing behind him. Don shrugged his shoulders. The client was a burly, hulking man in his forties, with lines etched into his forehead and at the sides of his mouth, but Callia still recognized the small child. His face was wet with tears. "Ma'am, I don't know how you do what you do, but I am so grateful. I've . . . I've had that nightmare where I'm hungry and lonely every night for thirty years. You broke the chain. I don't know how to thank you."

"I'm glad you enjoyed it," Callia said. She never knew what to say.

"Enjoyed it!" the man exclaimed. "So much more than that! I . . . "

"We've got to let her rest," Don said, taking the man by the arm and leading him out. "Sorry." Callia settled back. Thirty years. She shuddered. Extricating him from his nightmare had been a strain. She had probably done more than should have been done in a single session, but she couldn't leave until that pathetic child was happy, if only for a moment.

Don returned, fanning a sheaf of hundred dollar bills

in front of her face. The client had paid with cash.
Ninety percent of voyistes paid with cash. Some people
didn't want paper records of visits to a dream guide.
They'd rather have been caught paying money to a
storefront psychic. The other ten percent were itching
for notoriety or an argument with their insurance com-
panies for calling dream-walking nontraditional mental
therapy. "He's booked for eight more sessions, sugar.
And he'll send us a bunch of referrals. Congratulations."

"Good," Callia said weakly.

"You don't sound very happy," Don said, disap-
pointed. "You ought to be crying 'hallelujah.' "

"You don't know what this costs me, Don," she said.

"I know what it earns you," he said, tucking the
money into her hand and kissing her fingers. "If I wasn't
such an honest man, we could be living in a mansion in
the Bahamas."

Callia was too tired to argue. If she'd had her full
strength, she'd have walked out and gone to Tibet or
somewhere remote to get her head together. But those
days were over forever. She was so unhappy. She ached
to have the body back that she once had, the one she still
wore when she walked her dreams alone. Not a willowy
supermodel shape that so many of her older female
clients craved, but the very normal, athletic woman with
the tanned skin, well-defined muscles, and strong
wrists. Her real wrists were limp and feeble, like broken
flower stems too frail to hold her hands up. She looked
at them with loathing.

"One more session, and we'll be done for the day,"
Don said, brightly, deliberately breaking into her
thoughts. "Come on, sugar. Cheer up!"

"No, Don, please. I want to talk to you . . ." But he was gone.

The noise out in the corridor meant that he was bringing in a group. Hooked up to an adaptive relay, Callia could escort up to a dozen people at once to the dreamscape with her, a feat popular for special parties. This bunch were talking loudly about the usual fantasy full of naked women and flowing rivers of scotch. Don explained patiently to them that dreams weren't daydreams.

"Hey, we want to have a good time!" came a hearty voice Callia assumed was the host, or ringleader, as she liked to think.

"Pleasure comes in many forms," Don said, and got them settled in before coming to help Callia go into her trance state.

The men (they were all men) were very skeptical of lucid dreaming, right up until Callia got an intuitive hook into the fantasies of the ringleader. She guided them into an open field where an enormous, raucous picnic was going on. There were thousands of barbecues, picnic tables full of food, and, yes, beer. Animals made of jello and ice cream romped among the crowds with panniers full of spoons. Clowns handed out the keys to sports cars. As night fell, there was a fireworks exhibit. Callia sent the voyistes flying toward heaven on the backs of skyrockets. They laughed and yelled as they fell out of the sky with parachutes made of sparkling light, and ran back to be launched again and again. Callia kept them in line, making sure each one got his turn.

When the rockets exploded in the sky and shed their momentary brilliance on the night, Callia glimpsed at

the periphery of her vision scenes of hanging and dis-
memberment like horrible photographs. The shadows
were there, more of them than ever before, taunting her
with visions of what they would do to her. She felt
something sharp poke her in the back, and she jumped
away, looking for the source of the pain. The nightmares were massing, starting to surround the picnick-
ers. Callia feared that even the large group she was
guiding couldn't defend itself against the horde. As
soon as the light show was over, she hustled her party
toward the exit to the real world, looking behind her all
the while. They complained the whole way, not understanding why the dream had to end so fast.

Although some of them were still grousing when
Don went out to disconnect them from the machine,
Callia knew they were impressed and pleased by their
experience. One of the visitors stopped in to say so on
his way out.

"You are one hell of a good people-pusher," he said,
respect in his voice. "You are the pied piper. If you ever
want a job as a top management executive at my firm,
give me a call." He handed her a business card. She
smiled at him tiredly. "Well, I'll be back, anyway. That
was the greatest thing that has ever happened to me.
Can't wait to do it again." He raced away, calling for his
friends to hold the elevator.

"Hear that, sugar?" Don asked, fanning the bills as
usual. "Callie?"

"Don, those things were there again," she said.
"Thousands of them. I . . . we had to run away. They
followed us to the gate. They almost got us. I think
they'd have killed us, but we got out ahead. . . . "

"Sugar, they're phantasms," Don said patiently, pulling up a chair beside her couch. "Brain waste."

"I wasn't imagining them! I *felt* them. I can't do this anymore, Don. I can't risk anyone else's life or mine anymore. This is the end. I want out!"

"Everything will happen in good time," Don said, kneeling beside her and clasping her thin hands in his. "Don't quit now, sugar. You're at the top. Don't go away now. Please, Callie. Don't make a hasty decision. *Please*."

Callia sagged back on her cushions. She gave in to his pleading because she was too tired not to. Don took her back to her apartment, made her dinner, and left. He was always careful to give her her space. He had never made a hard pass at her, even though they practically struck sparks off one another every time they touched.

"One day," Don had once said, focusing those intense eyes on her, "one day when you're back to your old self, if you still feel the same way, we'll shake every wall in this building, but until then, think of me as Nursie. I won't sully the medico-patient relationship. When you're ready, you'll know it."

Callia found that frustrating. He never objected to her seeing other men, but other dates always seemed to turn out unsatisfactorily. They were fascinated by her celebrity or were looking for freebies. By the time the date ended, she hated them and herself. Dating was a nightmare. She hadn't remembered what it had really been like. Going back to work, and Don, was a relief. They were meant for each other, but not until she was whole again. If ever.

*   *   *

It was in the midst of her next appointment that the shadows struck. Callia had had a feeling that nothing good was going to happen that day. A new client had commissioned an individual dream. She led him toward his feeling of joy. They were enmeshed in a true adventure scenario, full of damsels in distress, chases, and narrow escapes under a hot yellow sky.

A red dragon, her personal symbol of overwhelming power and destruction, zoomed in on them. Beneath its wings she could see the sharp blackness of the shadows. They were coming for her this time. Callia grabbed the man by the arm and started to run toward her exit point. The dragon breathed out streams of flame that singed their heels. The next blast took her full in the back, burning her to the bone. Callia heard the clash of knives and axes behind her. Gasping with pain and fear, she picked up her client in her arms and flew out the door. It closed on a wall of flame that lit up the frosted glass.

Don and the client, a trim, tanned man in his thirties, were in the room when she came out of her trance. She was exhausted.

"That was great!" the man exclaimed. "It felt so real, more real than reality. I never have dreams like this myself!"

"Oh, you do," Don said. "You just don't remember them."

"No," the man said, grinning. "Wish I did. She's *really* amazing. May I come back again tomorrow?"

"No," Callia said, flatly.

They both looked down at her. "No?"

"We're booked tomorrow," Don said hastily. "Ms. Nelson is very much in demand, you know."

"Oh." The man looked at her with more respect. "May I have an appointment next week, then?"

"Certainly," Don said. "Same time?"

"Yes, good," the man said, eyes shining. "Man, I don't know how I'll get through a whole week!"

"That's what we like to hear," Don said. He returned from the outer office counting money. "I've got to see the accountant tomorrow." Callia sat up and took his arm.

"Don, please cancel all the appointments, not just tomorrow."

"I can't do that," he said. "We've both got bills to pay. Why, your physiotherapist *alone* . . . "

"I don't care. I nearly died in there today! I'm quitting. I don't know what they are, or where they're coming from, Don, but I'm scared. Sooner or later the piper has to be paid." Callia shivered. Don spread a shawl across her legs and tucked it in.

"Hell, no one else is complaining, sugar. You're just tired. I'll cancel all of the weekend's appointments, and we'll go for a drive somewhere, somewhere real." He grinned, his white teeth flashing. "Time you saw some scenery that isn't in your own head. Oh, hello, Mr. Carlson."

Callia looked at the tottering, old man in dismay. Poor Mr. Carlson came back week after week to commune with the image of his late wife. They just walked together and talked, never more than that. Callia worried about what would happen to him if the monsters charged out of the shadows when they were there. She looked at Don desperately.

"Don, I *can't.*"

He was diplomatic. "Could you come back next week, Mr. Carlson? Callie is sick."

"Oh, I'm so sorry," the old man said, with a kindly smile. "I just . . . I just wanted to tell Betty about our grandson's graduation. I hope you feel better, my dear." Don escorted him out and came in with the relay headset. He hooked it to her biofeedback unit and sat down beside her.

"All right, I want to see what you've been seeing." He tucked her hand in his and settled her on her pillows. Callia closed her eyes contentedly. Having him there gave her such confidence she melted into the dream state almost at once. She passed through the portal and found him waiting there for her.

The two of them stood on a grassy promontory overlooking a bay full of sailboats. Callia adored sailing. She used to live on the beach during the summer. She glanced at Don. He was watching her with a curious expression in his deep eyes.

"So this is what you really look like, huh?"

"No," Callia said sadly, looking down at that fit body. She was wearing a halter top and a denim skirt, her favorite summer clothes. "It's just a dream. This is what I used to be." Don shook his head.

"I beg to differ, sugar. This is the real you, inside. I'm sorry I never saw it before, but it doesn't matter. I love you the way you are outside, too."

Callia wanted to throw her arms around him right there, but she was afraid if she turned her back, the shadows would leap on them and devour them. She just took his hand and waited.

Gulls did an aerial ballet as the sky turned from blue to crimson to black. Callia kept expecting the hot breath of fear to envelop her, but all she could feel was a cool breeze on her skin and the warm pressure of Don's hand.

"Nothing," his voice said in the dark.

"They were here," Callia said desperately. "They've been here every time for months! They attacked me."

"Well, they're gone now. Come on home." He started counting her up out of trance.

"There's nothing in there but your wonderful imagination," he said, when she opened her eyes. "Maybe whatever's going on in there is just you." She coughed and he leaped to his feet. "I'll get you something to drink. Be right back."

Callia thought about what he had said. What she had been seeing could certainly have come from deep within her own psyche. Maybe the shadows were hers. Who was the piper that needed to be paid? Perhaps *she* was. She had never really dealt with her own frailty. Mortality had frightened the heck out of her, but Don had been there every step of the way since the moment she woke up. He never let her fall all the way into despair, but that meant she hadn't had to think seriously about the reality of her condition. And yet, it must always have been there in the back of her mind, at the edges of her thoughts, preying on her.

She had to go back and do battle on her own behalf. The analyst, the toy who had given pleasure to so many, the conduit to fantasy, had never enjoyed her own skills at problem-solving. She had gone rambling in the dream world, but she'd never been her own voyiste.

With difficulty, she threw her metal-braced legs over the edge of the couch and hobbled the few paces into the outer office. The healthy Callia that once had been could have covered the distance in seconds. Yes, this is what it would have been like if she'd been alone, no Don to support her every step. She needed to be independent again, or she'd never be whole. She locked the door. The delay while Don went to the super for a spare key would give her the time she needed to try.

Callia tottered back to her couch and turned on her machine, but she scarcely needed it. She knew the way. She turned her eyes toward the beryl sphere on the table and let the honeyed light envelop her.

The portal swung open on a twilight desert landscape full of sharp edges silhouetted against a bruised-purple sky. As soon as she set foot on the ground, the shadows she'd been afraid of flooded in around her, surrounding and smothering her. "Cripple," one of them whispered. "Fraud," another taunted.

Callia felt hot tears burning her eyes. Her body wasn't strong and healthy as it usually was in the dream state. She was weak, with twisted limbs and pale, dry skin. She gasped for breath as the weight of the shadows pressed her down into the sand until her feet were buried to the ankles. She was trapped. She would die here. The horde of demons was everything she'd ever been afraid of in her life since she was a child: strangers, heights, going fast, smothering, tight places, fear of loneliness, and fear of rejection. The little girl inside her had been pushed aside as she took every dare, faced every challenge, and leaped every hurdle, especially ones people told her she couldn't clear. That was how she'd wound up having an accident in the first place. She'd been careless and stupid. The weapons the demons wielded she had created herself from every mistake she had ever made. That grotesque, purple-brown imp was her disgust at her condition. That green one was her greed.

"You're just in this for the money," it sneered at her. "You'd be too scared otherwise."

"No, I'm not," she said, having to gasp for every breath. "I help people."

"You can't help yourself," grunted the purple-brown imp. "You're nothing anymore. Don stays because of pity."

"No!"

She could barely look at it, but it forced its way into her field of vision, prying open her eyelids to climb inside her. Callia struck at it. She snatched it from her face and threw it to the ground. With a sudden burst of strength, she pulled one of her twisted legs from the sand. Ignoring the pain she smashed her foot into the imp again and again until it sank underground. The greed-demon tried to scramble away as she came after it. Callia felt power returning to her limbs as she kicked the green monster far away. It exploded against the sky like fireworks. Callia seized her dreads one by one. They slashed at her, but she swatted the weapons out of their claws. She looked hard into the heart of each fear, recognizing the truth in it, before she tore it into tattered rags of black and threw it far away from her. She *did* have worth. She did help others. What she did *mattered*. She was worthy of love. Her nightmares couldn't keep her from doing what she wanted.

Don's concerned voice broke into her thoughts at just the right moment, as the last red-eyed banshee fled screaming off into the void. Callia dusted her hands together as she strode back toward the frosted glass door.

Her clients were right. That did feel good. She might have to do it again one day, but now she knew she could.

"Sugar, can you hear me?" Don was leaning over her, his worried face inches away from hers. She looked up at him, feeling warmed by the love and concern in his eyes. She no longer wanted to wait until her body had mended completely.

"Want to shake some walls?" she asked.

ROUNDED BY A SLEEP
by David Bischoff

David Bischoff is active in many areas of the science fiction field, whether it be writing his own novels such as *The UFO Conspiracy* trilogy; collaborations with authors such as Harry Harrison, writing three *Bill the Galactic Hero* novels; or writing excellent media tie-in novelizations, such as *Aliens* and *Star Trek* novels. He has previously worked as an associate editor of *Amazing* magazine and as a staff member of NBC. He lives in Eugene, Oregon.

I had a dream about my cat the other day.

She was a tabby, Rambles was. She died just short of her fortieth birthday. Rambles was having kidney problems and she was at the vet and they had her on kitty dialysis. A Techer goofed and the drip got turned on too high. Pets aren't a really high priority at the Vet-Center, and so the brain died, too, which meant I couldn't get her back in a bio-tank as a catfish. So that was that, and I had to pay the bill anyway.

Rambles liked to sleep right on the pillow next to mine. I had a hard time for a while afterward sleeping without her breathing next to me, or snoring . . . or purring.

I had a hard time, period.

Rambles was my mother's cat, and my mother died of lung cancer about ten years before the Rejuve Age gave us all the possibility of Faux Immortality. I'd think, if only Mom had hung on for another ten years . . . but then, what would it matter? Seventy . . . ninety . . . one hundred and fifty . . . They figured people should be able to live a lot longer, but they hadn't figured that something in the human unconsciousness that would want to click off. So we all got, what, maybe about seventy more years of life. We still snuffed it, we still died. It was like there was this switch in the collective unconscious that said, *Right. Out of the gene pool. Time for someone new.*

Anyway, Rambles died. I grieved.

Death is the great theme. Mortality rules, and all that.

One night, though, maybe a month after I got the kitty ashes back in a little cedar box, she came back to me.

I was sitting on a couch somewhere, reading a book of poetry. Rambles just sauntered in from the next room, jumped up on the couch, climbed into my lap, and proceeded to turn on her kitty engine.

I said, "You're dead, Rambles."

She was soft and warm, and she had that miniature leonine look that Abyssinians have. She had a gleam of peace and gentle awareness in her, that fed-cat look, sleek and self-satisfied and one with the universe.

"Am I?" she said. "Go back to your poetry, would you?"

I did, and I read some of Tennyson's *Idylls Of The King* to my dead cat. I petted her, and I had the impression of fleeting stirrings of other events flickering through the windows. Giants peering in. Pterodactyls flying by. I suddenly realized that I was naked, and there were a bunch of Victorian women having tea all around me. Then I remembered that I'd forgotten to go to my Psychology 201 class all semester and the final exam was tomorrow. Then the roof of the house flew off, and the Wicked Witch of the West flew by, cackling.

I petted my kitty.

"I miss you," I said. "I miss you so much."

My name is Brown.

Marvin Brown.

I'm one hundred and three years old. It's the year 2054 AD.

I live in an Assisted Living Environment in Iowa, just outside of Dubuque. Oh, I get around just fine, thanks. I play tennis too, and hike, and do all kinds of healthy things. I date the women here (who outnumber the men three to one), so I have a fairly active social life, I guess. I just don't have much money since I didn't count on living this long. The ALEs are the government's and the younger generations' way of putting us away somewhere cheap while they figure out how the hell to make their later years better than ours. I worked as a Bureaucrat for the State until they booted me out at seventy-six. Fortunately I painted and played guitar or I would have died of boredom very early into my retirement. I never married, which in terms of my longevity is a statistical anomaly, but oh well. . . .

I live, I grieve, I dream.

I have my robolacrum.

I think about my life and how I fucked it up. Sometimes I long for death, but I'm vaguely frightened of it. Instinct? Do not go peacefully into that good night? Death is such a cliché, and fear of death is as common as colds. But you know, it's a rather personal business, death.

Death is kind of like something you don't want to think about, the big question mark, the great Unknown. The Night. The Sea. The Chasm. The Dark and the

Cold. Whole industries in life run on the cogs of death, and they have fired more than my share of synaptical adrenal surges over the years.

What you do now, it is said, will create what fills that final void. But why is so much of that AfterStuff made to make the NowStuff so dreary and riddled with uncertainty and anxiety?

The doctor wasn't smiling when he came into the examination room. I still had my smock on, with my bare butt hanging out the back, and I was freezing. The exam machines, cold oddments gleaming in the fluorescent light, had their way with me today.

The dispensary smelled of swabbing alcohol and paperwork. I heard the hum of modern science in the walls, the beep beep beeps of monitoring machines. Coming here, I heard coughs and groans and boredom hanging in the halls, along with the scent of resignation and a faint touch of bedpan. The machines are amazing nowadays in these places, but the place where medical doctors dwell still strikes me much the way it struck me in the days of my polio shots a century ago.

The red striped tie sticking out from the white coat dangles as the doctor pulls up a metal chair. He's got a stethoscope on, but it's more a ceremonial ornament these days than anything else, what with the Nurse-machines. It's a kind of twenty-first century caduceus.

He's a young guy, with short, slicked back hair and a smooth firm chin. Dark eyes and a narrow face. He looked kind of uncomfortable then, like he was trying to remember his lines for a particularly tough dramatic role. He looked like a High Priest of Medicine come with a message from the Oracle.

I already figured the news he had wasn't good.

He examined the electroplate he had one more time, as though just to be sure.

Then he looked up.

"How are you feeling, Mr. Brown?" he said.

"Poked and prodded."

"I mean the head."

"Oh." I'd been complaining of headaches. "A little dopey. Painkiller's pretty good, I guess."

"Good. Good. Not the days of morphine, morphine, or morphine. We have a variety of options, depending upon the need."

Lecture, lecture. Ah, ain't medical science grand?

"Well, it's kept me alive for a long time."

"Hmm. Yes. Well, there's more time possible, Mr. Brown. . . . "

I suppose he thought I should suddenly break out into a great big smile and look all eager. I was still feeling cold, though, and good news or bad, these machine places fill me with a kind of existential dread that I can't shake off.

"So what's the diagnosis, Doctor?"

"Well, Mr. Brown. As good as our telltales are now, we can't detect everything. You've come in for regular medical checks. . . . Yes, and we've kept you ticking. Something's developed in the last few months though that was either extremely fast in development," he lowered his voice. "Or that we missed."

I felt an instinctual surge of fear. Something bad.

"Okay. I'm listening."

"It's a glioblastoma, I'm afraid."

I blinked. "You mean a brain tumor?"

He blinked. "Ah . . . you've heard that particular term."

"Yes. I had a friend. He died of one when he was forty-four years old. A long time ago." The words were coming out like nervous tics. "Actually, no. It was the chemo that killed him. But the tumor would have gotten him eventually. Nasty things." My mouth was a little dry. Even when you get this old, it doesn't seem like you're old and there's still that deeply embedded chill, that inner scream when cancer and tumors and terminal illnesses are discussed. "But that was a long time ago. Medical science has advanced."

I didn't care if I had some sarcasm in that. I was the one with the hunk of disease in my gray matter.

"So it has, so it has," said the doctor. "It's a primary tumor. Malignant. These things used to be terminal. Now they can be cured. It's just no fun, that's all." He smiled weakly. "And there are aspects of your situation we need to discuss."

"Oh?"

"Yes. We can cure you, Mister Brown. But because of the nature of the placement of the tumor . . . you'll lose the ability to dream."

I was sitting in a French cafe, talking to Stu about the relative merits of Throbbing Gristle.

We were sipping at large steins of brisk German beer and when the conversation turned to a song by The Residents, four guys in tuxedos and top hats with eyeballs for heads came out and performed the song for us. Stu laughed. It was a nice day and Stu liked nice days. He liked, he said, the way the sun warmed your face. When you lived in New York City and spent a lot of time up at night, you got pale, and Stu was pale. But he was Greek, and I guess he had a deep ancestral appreciation of the sun.

We finished our beer, got up, and started to stroll. Cobbled Paris avenues unwound before us. We walked into Denmark. Tivoli Gardens, with lights hanging in the trees, smelled of popcorn and baked pretzels. Somehow some Roman fountains had found their way into the center of it all, and there were beautiful women frolicking in translucent robes. Stu liked beautiful women frolicking.

It was a good night in Tivoli Gardens that night. The stars hung low and the air smelled of lavender and honeysuckle. I caught glimpses of old friends and family. My mother and father strolled past to the huge ferris wheel, strung with necklaces of lights. My uncle was at a booth, smiling as he sold huge ice cream cones to giggling children. The air was warm and summery, with buttery aftertones.

"Do you remember the night we went to see Genesis at the Beacon Theater?" I said.

Stu snorted. "Yeah. Good show, but still I would have preferred it with Peter Gabriel."

"I think in 1976, if some of the people knew where Phil Collins was going, there would have been a few rotten tomatoes tossed."

Stu cackled and a wicked light twinkled in his eye. He was dark and still slender, all in black, with a sharp black goatee. He looked like Che Guevera gone beatnik.

"Psst. Psst. Gentlemen. Over here," came a voice with a strong German accent.

There was a stand holding treats and candies. Behind it was a man with a handlebar mustache and slicked back hair. He was amusing himself with a game of solitaire.

He was my grandfather. He gave us a bag of caramels to share between us.

"When I came to America and had my candy cart, I would stand outside Carnegie Hall and listen to Jethro Tull sing."

"You mean Caruso," I said.

"Eh?"

"I said, you mean Enrico Caruso."

"Ah! Yes. Just so. Enrico Caruso!" He made an unpleasant face. "Phil Collins! Pah! Genesis should have gotten Enrico Caruso to replace Peter Gabriel."

Stu laughed in his cynical way. It sounded good.

There was a tug on my leg.

It was Rambles.

I picked her up and held her close so that her whiskers tickled my cheek.

"I should like some chocolate mice, if you please," she said, and then the music from the speakers hanging like Christmas baubles in the trees turned to tiny fairies and they danced and sparkled in a stream to the crescent moon.

"Marvin?"

"Yes."

"Marvin, I haven't heard from you since you went to the doctor. Are you okay?"

It was Daphne. I guess, of all the women I see, Daphne is the most special. However, I don't feel quite connected with her. Hell, I don't feel connected with anyone, anything.

"Oh. Sure. I'm just taking a little downtime, that's all, Daph."

"But you're okay."

"I guess."

"Marvin. Marvin, you're acting like an old man!"

"But, Daph. I am an old man."

"Oh, come on, Marv. You're in great shape. You beat everyone in tennis. You're the winner in the Longevity Pool amongst the Community."

We'll see about that, I thought.

There was a deadly pause.

"Look, Daph. Can you call me back next week? I really don't feel like talking now."

I could hear her about to rip into me. But the nice thing about keeping your options open as far as dating is concerned, is that a Significant Other doesn't quite have that strange power over you that allows them to totally speak their mind.

"Okay. Okay. But I'd like to get together and do something. I really would, Marvin."

"Okay. Talk to you later."

The robolacrum daintily spread my toast with non trans fats gloss and set them down before me. It poured me some tea and pushed a creamer full of fortified skim milk to my side, for easy reach.

"I understand that the clouds will lift at approximately two thirty in the afternoon," the robolacrum says. "Would you like to take some iced tea on the deck if that's the case?"

"Okay," I said. "You can cut the formality, Ralph. If I want a butler, I can stick in the Jeeves cassette."

The mobile companion takes this in. I suppose, if he

had lips, he would have pursed them. "Galvanic indicators present a low neuro-transmitter level, dude. Shall I get thee a hefty jab of anti-depressant insert?"

Sometimes I wish I hadn't programmed the smart-ass factor into my robolacrum. But then, it always reminded me of that reaping and sowing dictum.

"Sure. Why not."

Ralph's name is really not Ralph 124C 41+. I just named him after that famous old Hugo Gernsback book. When you're a hundred and four and you live in a reality that you might have read about in a Frederik Pohl or Philip K. Dick story, you tend to get a little bit free with your allusions.

The self-portable computer wobbles over to the med-cabinet of the apartment, gets his gear, and then comes over, efficiently humming with sterilizing servos even as he fitted the med-glove into his attachment slot. "Now let's see if we can get a nice fat vein up, eh?"

"I thought the A in AI stood for Artificial, not Arch," I muttered, grimacing down at the table monitor where I'd been reading some news stories. Colonies on Mars having financial trouble. Asteroid mining accident—twenty-six lives suddenly not on the longevity market anymore.

"I believe it stands for Asshole Incarnate, Mister Brown. Now hold up your arm please."

The insert wrapped around the bare arm and I got myself a spritz of heaven. Ah, who needs booze or illegal drugs when you've got brain boosts from medical science? True, they do nothing for your soul, but for short-term purposes, there's nothing like them for a lift.

I felt a pleasant tingle. Gursh of serotonin, oh, frabjous day . . . dances of endorphorin. Bliss! The docs have identified hundreds of different kinds of neuro-transmitters, oh yes. Funny thing, medscience. It took until the late twentieth century to figure out why people got pleasure and satisfaction from alcohol and other drugs. Pshaw! The drugs did what life was supposed to do, they pushed the buttons in the body to squirt out all the stuff inside that not only makes life more than a garbage heap of pain and suffering, but the stuff of joy and calm and happiness. Of course the problems were that they tended to mess up the synapses in the process and you got alcoholics and junkies and, heck, all kinds of social problems.

But, oh, now! Now we have no alcoholics, no junkies, no social problems. . . .

And every senior citizen has his handy dandy robo-lacrum as companion.

"Ah," I said, trying to fight the smile but not succeeding. "Ah!"

A satisfied light gleamed in the robo's eyes. "There now, Mister Brown. Isn't that much better?"

"Yes," I said. "Yes, I have to admit it is."

He stood up straight and tall, and looked proud. Today the robolacrum wore the Horatio Hornblower outfit that I'd gotten him on his six foot, trim and muscular frame, and I have to say, with the feathery blue hat and epaulets and gleaming buttons, he looked both magnificent and ridiculous.

"Good, good. Now then . . . " He took a spyglass and pretended to peer inside my ear toward my brain. "What neurosis and psychological boo-boos are bubbling around inside there that we can deal with?"

I'd like to think that my AI, my dear Robo-guy, has a real personality. At times like this, when the humor pops out at sixes and sevens to his mechanical companion and Dr. Feelgood functions, I realize again that I've done a damned good time programming him.

"Oh, you won't need that," I said. "They're fairly teeming."

"Having those grief problems again, then, eh?" The elasto-muscles worked in the jaw, making a wry face. "Hmm. They seem rather incapacitating. Now then, modern psychoscience hasn't quite perfected the proper mixture for these kind of problems that haunt the modern psyche. How about a little old-fashioned heart-to-heart discussion about your feelings. That way maybe we can stop those dreadful smaerds."

"Smaerds?" I say.

"Yes, dear boy," said the Robo. "Smaerds. Dreams in reverse. Modern psych jargon. Dreams are supposed to work out issues in the psyche. If they start invading the waking life, start to predominate—and take over, then they work to the detriment of an individual. They work in reverse. And those dreams become smaerds."

"Smaerds."

"Yes. Now then. Is it the death of your mother that's bothering you?"

"Yes, but it's more than that."

"Your father, then."

"Yes. More, though."

"The death of your cat, Rambles. The protracted and untimely death of your older brother. The death of your grandparents. The death of all your sisters and other brothers. The Holocaust. The death of millions in war so far this century. The billions of other human beings who've died this century. The trillions of human beings and beloved pets and friends and families of others who have met their deaths since the beginning of time?"

"I should have taken that sarcasm chip out of you, you know?"

The robolacrum shrugged. "I'm sorry. I only mean to jog you out of the morass of self-pity in which you wallow."

"Ah. I'm not sure I programmed you to say that."

Captain Robolacrum clacked his spyglass closed and walked over to the poopdeck to stare out at the ocean of grass of the retirement community. He put his locked hands behind him and stared out the window.

"For your approval—" The Robo began in his best retro-Rod-Serling. "—One retired bureaucrat, left out to pasture with nothing but goodwill from society and government. Marvin Brown. Born in beautiful South Carolina. Graduate of Duke University. A tax lawyer for the Iowa Treasury, serving with distinction well past normal retirement age. He's traveled around the world, both before and after his work. With a series of delightful and beautiful companions, he has never been truly alone—and now he has benefited greatly by the excellent robolacrum mobile program—as well as plenty of feminine companionship provided by his retirement community. Marvin Brown . . . who insists on constantly taking the trip past the light post straight up ahead—directly to . . . The Twilight Years Zone."

I clapped slowly but emphatically.

"Bravo! Bravo! You've been in my vid-master collection, I see."

He bows curtly. "Research into these things is always beneficial."

"Well, you've convinced me. I have no right to feel

depressed or repressed or pressed in any way at all. At a hundred and three years of age, with a future of leisure and delight and meaning ahead of me, I should have no problems whatsoever. I shall take everything into account accordingly."

The robo smiled slightly, with a little quirk in his expression, as though he were looking into whether my sarcasm chip had been thrown into over-activity.

"Good. Good. Equilibrium. Status quo. Survival," said the robolacrum. "We all must do our best to survive . . . and live a quality survival, yes?"

"Yes."

"What would you like for dinner tonight? I have an urge to prepare a ragout of lamb with plenty of garlic and a nice tossed salad of Asian herbs with some balsamic vinegarette. Or are you in the mood for some recreational cooking of your own? I could put on that new Henry Purcell cube. Or, wait—perhaps we should invite one of your lady friends over for an evening of televised entertainment?"

"Did I ever tell you I almost got married once?"

The robolacrum raised an eyebrow. Sometimes I wish his facial expressions had not been so finely calibrated. "No. I wonder why not?"

"Maybe I like to keep some things close to my chest."

"How can I be a proper companion and comforter if you don't tell me things?" he said. He looked hurt. I knew his feelings were merely simulacrums—no zappings of electro-chemistry, no quacking ducts of glands in him. But still, I felt a little bad about that. He'd been nothing but faithful to me, after all. He was just doing his job, and if his affection for me was merely a pro-

grammed illusory thing, often it was more than welcome.

I was quiet for a moment. He was respectful and
stood quietly above me.

"Her name," I said, "was Eloise."

The old Gothic buildings of the university rose up
from around the green mall with stately dignity and
with a touch of misty hauntedness. There are large flowers smelling sweet and exotic rising up from the grass,
and a taste of eternity hovering about the trees. A cool
breeze fluttered the dresses of the girls as they walk
along the sidewalks and from the open window of a
dorm room, a Yes version of a Verdi opera is flowing,
Jon Anderson sounding very odd singing all the vocals.

"I'm dreaming about you now," I said, as I lay on the
grass looking up at the galleons of clouds moving in the
sky. "Because I thought about you today."

A couple of the ships in the sky exchanged cannon
fire, filling the deep blue with stars and fire. Multicolored sparks drifted down, fading out like fireworks.

"Lucid dreaming can be nice," she said, her long
blonde hair spilling off the edge of her chiffon dress. I
got olfactory memories of her. I got gentle Ivory soap
and cinnabar. I got Prell highlights and gentle wit, and
knowing innocence. "But isn't it all a bit—mundane?"

"Hmmm?"

Her blue-green eyes started to glitter. Her sweet lips
smile gently and all my heart is in her peaceful, mis-
chievous smile.

"The song, Marvin, is not 'Lucid in the Sky with Di-
amonds.' "

The clouds began to drip mauve and silver dissolving

through the sky. The Gothic buildings sprouted candle flames and slowly relaxed into clumps and mounds.

I sneezed and got that tremendous orgasmic feeling of release.

Silver coins tinkled out of my mouth and nose, and I saw them, when my eyes opened, sprinkling down upon a beach smooth and white as a baby's rump.

I looked up. We were sitting on a beach in Maui. I recognized the condo in Lanai, the hills and mountains to one side, the surf and ocean to the other. A soft breeze played against my cheek. Medieval sea serpents cavorted in the distance and waterspouts roared up willy-nilly to dash spray against a helter skelter sunset.

La la la.

There was that fabulous Hawaiian feel, that amazing three-dimensional something that you never get from the garish colors of the pictures and movies. The scent, the vibration, the gentle calming smells, the taste of fruit, the gentle touch of sunlight, calm and tender life.

I smelled barbecued corn and pineapple, and I turned and saw that Eloise was there. She was older, with lines in her face and gray in her hair, but she had a feminine glow, a beauty that I'd never seen before in her because she had left me when we were so young. But she had a grace now, a beauty and a dignity that she'd never had before. I felt a wisdom and understanding—and a deep love in her eyes that was a cultured, tended, and growing thing, something that I had never imagined, let alone experienced.

There was a deep connection.

"This is nice, " she said.

"Yes."

"But I don't know . . . remember that month we spent

in Bali? I kind of preferred that in a way. So much more alien, so much more exotic."

I didn't remember. I searched back, but I didn't recall. I wondered if I should lie, should just play along . . . but that didn't feel right. With this person here . . . I didn't lie . . I couldn't lie. And that felt right in the deep wash of something intimate and communal in our relationship. Something rich but not at all strange. . . .

"No," I said. "I don't remember, Eloise."

I expected her to be sad and hurt.

But she wasn't.

Her eyes sparkled knowingly and mischievously, with that sexual element that seemed to say, *You're in for some playful fun and I, buster, am the one who's going to give it to you.*

"Of course, you don't, darling. That's another reality entirely. Purely of the alternate variety." Her eyes glittered. "But we can go back there, you know. We can be together. It's different here, you know."

"I never went to Bali," I murmured. "That's in Indonesia, right?"

"No, dear. I mean Bali World . . . off about a hundred light years that way," she pointed up into the sky, and suddenly stars sparkled on in the black canvas backdrop, as though summoned.

She reached out for my hand, and her touch was all I needed to know of any kind of reality.

The doctor frowned.

"I must admit, I don't understand, Mister Brown," he said. He leaned forward in his chair on the desk. Around us were bookshelves with old medical books—a hobby of the doctor's, he had told me. The room smelled pleasantly of old leather and aftershave—and maybe even a touch of pipe tobacco, with none of the usual medicinal flavor of doctor haunts.

"I've made my decision," I said. "I believe that any kind of analysis will find me mentally stable and that the decision will stand."

He scratched his nose a moment and then shook his head sorrowfully. "I must say, being in the business of prolonging life and health—to let disease take over . . . I guess it goes against all I've worked for in my profession . . . all that this society has fought for."

"I don't want the operation, Doctor. It's as simple as that."

He gave me a look as though I were some kind of lunatic. "You have years ahead of you, Mister Brown. Decades. And frankly, with the advanced work being done with nanotechnology, I'd say that within twenty years human beings will have shots at life spans of hundreds and hundreds of years. You're turning all that down? Your profile shows no particular religious convictions . . . or anything else for that matter that would indicate why you've made this decision. Please. I'd like to understand."

"It's simple," I said. "You say that in these procedures people lose their ability to dream. I don't want that, Doctor. I don't want to give up my dreams."

The robolacrum brought the tray with the tea and set it on the side table. He poured. The aromatic fragrance drifted over me as I lay on the recliner, a tasseled throw over my legs.

"Thank you," I said.

"Would you like some biscuits or some other kind of food?"

"No."

"You really should eat."

"I'll just take the nutrient drip, thank you."

"Any pain?"

"A slight headache, maybe."

The robolacrum bustled over and slipped my arm up into his attachment. I felt painless pricks and gushing and in the metal of his arm I felt hums and clicks of needles. A warm glowing peace washed over me. Without the pain and fear, there was a feeling of naturalness and destiny about this dying business, like eating or sleeping or falling in love. I felt the intimation of a peace that I'd never felt before.

Wasn't it Robert Louis Stevenson who'd said something like 'And lay me down with a will . . . '?

"There. Better?"

"Yes. Thank you. Your nursing abilities are astounding."

The robolacrum sat down in a chair. He looked puzzled. "I do not understand. They even offered you a chance with the new nanotechnoloogy devices. The doctors offered the chance of them destroying the tumor without any side effects."

He said it a bit peevishly, as though he was upset that I was going to leave him, and I felt touched and although he was just a machine, really, I felt I owed him an explanation.

"I'm ready anyway. I've had enough. And besides, my friend . . . I do believe most people look in all the wrong places for eternity and paradise."

He shook his head.

"I'm tired now. I want to go back to sleep."

"Yes," he said. "Watch out for the smaerds, though. Watch for the smaerds."

He came over and gently touched my shoulder, as I drifted away to a better place.

Eloise was there, and she was upset.

"Marvin," she said. "Marvin, Marvin. . . . "

Look, I'd told the robolacrum, what's the difference? You're born. Fact. You die. Fact.

You're here now, but you weren't here a few years ago, and you won't be here a few years from now.

We're talking nonexistence then, nonexistence later. It's the nonexistence later that has got the philosophates' pants all tied up in knots—but it's not like we all haven't experienced nonexistence before.

Dust to dust, ashes to ashes . . . and really can't be that bad now, can it? Deep down I think we all remember what it's like to not exist. How else can you explain the popularity of the Seraphiminator and the Deep-Downer? Hmm? Answer me that. What can Death be but the ultimate relaxation device? We all hunger for that.

Ah, said the robolacrum.

But what smaerds may come?

"Marvin," Eloise said in my dream. "Marvin, you're being a fool."

When I woke up, Ralph was waiting by my bed.

He smiled at me, and somehow it felt . . . real.

I had no memory of the surgery.

"How are you feeling," he said. "Any pain?"

"No," I replied.

The smile somehow grew brighter. "You'll be fine. The operation was a total success. The doctor will be in a little. And you know . . . as it happens . . . your friend Daphne has been in the waiting room quite a while."

I reached up and felt the bandages.

I felt no pain, but I did feel an emptiness.

"Have I been out for a long time?" I asked.

"You've been sleeping for a solid day," he said.

No dreams. No smaerds, either, for that matter. I just felt that emptiness . . .

And future . . .

And fear . . .

And then grief, vaster than I'd ever felt grief before. I would dream no longer.

All my loved ones were lost to me again, this time forever. I felt alone in a way I'd never been alone before.

Ralph touched me, and for the first time I realized how warm and soft his hand was. Perhaps, just perhaps, living totally in the now might have its good points. . . . "Daphne's been waiting quite a long time. Would you—?"

"Yes," I said. "Yes, Ralph. I'd like to see her very much."

NEEDLE AND DREAM
by Andre Norton

Andre Norton has written and collaborated on over one hundred novels in her sixty years as a writer, working with such authors as Robert Bloch, Marion Zimmer Bradley, Mercedes Lackey, and Julian May. Her best known creation is the Witch World, which has been the subject of several novels and anthologies. She has received the Nebula Grand Master Award, The Fritz Leiber Award, and the Daedalus Award, and lives in Monterey, Tennessee, where she oversees a writer's retreat.

*D*welling in the pocket of fertile earth that lies walled by the rise of Mount Tork to the south and the Sleeping Hills to northward, the villagers had little knowledge of the outside world. They did, however, have dreams; and, through the centuries they had been isolated from those who had once been their own kind, such night visions had become their one link with the Power Beyond.

The village folk did not dream often these days. Thus, when man, woman, or child spent sleeptime in a dream, they made haste to report it in the morning and were hurried off to the cottage of the Keeper. There, that guardian of the Old Ways would question them rigorously, noting down in his record book their descriptions of things they had beheld, of actions in which they had had a part.

Many of those sleep-seeings would prove a reliving of

*normal doings, though sometimes the daily round was
admixed with irresponsible behavior in scenes which
the sober Keeper had to shake head over. But dreams of
true foretelling had been sent, as well, and those were
entered into the charts and carefully consulted at need.*

*There had also come images from the Dark, and those
were like a poison in the body of the village. Hanker, the
smith, had dreamed of plague—and did it not strike
their valley from out of nowhere within two tens of days
thereafter? The folk who Dark-dreamed were shunned
by their fellows and forced to stand apart, and they were
given potions by the wisewife to make sure they did not
follow one such nightmare with another.*

It was a cloudy dawn when Krista awoke. Sweat
beaded her forehead, and her nightshift clung to her
spare body, which shook uncontrollably. She huddled,
drawn in upon herself, as though a monster padded
about the bed preparing to seize her if she put forth so
much as a foot.

The girl could not forget even a portion of her dream,
though much of it was strange beyond her understanding. At last, mechanically, she dragged herself from her
narrow bed and dressed for the day, but once she had
braided her hair she could delay no longer. All the rules
she had been taught to live by pushed her to her duty
now. She had never dreamed before, yet she knew well
the course that lay ahead for her. Luckily, no sounds
could be heard within the cottage—she alone had
waked.

Fog swirled around each of the small houses along
the lane, dimmed them to hulking shadows—forms
that, for the first time, Krista found menacing. The girl

shot wary glances left and right as she hurried to the last cottage at the very end of the village. There alone a lighted lantern hung, for it was the rule that any dreamer must seek the Keeper at the end of his or her seeing, even though the time might still be night. Raising fist against the door, the newest visionary smote its surface with what force she could.

Though Krista had been beckoned in by a wave of the Keeper's hand and sat now on a stool by the fire cradling a tankard of hot herb drink between her shaking hands, she still shrank from speaking. The loremaster, meanwhile, made ready the great recording book and set out a pen and a small cup of soot-black ink. He performed these tasks with great precision, as though he, too, were reluctant to break the silence. At length he turned his head to survey Krista, and the girl gulped, while the tankard threatened to douse her with some of its contents.

"Master Keeper," her voice sounded high and shrill in her own ears, "I have dreamed."

"And what have you dreamed?" he asked calmly.

His visitor set her drinking mug down on the raised hearthstone, then twisted her freed hands together in agitation, but there was no escape.

"Of the Dark—it must have been of the Dark!" The words burst forth in a near scream.

Krista expected her host to frown, to draw back in aversion, to order her from his hut with a curse, but the Keeper's inquiring expression had not changed. He was still merely expectant, not judgmental.

"Tell me, from the beginning," he said, as though he were greeting her in the village lane.

Her listener's attitude was soothing. Even though the young woman was still cold with fear. she found that she could, indeed, recount her vision from its start.

"I—I think I was at the inn. It was market day, and an outlander had come with a wagon filled with wares that were rich and strange. He did not cry aloud these goods—rather, he stood to one side and let the people look for themselves, with no pointing out of this or that item. Yet even without merchant's patter, the folk took many things, bringing out long-stored savings so that they might deal with him. But they did not need such monies, for the trader's prices were small—too small for what he had to offer. With each sale he made, I saw that his eyes looked like—" Krista took a swift breath, "like a hunter's watching a fook-hare nose at a trap!"

Shivering at the memory, the girl continued. "Most of the goods had soon been taken from the cart. It was as though no one thought the cost was set too low—they seemed not to wonder."

"But you did—and chose nothing from this wagon of strange wares?" the Keeper asked.

The dreamer shook her head vigorously. "I wanted nothing of what I saw; truly, I would have gone away, but I seemed to be held there."

Taking up the thread of her tale once more, she continued, "Soon all the money was gone, and the people had to bring items for trade to do their buying: hides, jars of preserves, lengths of weaving. At last the wagon stood filled once more, this time with the work of our neighbors' hands. Then the trader turned and started onto the mountain track. Yet none watched him go—they were all too busy comparing their bargains, boasting of their good fortune. But—" The young woman shuddered, raising hands to cover her eyes as if she could thus blot out an evil sight before her.

"But—?" the loremaster prompted gently.

"It was as though all they had taken from the stranger had been dipped into the blackest of shadows, and those shadows had passed into the folk themselves."

Krista halted, but her host continued to look at her, evidently awaiting more.

"What was then shown to you?" he asked.

"I—I went after the merchant up the mountain trail: again. something made me act against my will. And I found myself holding," the dreamer stretched forth her arms, gazing down on them as though they still held a burden, "my marriage quilt, the bride-piece I have stitched on ever since Gregor spoke for me before he went to the summer pastures.

"The quilt—or all I have done so far—is of patch-work. It has red in it, and yellow, like to those flames yonder." The young woman gestured toward the embers. "And it seemed that, when I held up the fabric, the colors blazed as does a fire newly fed. The quilt twisted in my hands; then it tore away from me and floated toward the trader and his cart. He and the wagon together turned black as a dark o' moon night until the cloth flapped down upon them both.

"There came fire at that touch, not the clean blaze of a home-hearth—this was black in flame. But it did not consume the quilt; rather the quilt smothered it. Then I woke, but a terrible fear was with me that that shadow-stuff had taken me prisoner also. This was a dream of evil, Keeper," the girl finished in a low voice, no longer daring to look at her host, and waiting for his judgment.

However, instead of accusing her, the loremaster

asked a very unusual question. "Of what, Krista, is your bride-quilt made?"

His visitor shifted on her stool, relieved and also irritated—why ask about matters that had nothing to do with the coming of Evil?—but she answered.

"Because I am the only girl of our house, my mam and my aunty opened an ancient chest, long stored, for my use. They brought out odds and ends of fair finery and of other bride-pieces stitched long ago. Then my mam drew forth a pattern, clearly drawn, which she said my grandmam's mother had lined because she had seen it in a dream—"

Startled by her own words, Krista stopped. For the first time she remembered Mam's tale. As she pondered what it might mean in the light of her own dream, the Keeper pushed the ink and pen a little away and began leafing through the record book. Shaking his head, he arose quickly to reach down another such volume from a nearby shelf, then began flicking through its pages.

"Your great-grandman was Mistress Magda." He put down the book, opened to a mid-point page. "That was in the time of Keeper Whitter—near to a hundred year-lengths ago. He noted her vision carefully, for he was certain it was more important than it seemed. Indeed, it must have been a true foreseeing."

Setting the record aside, the Keeper turned directly to Krista. "You have dreamed of evil, yes, but you have also been shown a weapon—"

"A *quilt?*" she exclaimed.

"All defenses are not arrows, swords, or axes, maiden," he replied, smiling at her bewilderment. "The Powers Beyond at times use other tools. How near done is your bride-piece?"

"I have the backing of the patchwork side, then the quilting itself to finish," the young woman answered. "There is still much to do—it is my rest-time work, you see."

"No," the loremaster shook his head. "It is your true work, and from now on you will sit to it every day. Through you, we have again had a fore-glimpse of the future, though that may not run in the same path shown in your dream. The Powers have granted us a warning, and we must abide by it."

Nothing was told to the village concerning the subject of the latest dream to visit the people; yet Krista had, each day of her work with thread and needle, an audience that came and went. A few of the men paused to examine her labor, and, while they could see no sense in what she did, they did not gainsay the Keeper that it should be done. However, all the women and girls, down to the smallest tot holding to her mother's skirts, came and watched, went and came again. There was always a cushion close to hand full of ready-threaded needles, and most of the womenfolk who viewed her work would add to that supply.

Each stitch must be set by her own hands—that Krista somehow knew without being told. Hers was not the lighthearted task that a bride's work should be—in fact, the girl no longer considered that her quilt was destined to serve any purpose of her own. Still, the design was bright and cheerful. Shades of red formed the hearts that promised joy to a new-wedded couple, and bright gold backed those symbols of love, each set into its proper square. The quilting lines themselves, though, were strange. and the young woman had to concentrate intently on the placing of nearly every one. The pattern was like no other she had ever tried, and several times she saw Mam and Aunty shake their heads over those swirling lines made up of tiny stitches.

The dreamer kept at her task, though her shoulders grew sore from continual bending over the frame set up near the hearth of the cottage. Sometimes her head ached, too and, when she closed her eyes for an instant, those lines appeared before her once again, running red as threads of blood. At first she expected to dream again, but when she stretched wearily onto her bed at night she slipped quickly into a sleep that was untroubled.

At the second seventh day after Krista had begun to work at her stitchery full time, from overmountain came a curious arrival—not the trader's wagon she feared but rather a ragged straggle of folk. Mothers trudged along, gaunt from hunger, striving to nurse infants who seemed close to the Lasting Sleep. Here and there among them limped a man held up by a crutch, or one who stumbled blindly, guided by a woman or a half-grown child.

Nothing of the Dark clung about these unfortunates— indeed, they were so far spent that they could not remember what had happened to them. But it was plain that an action of the Shadow Power had driven them into the valley.

On the twentyday after she had begun her work, the girl at last overheard one of the strange women, to whom Mam had opened the door, stammer forth some of the story. Beyond the mountains, the newcomer said, disease and death had ravaged the earth and all who walked it. Hope was at its lowest ebb when a fine lord had come riding into the town with many liveried men in his train. He had offered true gold for land whereon to build a dwelling, and he had been very free with his riches.

Joyfully, the men, and the women as well, had gone to labor on his walls and towers. When they had finished, a feasting had been appointed. To this, too, they had gone eagerly—only—

The woman who spoke shook now, holding close her silent baby. To that celebration had also been summoned Something *Else*. The fair nobleman had become foul, drawing about him black clouds, and from those—though it was the height of summer—fell pellets of ice. The trees drooped and died. Then his underlings had come among the people (who had found they could not escape) and sorted out all the men who were hardy. Meanwhile, monsters issued forth from the unnatural darkness to torment and herd all the other folk over now-blasted fields, past dead horses and cattle, to the very feet of the mountains. And the lord himself came to the place where the townsfolk huddled and laughed hatefully, boasting that more power existed in the world than those dolts could ever know and that he had seized such might and made it obey his will. He then pointed to the mountains and swore that not the rocks themselves would hold from him what he wished.

As the fair-foul one rode away, his shadow monsters moved in once more, and the outcast people strained to climb above the sad twilight that held them. Thereafter they had wandered, for how long none of them could count.

This tale was, indeed, the meat of an evil dream, but it did not contain the mysterious merchant and his wagon. Krista raised her voice: "It was a lord who used you so? Not—not an outland trader?"

The woman started, as though the question had pierced through a mist in her mind and a memory had suddenly become clear. "There *was* a merchant, but in an earlier season," she answered hesitatingly. "He brought many fine wares and was eager to trade—so eager that he asked under-price for what he offered. He took, in the end, bags of grain from the fields and fruits dried and preserved. Those goods he loaded into his wagon and was gone with the dawn, and we never saw him again."

Now she frowned, sitting up straighter, and fixed Krista with an oddly compelling stare. "He had strange eyes—" She paused, then added, "So did the evil lord and his men. Why do I think of that now?"

"Strange eyes?" The Keeper had come in and was standing behind the woman, listening. "In what manner were they strange?"

The speaker shook her head. "I do not know why— that is gone from my recalling."

The loremaster turned to Krista. "How near are you to your task's completion?"

The young woman surveyed the frame-stretched quilt. "Perhaps—yes. I shall finish by tomorrow's eve."

"I think." he said then, "that our time grows short. Why this Dark One hungers for land I cannot tell, save that the Shadow, which is lifeless, is ever greedy for what can bring forth things truly living. I doubt that these who have already suffered at the hands of the fair-seeming lord were meant to reach us; yet perhaps

the Great Power wrought their fate so, even as It fore-
warned us with two dreams, separated by ten tens of
years. Stitch well, Krista—the weapon must be ready
when the enemy appears."

There was much stirring in the cottage after he had
gone as the woman from overmountain was pressed to
tell all that had occurred. Her audience grew and grew
until they threatened the quilt-frame, and Mam had to
urge the wayfarer and those who would hear her outside. Then Krista's mother came back inside and stood
looking down as the girl set one precise stitch after another.

"You dreamed," the older woman said after watching
the work for a few moments, "and the Keeper has said
your vision was a foretelling. We know of old that such
night-seeings can be hard to understand, for they seldom show what *must* be—only what *might* come to
pass. In truth, I know not how a maid's stitchery can aid
against a great servant of the Dark, but—" Laying her
hand gently on Krista's head, she ended, "do what must
be done, daughter. You have the skill to do it well."

But do I? the young woman asked herself silently as
she straightened shoulders stiff from bending over the
quilting frame. Her many-times-pricked fingers were
sore, as well, yet she dared use no ointment on them lest
it stain the cloth. Her bride-piece. Krista pushed her
chair back a little and looked at the design measuringly.
Why had she thought the pattern so fine? Now the colors seemed to clash, and she knew she would never
want so gaudy a spread of stuff across her marriage-bed.
Marriage . . . she did not seem even to remember clearly
what Gregor himself looked like, how his speech
sounded—it was as though *he* were a dream long past.

(Take another threaded needle between thumb and finger; place another stitch with care.)

That night Krista worked as long as she could by the light of the five candles her mother had brought; and, just as her tired eyes blurred, she knew she had achieved her goal. Save for the edge-binding, which was the last and easiest task of all, the quilt was finished.

The same heavy sleep that had followed each day's labor on the bride-piece descended upon her, and once more she slept with no troubling dreams. When she awoke, she found her workday clothes gone from the chair where she had left them; in their place was her feast-day finery. She was starring at these rich garments blankly when Mam came in, a cup of new milk in her hand.

"The Keeper has sent word," the woman said breathlessly. "Two of the outcast folk who built a hut up-mountain have seen what we await. The trader comes!"

Krista half staggered to her feet. "The binding—"

"It is ready, dear heart, save for the last stitches. Drink now, and dress in your best, for this is the day toward which you have labored."

And the binding did go forward smoothly—even the pain in the girl's fingertips did not delay those straight and simple stitches. She put in the last of them just as the noonday sun placed a golden patch of its own on the floor within the edge of the open door.

That light was eclipsed as the Keeper came swiftly in. He did not seem to see Krista but had eyes only for what she held. "It is done? That one is coming past the mill—"

The young woman began to fold the quilt, Mam aiding her in trueing up the edges of the bulky square.

"It is done." she answered, hugging the bundle to her and stepping toward the door and the waiting lore-master. If the merchant was as close as the mill, then it was certainly time they were gone. Mam had assured her that the overmountain folk had all hidden themselves well out of sight so the trader would see only what he expected—a small village busied with its own affairs.

Then the girl was out in the sun, caressed by summer air. Her back straightened as she moved away from the cottage with her mentor; somehow she was sure of the worth of the work she held.

There was, indeed, a tall canvas-topped trader's wagon just pulling to a halt before the inn. The beasts that drew it—four of them—were certainly not the oxen that the villagers knew, nor were they true horses. These creatures had rust-red coats now matted with road-dust, and horns sprouted from their heads, short, stubby, and black—black as the hooded cloak their driver wore.

Though the day was fine and warm, the new arrival had wrapped that cape about himself as though he felt deep winter's bite. But the hood shifted a little as he moved to the rear of the wagon to loose the ties of the canvas and open to sight his wares.

The villagers surged forward as if they had been summoned by hunting-horn, fully intent on what was now on display—and that which lay within the cart seemed truly a hoard of treasures. The merchant stood to one side, merely watching the people as they milled about, pointing, reaching, urging each other to look at this wonder or that.

Fighting the pull of a strong desire to join them,

Krista broke free of that surge of folk and moved nearer to the trader. Then she might have called to him, for he swung around and faced her directly. His *eyes*— At once the girl recalled what the exiled woman had said. Neither blue, nor brown, nor gray, nor green was orbed there—rather it seemed as though two coals, black save for a spark of fire in their hearts, had been set into his skull.

The young dreamer did not know what was expected of her, but she shook the quilt out of its folds, and the gold and scarlet blazed in the sun, even as did the outlander's coals of eyes.

Two strides he took toward her, then stopped abruptly as the heavy length of cloth unfurled. dropping a corner at his feet. For the first time, he shrugged the cloak away, revealing a jerkin and breeches the dusty gray of wood-ash. About his waist was a broad sash-belt divided into pockets. With his eyes still fixed on the girl, his fingers sought one of those compartments, fumbled within (for he did not look down), and withdrew, a-glitter with gem-hung chains of silver and red gold.

The outlander did not speak but dangled these baubles at eye-level before her; however, when Krista made no move to take his bright bait, he abruptly dropped the necklaces into the dust of the road as if they were worthless trash. Again he opened a pocket in his sash, and this time—

He seemed to have caught the end of a rainbow and tossed it out onto the air. So fine was the substance of the shawl-scarf he now displayed that a goodly length had been folded into the belt-pouch before being freed to expand and float in the breeze.

The young woman gasped before she could control herself. This web was out of dreamland itself! The trader whirled the stuff closer, wordlessly urging her to take it—and this time he also made clear his own desire by pointing with his other hand at the quilt.

This time Krista found her voice. "No—this is not for trade."

The glowing embers of the merchant's eyes flared, and his lips twisted in what was close to a snarl. Loosing the scarf to the pull of the wind, his hand sought yet a third pocket.

What he drew forth this time was neither gems or fine fabric but a book. The girl's gaze was drawn to the scuffed hide that served as its cover, the symbol set thereon in dark metal—a design like to, yet unpleasantly unlike, the one graven into the door of the Keeper's cottage. Though her tempter made no move to open the volume, the young woman drew a deep breath.

Dream power—lore long forgotten in this land! She knew without explanation that this was the gift he was offering her now: such might as a great lord—or lady—could wield to gather all the world into an iron grip.

Krista swayed, her body striving to betray her. An unseen force was cloaking itself about her, pushing her closer to—

"NO!" She spoke her denial aloud, and in the same moment she was aware of new knowledge. This one—no true trader—was here to play on the greed of the village. Indeed, those of the company surging around the wagon (though some few had stopped, torn themselves away, and were watching the two who stood apart), looked like folk completely overcome by desire.

The outlander was smoothing, almost stroking, the cover of that noisome book, which seemed to Krista to waft forth an ever-growing foulness. Again she braced with all her spirit's strength against taking what he had to offer. The volume of vision-lore use was truly the most valuable thing he possessed; but by offering it to her, he had, in his arrogant assurance that she would be unable to resist, resummoned her dream—

Again Krista moved, not to step toward the merchant but rather to shake free the quilt that hung limply before her. Strength whose like she had not known she could summon flooded into her arms in that moment and, even as the scarf had lifted weightlessly into the air, this far heavier work of her hands rose. The red of loving hearts. the gold of good fortune flashed brilliantly in the sun. She whirled the bride-piece out, fearing suddenly that she might not have the agility to make it reach to where it must go. But—

The trader, who had opened the foul book, snapped it shut again as the cloth reached him. From its pages puffed up a black dust—and the girl knew that he used, now, his ultimate weapon.

Even as that murky powder thickened, the quilt tugged itself loose from the last fingerhold Krista kept upon it. She heard fear-stricken cries, answered by harsh orders barked by the Keeper. The villagers turned as one and stumbled away as fast as they could, women dragging screaming children, men waving staffs and walking backward as though to put themselves between the merchant and their kinfolk.

Red and gold—warmth of heart and truth of soul—

the two were mingled together as the quilt found its
prey. So brilliantly did the colors blaze that Krista's
eyes were dazzled until she was near blinded.

The bride-piece settled. Through its bright expanse
nothing could be seen of the outlander. Down, down, it
fell; then there was no sign of any wandering trader—or
Dark One.

Fire flared, leaping to the canvas of the wagon with a
roar of what might have been vengeance. In the same
instant vile odors arose, and tendrils of sooty smoke
coiled out, seeming wishful of trying to reach those who
watched.

There was a last burst of raging flame, and then the
fire was gone. Where the wagon and beasts had stood
was nothing save withered grass, but where the malevo-
lent merchant had paused to confront the maker of the
quilt lay a circle of scorched earth.

Krista sank to her knees, her face buried in her oft-
pricked hands. She had trifled with a great Power—and,
by the traditions of her people. payment would be demanded for this day's work.

Then hands were on her shoulders, supporting her
and drawing her to her feet.

"Have no fear, daughter—you have destroyed the
Dark in one of Its guises. True foretelling, Krista, a true
foretelling dream!"

The girl turned her head a little so she could see the
Keeper's face. In it, she read concern, but also pride—
pride in her and her ability with the needle.

She summoned a wan smile and, within her, peace
and belief were warm. Then she glanced to where the
work of her hands had become a weapon, and she said,
with a small catch in her voice,

"It seems that I must needs set to work again, or there will be no bride-piece come oathing-day."

Another quilt, yes—but one born of a dream of heart, not head.

HOLY, HOLY, HOLY
by Jane Yolen and Heidi E.Y. Stemple

World Fantasy Award winner Jane Yolen has written well over 150 books for children and adults, and well over two hundred short stories, most of them fantasy. She is a past president of the Science Fiction and Fantasy Writers of America as well as a twenty-five-year veteran of the Board of Directors of the Society of Children's Book Writers and Illustrators. Recent novels include *Child of Faerie* and *Welcome to the Ice House*. She lives with her husband in Hatfield, Massachusetts, and St. Andrews, Scotland.

Heidi Stemple lives with her husband and two daughters. Other short fiction by her appears in the anthology *Mob Magic*.

So I was sitting in front of the TV, closer than my mom thinks I should sit—beta rays or gamma rays or laser rays or some such—boring into my skull. Mind candy on the screen and I was halfway through an entire pint of rocky road.

That's when I had the vision.

No, I wasn't stoned. Not drunk. I don't actually do drugs or drink more than one beer. Okay, maybe two, but it has to be at a friend's house and me not driving home. Not after what happened to that idiot Jeremy last year.

And this woman suddenly appeared before me. You know, like Princess Leia to Luke, only she wasn't in miniature. Not a hologram.

This was more like a holygram.

OhmyGod! I thought. Holy, holy, holy. . . .

Now, it wasn't whatshername—Mary. That would have been bizzaro as I am, sort of, Jewish. I mean my folks are Jewish, but we go to the Unitarian church in Northampton. Which means we pray to whom it may concern.

That's an Unnie joke, guys.

Not Mary. Not dressed like that! Unless Mary's shopping Victoria's Secret these days and walking the streets of Holyoke looking for a pickup.

So there I was. Sitting, minding my own business, channel surfing. And seeing something that was obviously not there.

What's a girl to do?

Call Ghostbusters?

Call 911?

Call the funny farm?

Probably the last option. Immediately. Have them send the wagon and a white coat. I'm seeing visions, so I must be nuts. Oh, and by the way, I have an algebra test tomorrow that I haven't studied for.

Come to think of it, that would have been an added bonus. If I was locked away, I couldn't very well be marked down for missing the test.

But if I was stuck in lock-up, I'd have to miss Leah's big party as well.

So I thought: Maybe I'm not crazy. Maybe I'm just tired. Maybe all this school stuff has simply fried my brains.

So I called Leah. Leah Clemente. Not only is she my best friend, she's Catholic. And as Leah said when I told her, *Visions R Us*.

She came right over. Sat with me in front of the TV. Finished the rocky road and started on a box of Oreos. The double stuff kind.

And halfway through the second section of the Oreos, Ms. Vision showed up again. Only this time she was in a prom dress, one of those old-fashioned ones with too many petticoats, like some Disneyesque princess. Where she got it I haven't a clue. Slimline, slinky formals are in this year.

So I said to Leah, "There. Do you see her?"

She looked where I was pointing, about a foot in front of the screen. Even forced her eyes down to a squint.

"Nada," she said at last, which means "Nothing." Leah's taking Spanish. "This vision is meant just for you, Ashleigh."

"Right," I said.

"No one could hear Joan of Arc's voices but her," Leah said. "And remember the kids at Fatima? Only they could see the vision of Mary. Everyone else has to take the visions on faith."

"Faith? But why me? I am not a Faith kind of girl. And what does it mean?" I wailed.

She shrugged. "It wasn't a Catholic vision, so I can't help you there."

"But . . . Unitarians . . . we don't believe in visions."

She shrugged again. "We could always ask my priest, I suppose."

But neither one of us thought that was a good idea.

At least Leah didn't think I was crazy. That was something. She didn't dismiss my vision out of hand. But then, Leah believes in angels and the healing power of crystals (behind her Catholic mother's back, of course). She believes that prayer can help you win a ball game. (Though if both teams are praying, who is God going to listen to?) She believes that Jason O'Connell will ask me to the spring dance.

Basically, Leah believes in *everything*, so maybe she wasn't the most discriminating person to ask about my sanity. But at least she was on my side.

We finished the cookies, more ice cream, and some cold pizza in the fridge. Then Leah had to go home. It was a school night, after all.

The vision showed up again when I crawled into bed that night. It was dark and quiet and just after eleven. My parents were asleep already, my father snoring with those funny little pop-pop-pop sounds that makes Mom use earplugs. My little brothers were long gone into dreamtime. I had just hung up the phone a full hour after my phone curfew, but who's counting. Not my snoring dad. Not my mom in her plugged-in state.

I pulled the covers up to my nose, something I've done since I was a toddler, and was about to close my eyes.

And there she was. My vision. At the foot of my bed.

This time, though, she was in a long, black power suit, her hair skinned back in a French knot. I'd seen that outfit in Mom's Sak's catalogue. Not even Ms. D'Amboise, our French teacher, could have pulled *that* one off.

"Okay," I told her, sitting up and dropping the covers. "That's three times you've come visioning without a permit. Three. Like in magic. Or myth. Or fairy tales. Three Little Pigs and Three Bears and all. Only I don't get it. Who *are* you? What do you want?"

She was as silent as an old movie. A *really* old movie. Only she was in color, not black and white.

She held out her right hand.

Something glimmered in it in the semidarkness.

All right, I admit I was getting three things: Annoyed. (Wouldn't you be?) Scared. (For my sanity, of course.) And curious.

I closed my eyes because of the first two. And opened them again because the third—curiosity—won out.

She had a gold key in her palm.

I stared at her and she stared right back, as if waiting for me to do something. Like take the key.

"Now, hold on," I said. "You're a vision. A dream. A holygram. You can't expect me to do anything but see you, or else this is getting seriously spooky."

She got a kind of annoyed look, like Mom sometimes does, with those little snaky lines between her eyes. Her mouth grew thin, the lips hard together. Like a dash in one of Emily Dickinson's poems. She shook the hand holding out the key, as if emphasizing what she wanted.

I shrugged. Just what I needed. A vision with attitude. I leaned way over toward her, fully expecting my hand to go right through, and something cold dropped into my palm.

She disappeared. Not a wrinkle on the suit.

I looked down and there was this tiny key, dollhouse size, in my hand. It almost disappeared in one of my palm creases.

What was the key for? Why did I need it? Where could I find a door that it fit? All these questions—and the vision was nowhere to be found.

I reached for my phone to call Leah. Leah would know what to do.

But her mom gets super-cranky if I call after nine. And it was closing in on midnight.

Besides, I had a feeling that with this one, I was on my own.

What would a good church-going Christian do?
Use the Bible.
Maybe that was the solution. Some people believe that all the answers to life are in the Bible, though not us Unitarians.

I have two Bibles. A Jewish Bible which my grandmother gave me when I was born. Little did she know! And a Christian Bible I got when I turned thirteen, from the last minister but one at our church who Mom said had Congregationalist leanings and stayed only long enough to hand out New Testaments that he bought the sixth graders with his own money. Instead of a trip to Sturbridge, which is what the sixth graders usually got.

Two Bibles.
Three visions.
Why not?

So, I found the Jewish Bible, with its white-and-gold cover. It creaked when it opened, leaving me feeling a little guilty for never really looking at it before. It wasn't like there was dust on it that I had to blow off, or cobwebs growing, or mold, but that's how I felt. Good old-fashioned guilt. Like Mom uses to get me to stick to my curfew or not smoke.

I couldn't find the other Bible anywhere.

So I started reading. Well, skimming at first. I mean, it's kind of like Shakespeare, with old-fashioned words and people worrying about stuff no one worries about anymore.

I read a few pages, tried to figure them out, read a few more, figured those out, went back and read them again.

But though there was stuff there about the beginnings of the world—and the end—and lots of *begats* and *shalt nots*, there was nothing about a little gold key.

I must have fallen asleep. I think I remember my mom coming in to tuck me in and gently slide the book from my hand. She usually makes rounds about two in the morning, checking the lights, the stove, the windows, and us kids. I am pretty sure I heard the soft click of the light switch and the creak of my door being closed.

But I was in a dream. The kind of dream that you don't want to wake up in the middle of. The kind of dream that if you do wake up, you don't dare open your eyes because you think if you just try hard enough, you can fall back asleep and pick up where you left off.

Yes, I was definitely dreaming.

And there was my vision. This time she was wearing only a leaf. Well, three leaves. In strategic places.

"You know," I told her in my dream, "I am not a vision kind of girl."

She didn't say anything.

"You know," I told her. "You need a better place to shop. I could take you to The Gap. Or J. Crew. Or. . . ."

She still didn't say anything.

"You know," I told her, "you probably want a real Christian. Not a Unitarian like me. A half-Jewish Unitarian."

She smiled and made a motion with her hand as if unlocking a door.

"The key?" I asked.

She nodded.

"To what?" I asked.

But just like that she was gone and I was wide awake. Sitting up. Not sleeping or sleepy at all.

I turned on the light and there, beside my lamp, was the little key.

"I bet I'm supposed to feel like Joan of Arc," I said aloud. "So why do I feel like I've fallen down the rabbit hole?"

No one answered.

I swung my feet over the side of the bed and picked up the key. The very real key.

I stared at it again. Trying to find any meaning.

Any connection.

Any anything.

Nothing.

Frustrated, I went to set the key back on my bedside table. But in the exact spot where the key had just been was a wooden box. It was bigger than a jewelry box, but smaller than a shirt box. The wood was a light, golden color, and the grain showed through. There was a teeny, tiny keyhole that looked as if it fit my key.

"I should have noticed that . . ." I thought out loud, then my voice trailed off. I was pretty sure the box hadn't been there a second before.

Maybe my mom had snuck in while I was asleep and left a present.

Except my birthday was months away. Christmas and Chanukah even further.

Maybe my brothers had been playing a trick.

But they were three and five years younger than me and had been asleep for hours.

Maybe. . . .

But I was out of maybes.

There was only one way to find out about that box. I took the key, slid it into the lock, turned it once and a half to the right, and the box lid lifted open.

Silently.

Easily.

I put my hand in, expecting to feel something.

Nothing.

The box was totally empty.

But then I looked in.

Empty—but full. Full of stars, planets, nebulas, galaxies winking and blinking up at me. It was like looking into a window into the universe. Not Joan of Arc, then. Not Wonderland either. More like *Star Wars*.

I must have stared into the box for hours, trying to make sense of it all, fascinated by the glittering and very real display.

Sometime later someone knocked on the door.

I looked up at the sound and when I looked back, the box, the key, and the night were all gone. Daylight was tinting my window rose.

Oddly—for someone who had had no sleep at all, I wasn't a bit tired.

Mom stuck her head in. "Time to wake," she said.

"Never been more awake in my life," I told her. Because suddenly I knew what the visions meant.

The key hadn't opened the Bible or a church or a synagogue. It hadn't opened Commandments or creeds.

The key had opened me. To a world larger than a box of Oreos or the latest dress fad. Bigger than a party or a date with a cute boy.

It had shown me infinity. Possibilities. A universe full of them.

I picked up my algebra book. I still had time to study for my test. I had time to study for *all* my tests, because knowing what I now knew, I would not let such an enormity go.

ON THE EDGE OF SLEEP
by Jane Lindskold

Jane Lindskold rarely sleeps without dreaming vividly and in great detail. In fact, her first efforts at storytelling were probably attempts to relate some of those dreams to her very patient sister, Ann. Her more recent works include the novels *Legends Walking* and *Changer*. She has also completed two novels—*Donnerjack* and *Lord Demon*—for the late Roger Zelazny. She lives in Albuquerque with her husband, Jim, the only person she's met to have dreams as weird as her own.

L ions.
     A woman: tall, capped with short, dark hair. She wears a bright red leotard that clings closer than a coat of wet paint, that licks lasciviously about her torpedo breasts and jutting behind. The music she's dancing to has a hard, bass beat.

Angry.

Angry the way a thunderhead seems angry, brooding with raw elemental wrath, thudding to that interminable bass beat. She dances like she's fighting, no clean or smooth form either, no karate or aikido, no fluid grace. Boxing comes closer to what she's doing: hard, jutting stabs of arms that end in clenched fists. Feet that march or stamp yet paradoxically glide. It's impossible to really stamp when you're dancing on clouds.

Maybe that's what she's so angry about.

*   *   *

Lions: no soft-bodied creatures these, not the flabby, loose-limbed creatures that loll in zoos or perform in circus acts. These have the sleek, hard bodies depicted in ancient Assyrian art, muscles rippling under coats of shimmering tawny plush. Their eyes are faceted topaz, ripped top to bottom by a narrow cleft of glittering obsidian black. Looking at these great, shaggy-maned beasts, you know why hunting lions was considered the sport of kings and heroes.

Obscurely, you're glad that you're neither.

Nightmares are born blind, otherwise they'd perish from pure terror at the sight of themselves. Being blind, they're completely encapsulated within the chill certainty of themselves. Nightmare blindness is akin to being a god, an island of perfect knowledge unchallenged by trivial considerations like contradiction or the limits of reality.

Remember the story about the blind men and the elephant? One felt the leg and said an elephant was like a tree. Another touched an ear and said an elephant was like a great leaf. A third touched the tail and insisted an elephant was nothing more than a twig. The fourth, who fondled the trunk, couldn't be shaken from his conviction that an elephant was merely a giant snake.

The mind of a nightmare knows that an elephant is exclusively yet simultaneously twig, snake, leaf, and tree. It perceives no paradox in this contradiction, yet the nightmare is terribly and intensely sane.

Sanity is highly overrated.

Elsewhere or perhaps not.
Lovers, arms twined around each other, legs, too.

Softly converse, words meaning less than the gentle laughter, the exquisite sense of closeness that persists even after loving has given way to holding and idle caress. Yawns of deliciously relaxed weariness intrude into the attempts at conversation.

"I'm so tired," Brent says, "but I begrudge sleep."

Cecily laughs. "I know. My eyes can hardly stay open, but I don't want to part from you."

"I wish," he says, stroking her fondly, "we could be together, even in our dreams."

"That would be nice," Cecily agrees, snuggling her head more securely into his shoulder, "I wish. . . ."

She drifts off before she can finish the sentence. Brent is barely a breath behind her. Unknown to them, someone is listening. Wishes made on the fringes of sleep have strange power.

Dark grayness, thick and soft as the tightly budded fluff of a pussy willow. Above? Why not? Such conveniences make belief easier, though in this place they do not really apply. Below is light, powdery green, the color of bottle glass rubbed by restless tidal motion for fifty-seven years against the ocean floor.

Out of the gray above drift two stars, bright sparks from leftover fireworks. They float toward the smooth powder green, resolving into two forms as they touch.

One is a girl, maybe fifteen. She has the unfinished look of an adolescent, yet there is an uncertain coltish grace about her as if the balance of her newly budding body is maintained at some cost and might fly to pieces at a whim—a whim most definitely not her own. Her silky brown hair is tied back with no attempt at style.

Silky brown lashes curtain eyes that are almost amber gold.

If you stare at her for too long, you get a queasy feeling, similar to gazing into a fun-house mirror, a sense that the image will warp, change, distort at the merest shift of light.

The second star becomes a sturdy, cobby boy of about eight. His sun-bleached blond hair is a velvet bristle. He is clad in shorts, a dark blue T-shirt, and grubby sneakers. Intense curiosity glows within eyes whose color was borrowed from a summer afternoon sky. He hooks his thumbs in the belt loops of his shorts and stares impudently at the girl.

"You're not wearing any clothes," he says to her, his voice clear and piping.

And she isn't. Had she been naked before? There is no way to tell. Time—convenient little designations like "before" and "after"—seems remarkably fluid. Memory plays tricks.

The girl stands naked to his blue-eyed gaze, wondering why she isn't more troubled. Normally she hates for anyone to look at her body. Ever since it started changing, such inspections bring nothing but criticism: stand straight, don't slouch, wear a bra, don't stick your chest out, don't swing your hips, be modest, be proud, don't run, don't dawdle, don't scowl, don't. . . .

There is something very familiar about this boy, yet she knows she has never seen him before. She forgets that minor inconvenience in quiet envy, wishing she were eight or ten again and happy in her shape.

And as quick as a thought, she is, a flat-chested, skinny imp of a girl, agile and wiry as a monkey. She wears clothing much like the boy's: khaki shorts with lots of cool pockets, a T-shirt (hers is white but bright with violet flowers); her feet are bare. She curls her toes in the thick green grass, enjoying the cool feel of the earth beneath, never wondering that there is grass or earth where before there had been nothing but smoothness.

Above the sky is the color of the boy's eyes. The sun that glows benevolently upon them both holds the amber of the girl's own.

Without saying a word, the boy digs a round rubber ball from his pocket and tosses it to her. They play catch for a timeless interval, never noticing as the green field becomes dotted with trees, nor when the trees grow thicker, taller, closer, until boy and girl are surrounded by a jungle hung with vines and decorated with odd, bright flowers, each blossom holding the scent of a different bottle of perfume. A buzz like that of cicadas in late summer comes from jewel-toned enameled beetles clustering thickly on the branches and vines.

Then the ball bounces off one of the tree branches, scattering beetles into humming indignation. As one, the children notice the alteration in their landscape. The round, rubber ball is forgotten, vanishing in mid-arc.

Boy and girl draw close to each other, shoulder touching shoulder. Hands reach out blindly, fingers intertwine in a comforting clasp. The boy thinks he sees a flash of something tawny in the underbrush and croaks in a voice hoarse with fear:

"There are lions in places like this. Big ones with fangs like razors and claws like swords. They leap on you and drain your blood, then drag you off to their lairs to feed your flesh to their cubs."

The girl shivers, captured by his fear. Yet some part of

her seems to recall that lions live on plains as tawny as their fur, not in jungles. Tigers live in jungles. Tigers and snakes and spiders as big as your hand.

The jungle writhes accommodatingly. When the boy's lions slink forth, green-eyed tigers flank them just a few steps behind. Every eighth vine metamorphoses into a boa constrictor tasting the air with a flickering tongue. For variety, some vines become pig-fat anacondas or hooded cobras who dance to the shaking of a rattlesnake's tail.

"Spiders," the boy says, somehow knowing the girl's fear though she has not voiced it, "hide under rocks or big leaves or in the bells of the most beautiful flowers. Their eyes see in all directions and their bite feels like fire and makes you swell up like a grape."

The girl releases his hand, leaps away from a fluorescent pink hibiscus blossom dangling just over her head. As she does this, she notices that the flower is grasped in the fangs of an anaconda whose hissing laughter resolves into words:

"A corsage for your pretty breast, my dear. Take care. There's a pin in the hand that holds it, a prick in the pants that give it. Pinning the flower is fine, but beware the prick."

The flower hangs dangerously close to her face, for the girl is suddenly taller, standing almost eye-to-eye with the furry-limbed spider that leers at her from the flower's pink cup. She feels something pressing intimately against her newly budded breasts. Shoving instinctively, she discovers too late that the boy's velvet head is the intruder, that his stumbling retreat from the lion has brought him up against her.

Only as her push sends the boy reeling toward the

foremost lion, a big brute with sabertooth fangs and a heavy black mane, does the girl realize the depth of her betrayal. She screams, wanting to run. Away? Toward?

Vaguely aware of her scream, the boy staggers right into the lion's jaws. He crumples and falls, then collapses, pinned beneath the lion's paw. He can feel where the lion's fangs are buried in his throat. The rank darkness of the lion's mane beards the boy's face. Yet the boy is aware of an anomaly. Rather than sucking out his blood—as he had wholly expected—the lion is filling him with something. The vein in the boy's throat throbs, a hot burning sensation as if some fluid is being pumped into him through a fat syringe.

His throat grows tight. The pressure within it builds. He is the flapping length of one of those long, thin balloons that are almost impossible to inflate. The pressure mounts and mounts. The lion vanishes, all but its mane which grows into the boy, becoming beard, long hair, fur on chest and arms and groin. Just when it seems that his throat must split open, the boy feels a dam within him burst.

As the lion fluid courses into his body the boy swells, grows, becomes a hairy creature, man in shape but containing all the lust of the animal. Lust projects out from his pelvis, providing him with a fang of his own.

Clothed only in his hair, the boy become manimal lurches to his feet. Growling deep within his throat he casts about for his prey—for surely if he is hunter, then somewhere there must be the hunted. He finds it in the slender young form of the girl, cloaked now only in her loose, silky brown hair.

Vaguely, like a voice whispering in his mind he remembers: *She did this to me. She pushed me into the lion. Now she must accept what the lion has made me.*

Roaring, the manimal leaps at the slender naked figure. Wheeling, her mouth open in a silent scream, the girl flees; her slim white legs flashing out beneath the curtain of her hair lure him on.

They become nothing but pursuer and pursued. Neither notices as the elements of the jungle merge into the twisting corridors of an enormous house with a seeming infinity of corridors. Most of the doors that line these corridors are closed. Those few that are open show furnishings from a Victorian melodrama: thick carpets, mountains of bric-a-brac, fat cushioned sofas with short legs discreetly screened by ruffled skirts, tables clad in longer skirts. Even the beds are curtained.

The girl flees, knowing that to enter one of those cluttered rooms would be to invite the hairy man who chases her to have his way with her, to rend her softness with his fang. He shouldn't do that, should he?

As the pursuit goes on and on and on, something whispers to her that she need not flee blindly, that there is some safety she can seek. Thereafter, as she runs, bare feet slapping on marble, thudding against polished wood, making no noise at all on carpet, she is searching for that something, though what it is she knows not.

At last, over the rhythm of her running feet she hears a faint, throbbing noise, a beat as of distant music. Unconsciously, then consciously, she orients toward the sound.

In her peripheral vision she glimpses door after door as she pounds down the corridor, the manimal panting so close behind her that she can feel the radiant heat of his body, smell the stink of his sweat. Each door is dif-

ferent in some detail: doorknob of white ceramic,
faceted glass, rounded brass, cylindrical gold; wooden
surface carved, inset with stained glass, barred with
metal, encased in steel; windowed, peepholed, painted.
Door after door after door. . . .

None is the one she seeks. Behind her the manimal
gasps, leers. She has forgotten the boy. He has forgotten
the girl. All is forgotten but this eternal flight, eternal
pursuit. Within each grows the sense they are caught
within a trap from which they cannot escape. He is an
ache, a lust. She is a fear and, conversely, a longing.

They run on forever in this fashion. Then she spies a
door made from diamond-shaped panes of ruby-red
glass. Each panel is a different size, yet somehow the
hodgepodge lot manages to fit together. The panes vi-
brate to a familiar rhythm. Lights flicker on the other side
of the ruby glass, lights that are strobing in time to an
angry bass beat that reverberates even into the corridor.

With a triumphant shout, the girl presses down on a
latch shaped like an extended hand dipped in gold. She
leaps through the opening.

The hairy manimal, though right behind her, somehow does not get through before the door slams tightly
between them. He pauses, panting, listening. At the
sound of the music, fear touches him, cooling slightly
the urgent animality that is his blood. Then, urged by the
arrow sprung from his loins, he follows her. Fear drains
away. Again he is shambling, prowling, confident. He
has run her to earth and will have his satisfaction.

The room behind the ruby paneled door is full of
throbbing light. He must squint to see at all. As he casts
about for his sweet, slender girl, imagining lifting her,
pinning her, impaling her, he freezes in shock. Shock

becomes terror so acute that his skin tightens into goose pimples. His hair sheds from his contracted flesh, leaving him naked and afraid.

The silken-skinned, curvaceous female shape who had fled from him, enticing him on with glimpses of white buttocks through her long fall of hair has vanished. On a low stage before him stands a woman of a breed who only exists in comic books—or in dreams.

Though she looks nothing like the woman he had pursued, somehow he knows she is one and the same.

Huge breasts—high, firm, and rounded—demand immediate attention—even instant worship. Their only covering is a lick of opaque red fabric that barely covers two perfect nipples. The red fabric descends to hug a waist spanned by a tight golden belt, emphasizing the woman's slimness. Her lower torso—coated by more of that red fabric—is muscular and firm, yet somehow invites stroking. She stands lightly balanced on impossibly long legs. Her feet, incongruously, are bare.

Beneath a cap of dark hair, her features hold the enigmatic perfection of a goddess. Her smile is cruel and knowing, but that cruelty is not directed toward him personally. Indeed, she hardly seems to see him as she spins and stamps to a throbbing bass rhythm. He is reduced by that disregard—and preserved.

Bile wells in his throat as he accepts that against this vision he is impotent, predator becoming nothing but a man, a man who watches, but cannot act.

And before him, the woman dances and her dance is a battle. She fights with herself, with unseen forces, with contradictions she has never learned how to resolve. Though she never looks his way, she is acutely aware of the man who crouches in sudden humility before the stage. In her ears drum the lyrics to every song that ever celebrated the sexual vitality of woman—a vitality that morality denies, ironically seeking to preserve untouched something that only becomes real in the taking.

Amazonian yet solitary, virginity on steroids. Her breasts are torpedoes, ready to fire. Her cheekbones are high, edged with knives. Even as the woman marches and twirls, punches and boxes, battles opponents woven from air, her amber eyes hint at the misery behind the defiance, behind the anger. They voice a silent warning, a hidden plea:

Touch me at your own risk. But touch me. Touch me.

Yet the man kneeling on the floor is unable to raise even a finger, as frightened and repelled by this impossible possibility as the girl had been by his lion-bred animality.

Stalemate.

Which one of them hears the laughter first? Perhaps it is he, unentranced by that angry bass rhythm. Perhaps it is she, aware of a dissonance, a sound that doesn't match the throbbing of her own pulse.

Eyes amber, eyes azure lift and look.

Built by the strobing lights, taking shape from the darkness between the flashes is a figure that thrills the soul. Vaguely equine, it rears, pawing the air with hooves shod in static. Filmy mane and tail of thin steel wire snap, cracking like a bullwhip or like thunder if thunder had but one voice.

This equine figure is not solid black, as one might imagine, but black merely in outline. Within the outline swim splotches of vari-hued light, pinto patches on a crazy-quilt pony. Each of these patches holds a daydream, a dread, a desire. Each is glimpsed only for a moment, then vanishes. Only one thing about the horse-like figure is solid—the eyes, opaque with the opacity of blindness.

Watching the replay twisting through the images glimpsed on the figure's coat, boy knows girl and girl knows boy. They recall the idyllic meadow, recall tossing the rubber ball back and forth, the sun warm in a clear sky. They recall the jungle and the beasts that crept from their hearts into its. And the girl—no longer defiant Amazon, but neither vulnerable nymph—and the girl gasps:

"I pushed you!"

And the boy—no longer beast, but no longer sexless innocent either—and the boy cries:

"I chased you!"

Hands steal out to grasp in ample apology, but before they can touch the nightmare laughs:

"You wished!"

And neither boy nor girl—now youth and young maiden—have the least idea what the creature's cry means. Nor do they know each other beyond who they are that moment, a moment flavored by some whisper of the past they shared as boy and girl, pursuer and pursued, predator and prey.

"You wished!" laughs the nightmare. Blind-eyed and particoated, it leaps into the light between the flashes of darkness.

It is gone.

Boy frowns, "We wished? For what?"

"Not for that!" The girl's shiver encompasses all the terror that has just ended. Her amber-brown eyes cast here and there, uncertain there might not again be a flicker, a reshaping of reality.

"Not for that," the boy agrees. He still clasps her hand in his, thumb gently caressing her fingers.

"No," she says thoughtfully, "but if not for that, then for what?"

He shrugs. "Should that creature make any more sense than anything else?"

"Oh, Brent!" she says in loving exasperation, then starts. Slowly she says, "You're Brent!"

Realization dawns in his blue eyes and as it does the bones of the youth's face firm into adult lines, his shoulders broaden. His hair, which had been long and golden after some idealized, even asexual, image of youth, is shorn into the modern style dictated by most respectable workplaces.

"Cecily!" he exclaims, crushing her to him.

The woman who returns his embrace is no longer the doelike creature of pale skin, wide eyes, and virginal mien. She is become the polished, even elegant lady who had caught his attention at a company party and later won his heart. Only the light brown hair, soft as silk, and the amber eyes are indisputably the same.

They kiss. Comforted by that kiss, they solidify further into themselves, enhanced by their mutual images of each other.

"If we didn't wish for what we've just been through," Cecily says, returning to the issue at hand with the same tenacity that has brought her to the top of her profession, "what did that horselike thing mean?"

Brent frowns, drowsy memory returning. "We did wish that we could stay together even in our sleep."

"That bastard!" Cecily exclaims, the air about her becoming turgid and blood red. "We wanted to be together. We didn't wish for nightmares right out of a Freudian analysis session."

"But if that stuff is what we would have dreamed. . . ." Brent says doubtfully. "I mean I did have terrible nightmares about lions when I was in grammar school."

Cecily shakes her head. "I wouldn't have dreamed that junk. Maybe when I was younger, but I don't think even then. So what if you used to have nightmares about lions! Do you have them now?"

"Not for years," Brent replies decisively. "What about you?"

"Nothing like that running naked stuff." Cecily blushes. "Though that Amazon did bear a distinct resemblance to a fantasy figure of mine when I was younger. I guess I was really angry. Imagining her hitting things helped me cope."

"But you don't daydream about her anymore, do you?" Brent says, his tone playful, but his gaze perhaps a little apprehensive.

"Not a bit," Cecily assures him, but in the haze cast by the bloody air, she does bear a certain resemblance to that formidable vision.

There is a power in the moments between waking and sleeping. There is also a strange power in lies, especially half-lies, for like dreaming itself, they warp reality.

Across the veiled realms of dream pads a vision of vengeance, a woman in red astride a huge, black-maned lion. It's amazing what happens when you claim your fears for your own.

*   *   *

Nightmares are terribly and intensely sane. They must be, since illogic and irrationality are their stock in trade.

Sensing a diminishment of the power that had been coursing through it, one particular nightmare—its crazy-quilt coat awash with images in blue and amber—pauses. Being sane, it does not panic. Being logical, it immediately deduces that something must be interrupting the flow of psychic energy. Being practical, it focuses, intent on finding the source of the blockage and cleaning it out. Being reasonable, it suspects one of its own kind. What else could it be?

It sniffs the dream ether. Imagine its shock when—instead of scenting the nightmare odor of trapped anxieties and buried fears—it encounters the rank scent of lion blended with a perfume that might be called Aggression.

Fear pangs within the nightmare's heart—a sharp sensation that would set the heart pounding and the blood racing if nightmares possessed either hearts or blood.

Since nightmares are eminently sane, reality twists. Instantly this nightmare possesses both heart and blood—reality even tosses in a circulatory system. Beneath the shrouding of images that color its coat, the coursing of red blood is horribly visible.

The nightmare gasps in shock at the transformation and because one cannot gasp without lungs, throat, mouth, and nose each of these organs form—not the images with which a nightmare clothes itself, but real flesh and blood counterparts.

Part ethereal dreamstuff, part solid, the transforming nightmare casts about. It feels stirring in the air, hears movement. A voice deep and masculine, a voice light and feminine share soft laughter. Instantly, the nightmare becomes angry. It lunges at the source of the laughter, finds nothing, but a sharp pricking on its rump, as from the impact of four distinct and terribly sharp claws, draws a trickle of hot blood.

Instinctively, the nightmare flees from the sensation. Because ethereal hooves cannot bear flesh and blood, further transformations occur. Feet, ankles, and legs— each with the necessary bones, sinews, and all the rest—coat the nightmare. A nervous system is thrown in *gratis*, and as it comes into play, the nightmare realizes that the pricking at its rump is pain.

It runs to escape the pricking of lion claws and the nipping of lion fangs and with each step the nightmare becomes more and more solid. Something must hold all these organs together, so tissue forms in between. Skin grows to cover the entire body. Each progression is completely logical and rational—each traps the nightmare within a solidity that makes it (accustomed as it is to continual shifting and change) increasingly claustrophobic.

At last, transformed into a solid human, it runs blindly from its pursuers. Only its gender is unfixed, shifting back and forth as first male, then female impulses touch it. There is some comfort in this normal instability, but not enough for the nightmare to regain control.

Beneath the tender skin of new feet the surface changes with every few steps: rough stone, plush carpet, smooth wood, hard tile, rasping concrete, slippery mud. The temperature shifts, gusts of wind bearing not only varying degrees of heat and cold but a host of odors.

Hearing is bombarded by a thudding, angry bass beat and by mocking, bi-tone laughter.

Mouth dry with panic, the nightmare strains to anticipate what will come next. A terrible ache wells up behind the blind eyes, a thudding in the center of the forehead. If only it could stop for a moment! But the pursuers are as relentless as a nightmare. Each pause, each attempt to rest aching muscles is met with claws across flayed buttocks.

The nightmare begins to weep. Hot salt tears gush from newly grown tear ducts. Steady as rain, they wash the blindness from the nightmare's eyes, rinsing away the opacity. Flakes—or perhaps the classic scales—fall from the blind eyes. For the first time in its existence, the nightmare can see.

It wheels to face its tormentors. Two indistinct figures spread their arms. The surface between them glows as brightly as a polished mirror. In this mirror the nightmare sees only itself—itself as it has always been.

Nightmares are born blind, otherwise they'd perish from pure terror at the sight of themselves.

But nightmare blindness is akin to being a god, an island of perfect knowledge unchallenged by trivial considerations like contradiction or the limits of reality. Therefore, this nightmare stares at itself, at the shifting images within its patchwork coat and it considers that it has not perished.

Yet.

And the images within its coat move—puzzle pieces shifted by invisible hands—until they form one image: lovers on the verge of sleep, naked limbs intertwined, the woman's head pillowed on the man's shoulder.

The woman is saying, "I don't want to part from you."

"I wish," the man says, stroking her fondly, "we could be together, even in our dreams."

"That would be nice," she agrees, snuggling her head more securely into his shoulder, "I wish. . . ."

She drifts off before she can finish the sentence, the man barely a breath behind her. Wishes made on the fringes of sleep have strange power.

Time, like everything else in dreams, is fluid. The nightmare considers that it may have wronged the two sleepers. Perhaps it has become more sympathetic due to its own venture into nightmare, perhaps it merely admits that it may have obeyed the words but not the spirit of the wish.

Once again, wish power teases the nightmare, entices it to pick up the thread and play. This time, however, the nightmare turns away, deliberately renouncing that possibility.

And time spins, reestablishing reality as it had been before the nightmare had meddled. The scales encrust the nightmare's eyes, bringing forgetfulness with darkness. The last thing the nightmare sees before comfortable blindness seals it once more into certainty is the soft rose pink and gold of an approaching dream.

Wishes made on the fringes of sleep have strange power. Sometimes they even come true.

DREAMFISHER
by Nancy Springer

Nancy Springer is a lifelong fiction writer, author of thirty-three volumes of mythic fantasy, children's literature, mystery, suspense, short stories, and poetry. Her latest novels are *Plumage,* contemporary women's fantasy, and *Sky Rider,* a ghost story for children. Recently released was *I am Mordred*, a young-adult Arthurian fantasy from the point of view of Arthur's illegitimate son. A longtime Pennsylvania resident, Springer is an enthusiastic, although not expert, horseback rider, and a volunteer for the Wind Ridge Farm Equine Sanctuary, a home for horses that have been rescued from neglect or abuse. She lives in Dallastown with several psychotic cats.

> "... *except for the inhabitants of a nameless mountain in Barbary, who themselves have no names; nor have they dreams.*" (From a fragment attributed to Herodotus.)

They lived on the mountainside very simply, the men hunting meat, the women gathering roots and nuts and the seeds of mountain grasses, the children playing at being men or women. They spoke names of things, of course, to say "Bring me sticks for the fire," or "I am going to hunt deer," but these names had come down to them through generations, bestowed by some creator at the beginning of time. Fearing to take upon themselves the function of gods, they did not name one another;

they were few enough, and needed only to point at a
person, a hut, or a direction taken. To say "that man"
would have been impolite, and to say "the fat man" or
"the bent old woman" would have been very rude. Children learned early only to point. They learned early to
kill rock rabbits and skin them and cook them and eat
them. They learned to throw stones and gather fire-
wood.

All the children learned these straightforward ways
readily, except for a certain girl.

She looked no different than the others—dark eyes
and shaggy dark hair, tawny skin, bare callused feet—
but wrong things came out of her mouth. It began when
she was very small. "Cake!" she cried, pointing her
pudgy finger at the round russet disk of the setting sun,
one edge hitting against scalloped clouds. "Cake! Yittle
girl eat it!"

"No, no!" her mother whispered to her, glancing
around to see whether anyone else had heard. "It is the
sun." Sun was sun, not a round flat cake of seed meal
baked on the hot stones by the fire.

"Yooks yike cake!"

The mother should have punished her then and there,
the others declared later. But the mother was too tender-
hearted, and the girl went on in her wrongheaded ways.
"Yooks yike flower!" she would cry, pointing at a rose-
and-white cloud when she should have been gathering
sticks for kindling. And as she grew, "See, the shadows
in the moon, they look like a rabbit sitting up on its hind
legs!" But the moon was the moon, not a rabbit. "See
that yellow flower, it looks like a dragon's head!" And
the wrongnesses she said grew more perilous day by
day. "That's a fire flower, see, and that one, it's a blue

butterfly." But a flower was not a fire or a butterfly! The girl did her chores well enough when she was not staring foolishly at a cataract or something, but she said such frightening things that other children stayed away from her, or were ordered away, and adults muttered when they saw her coming, for soon she would be grown, and then what?

All too soon the girl began to experience the monthly courses of a woman, and it was time for her to find a mate.

Often this process took care of itself, but not in the case of this girl. Boys her age kept far from her despite the attraction of her slender body, her fresh smooth skin, her bright-eyed face—she was comely, that girl, but too much one to say untoward things. Too strange.

Therefore her mother acted in her behalf. Discreetly, the mother arranged matters with an older man who averred that he could handle a slip of a girl and teach her to keep her mouth closed. Although respected, this man had no woman, because—well, it would have been very, very rude to say, but—

"No! He looks like a bear turd on feet!" the girl cried when her mother brought the man to her by the village spring, where everyone had gathered for the rite of joining. "No, I can't! I won't!"

The man's lumpy brown face flushed even darker with anger. "Be silent," he ordered.

"No! You *are* a giant turd!"

"Turd," some youngster in the back whispered, snickering.

The boy's mother turned and boxed his ears till he howled, but the damage was done. Folk gabbled with terror; what unknowable craft was in this girl? The man now called Turd picked up a stone from the ground and hurled it at the girl who had named him.

It hit her on the chest hard enough to stagger her. Others roared with echoing wrath and joined in, elder men and women throwing stones the size of their fists. If any had caught the girl on the head they would have felled her, but they struck her body and legs, cutting and bruising her and making her cry out. She looked for her mother and saw her standing to one side, weeping but not trying to stop the others as they all joined in, shouting and chanting and stoning the girl in a frenzy, boys grabbing the largest rocks they could handle, children hurling—

Smaller stones flung by children hit the girl in the face. She turned and fled down the mountainside until she could no longer run and she fell to the rocky ground, sobbing.

She awoke at dawn, shivering from lying on cold stone, stiff and bruised, with no memory of how she had gone to sleep.

Blinking, she sat up to rub her eyes, but winced when she touched her sore, swollen face. Then she winced anew at the memories, and her heart hurt worse than her body or her face.

Close at hand lay a deerskin bunched into a bundle. The girl stared at it a moment before she fumbled it open. Inside she found a few rounds of cake and three strips of dried venison. And a stone even larger than a man's clenched fist.

The girl flung the rock away, but its message stayed with her, all too clear: she was not to return.

But at least someone cared whether she might starve.

She stared at the flat cakes. They looked like the cakes her mother made. But then, all cakes looked much the same.

Her throat closed against the sight of the cakes, but she felt thirst. Water. She needed to find water.

Many nameless shallow streams and cataracts sprang out of that mountainside, running down over rocks to no one knew where. Looking into the distance down-mountain, the girl, like her elders, had never seen anything more than mist the color of frosty moss. Anything could hide in that mist, folk said. And the tacit wisdom of her people was that staying alive meant being wary of hidden things, demons and angels unseen in the night, fanged dragons unseen in caves, unknown dangers unseen in the distance. No one went where hidden things were.

The girl took the deerskin laden with provisions and walked aimlessly until she heard the trickle of water. When she found the rill—it could have been any mountainside stream, perhaps a few fingers deep and no broader than her slender body—she cupped her hands to drink, then splashed water on her face. Its cold touch stung her cut lips and reddened eyes, yet soothed her soul.

Then she started downmountain, following the rill.

She had no reason for doing this except that she had to go somewhere, and the rill would give her water to drink.

None of her people ever ventured downmountain.

But they were not her people anymore.

*   *   *

She walked through days and shivered through nights until all her dried meat was gone and her bread gone except the last half a cake. She had found a few groundnuts to eat, but little else, and she had seen many deer but no folk, nor did she expect to find any; she presumed no people in the world but those—those who were no longer her people. She presumed even less to find any other folk now that she saw how vast the world was. Each day she thought she should have walked nearer to the white-gray mist, and each day it looked as far away as ever.

The day she ate her last half round of cake was the day she came to the place that changed everything.

At first she saw only that the rill she was following ran through a cleft of stone too narrow for her. She would have to climb over the rift of rock in her way, just as she had climbed over many others. But this time, as she reached the top, she stiffened to a halt, dropped to a crouch, and stared.

"What is it?" she whispered, for never had she seen such a shining mystery before.

A dark bright bigness filled a hollow of the rocks, a gleaming round that gave off sparks of white light amid colors—she had never seen such colors, sky stone tree all blended like a dusky rainbow. What was it? And where had her rill gone?

For a long time she froze like a baby rabbit and just listened and looked, only her nostrils moving to catch any hint of danger. When she dared to move, she clambered to the cleft where the rill ran and peered down, tracing its shadowed course.

"Water?"

The great bright rainbow round had to be water, it

grew out of the rill and therefore must be water, yet—
she stood atop the crags at a cautious distance and
stared—yet how was it water? It seemed packed or
piled in such a way as she had never seen, so much
water in one place that it seemed to thicken and change,
she could not look through it to whatever lay under-
neath. Perhaps there was no bottom? But there had to
be. Stone held it.

"Like when I hold water in my hands to drink," she
breathed. The mountain held this water in one place?

Slowly, slowly she walked forward for a better
look—then leaped back, for she had seen the form of a
person moving on the sheen of the water. Her knees
weakened. She sat trembling atop the rocks.

Yet she did not leave. She whispered, "It looks like—
like . . ."

She had to know what it was, this place that made
water look like other things.

Still trembling, she eased forward on her hands and
knees. Crouching over the stillwater wonder, she gazed,
gazed, and in the muchwater she saw intimations of
light, dark, shift, change; the personform was only a
shadow now, blended with darker green shadow that
hinted of tree. After a time fascination put an end to her
trembling, and she surrendered to her wonder, sitting
atop the rocks with her legs dangling over the edge,
staring down into enigma.

It looks. . . . like. . . .

Like the surface of night sky, glossed with tricky
shadowlight behind which she sensed depths she could
not guess.

Hunger pain interrupted her thoughts. Barely aware
of what she was doing, she reached for her last half-

round of cake and bit into it. A tiny crumb fell from her mouth onto the top of the muchwater—

A flash, a splash, a glimpse of something so shining she blinked, and then she sat stiff with awe watching circle circle circle open wider and wider like her own eyes.

Circles faded and ceased. Muchwater lay still again. The girl stared into glimmerings, shadows, hints of movement. Something stirred in there, under there. What had been that sudden shining?

Without giving herself time to be afraid, she dropped another crumb.

Flash, splash, an arc of something that gleamed like cold fire. She squeaked with wonder and terror but kept her eyes open, gazing intently, and she thought she saw something flitting away under the surface. More than one something. Something that flies in the water, she thought, like birds in the sky. Something that soars down in darkness like angels and demons in the night. She felt herself quivering again, but she had to know, she had to know, she dropped a whole scattering of crumbs, then gasped as the surface was broken by brightnesses flying up like great sparks, by bubbles and flashings and circling ring ring rings and more mysteries skimming just beneath sight.

It was such glory, such beauty, that she calmed; muchwater calmed also. She sat still and rapt; muchwater lay still and shining. She gazed down, and from the water a dark-eyed girl gazed up at her. Within the face of that shadowy girlform she saw something scud bright, like thought.

The girl gasped, "It's like me! It *is* me!"

The wonderwater was her self, her soul, her mind, a

bright dark mystery out of which odd and frightening things flashed then vanished—until the next time.

Something roiled like thunder just below the face of the muchwater. Something roiled like thunder and lightning and freshets after a springtime storm within the girl's selfhood. She stared at the bread in her hand without recognition. She stared at the muchness of water. She shredded the bread and tossed it so that it fell like snowflakes into the water-like-a-night-sky below her. With a soughing sound like hard rain the surface burst into lightning rainbow arcs like—like. . . .

Long after the wonderwater had stilled, the girl sat gazing, gazing. What was the name of this darkling strangeness, water yet not water as she knew it? What were its brightflash emanations? She had to know, she had to know this place, she had to know herself.

For days the girl camped near the muchwater and did not quite starve. There were rock rabbits; sometimes she managed to snare one and char it over the fire she cherished on a hearth of stone; the fire had taken a whole day to start, so she never let it go out. In the chill nights she curled by the fire with her deerskin wrapped around her shoulders. At dawn she would look at the muchwater, awed anew each day to see it breathe mists of steam, living thing that it was. She grubbed for ground nuts, robbed a rock rat's nest of its pine seeds, found some sour bunchberries to eat; the bunchberries mattered most, for she dropped one on the wonderwater and found that it brought forth a bright swirl out of the darkness. She dropped a pebble, and it only splashed and vanished. The bunchberry did something the pebble could not. After that the bunchberries were for feeding the mystery, not her.

Day after day, whenever her hungry belly would let her, she studied the shadowshining water, in rain and sun and twilight and starlight. Atop the lowest rock to be closer, gazing into the round of water as if into a lover's eye, she still felt not close enough. There came a blue-sky day when, instead of sitting, she lay belly down on the rock with her head stretched over the lip, her arms reaching for the water, bunchberries in hand, yearning.

She dropped a bunchberry, watching intently as it made itself a bed on the face of the water which was also her face, shadowy eyes staring back at her with the bunchberry lying red like a wound in between; why was it that bunchberries did this thing and pebbles did not? A moment later there came the flash, the shining, and oh, oh, this time she had glimpsed a gleaming maw and eyes, red eyes like wet fire, it was an angel demon out of deep dark girlself mind, almost close enough to touch. If only she could touch it, hold it in her hand a moment, then she would—maybe she would know. Maybe she would understand the wrongness in herself.

Maybe she would be able to go home.

Her chest heaved with wanting. Wriggling on her belly like a serpent, she pushed herself closer to the water, head and shoulders and half her trunk over the lip of the rock, arms stretched down. Almost—close—enough—to—touch—

Making herself as long as she could, like a willow wand, she dropped a berry. She saw the mystery flash up out of darkness and oh, oh, it shone, and the sight of it so near quivered her whole body and sent her lunging toward it, her hands opening like stars—

She heard a great roaring splashing commotion as she flew down into the water-like-a-night-sky, and it was very very cold, its icy coldness thick all around her and in her ears, and she could not breathe.

She choked and thrashed when she tried to breathe the water, and it hurt very much. But then it became like sleeping, dark and blurry, like the inside of her mind when she closed her eyes. Some smudges of color like distant stars and muted sunset sky, but that was all.

Then there was not even darkness. It all went black.

She awoke to find herself lying beside a blazing fire, shivering even in its warmth, wrapped in—what was this thing?

"If you desire to go fishing, young woman," said a man's gruff voice, "you should do so by means of the proper equipment."

She was home, somehow, with one of her people? But—whoever he was, he spoke her language, yet she could not understand what he was talking about. Fishing? Means? She sat up to peer at him over the flames of the fire.

He was not one of her people. She had never seen him before, a strong old man with flossy white hair and beard, his skin lizardy and much lighter than hers—that frightened her, and so did his eyes, pale like a watery sky between saggy white lids. She had never seen such sky-colored eyes. But they seemed not unkind, although it was hard to tell in firelight.

Firelight? Why was it night already?

The pale-eyed man nodded at her as if she had done

something good by sitting up and gawking at him. "Greetings from the civilized world," he told her. "I am Herodotus, at your service. And what might be your name?"

There it was again, he spoke and she understood, yet she did not understand at all. Civilized? Name? Herodotus? She felt herself frowning from listening to him.

He nodded again. "It is a pleasure to meet you also," he said. He turned the spit he had rigged up over the fire, upon which something sizzled. It smelled good, the girl's belly noticed, but she did not think to wonder what it was; her mind was all taken up with the stranger. Where had he come from?

"I first became aware of your whereabouts when I sighted your fire," the old man said as if he heard her thinking. "For the past two days I have been observing you at a discreet distance. But when you performed your remarkable feat of fishery, I essayed to pull you out. I did not care to let a perfectly good barbarian drown."

The girl gave up listening and only heard, her eyelids drooping, no longer trying to understand but only to know what he was like, as she had learned what the wonderwater was like.

"Up you popped," he went on, "hanging onto an exceptionally large, exceptionally placid trout with both your little brown paws. I jumped about, I offered you a hand, I called to you, but you would not let go of the confounded fish. Not even when you went under again. I had to grapple you out by the hair. You are fortunate to have such long, strong hair, young lady."

He was like . . . he was perhaps a god? One who gave names to things?

Oddly, despite this thought, she felt not at all afraid of him any longer. He had made her campfire large to warm her. He had wrapped around her a large warm something, not a deerskin. He was Hero—Hero—what had he said he was? It did not matter. She lay down again and closed her eyes.

The next thing she noticed he was shaking her by the shoulder to awaken her. "Dinnertime."

She peered at him.

"Time to eat."

She sat up. The old man, what had he called himself, a hero dotus? His clothes were pale like his skin and eyes and very odd, made of some sort of thin droopy hide that was not hide, for no hide was colored so white, as white as his hair. It did not matter. He brought something on a dock leaf and laid it on the ground beside her. It smelled good, fatty, like meat, but it did not look like any cooked meat or fowl she had ever seen.

"What's that?" she whispered.

"Eureka! She speaks!"

She stared at him.

"Excuse me. I beg your pardon. Dinner is your precious trout, that's what it is, the most enormous trout I have ever seen. More than large enough for both of us. I'm obliged to you for catching my supper as well as your own."

"Trout?"

"Fish," the hero dotus said. "Eat it."

She understood nothing except the last two words. Eat. Yes. She felt weak and faint, her gut ached with hunger, and whatever the flaky white meat was, it smelled wonderful. She ate.

A young man so beautiful he must have been a god or an angel, a young man with sky-colored eyes and skin that shimmered like the wonderwater, held her in his arms. Just looking up at the soft corner of his mouth made her groan with love of him. He embraced her close, close, with her head nestled next to his, and he flew—great wings sprouted from his back, butterfly wings, eagle wings, no, now they flowed up the color of springfreshet waterfalls and he was flying, flying, she was being carried along with him, and there was no up or down it was all night sky wonderwater rainbow shining—but then he was still beautiful but no longer human, he was a gleaming serpentine presence she could not name, he no longer had arms he no longer held her she was falling, falling, she thrashed and screamed—

"It was just a dream," said a man's gruff voice. As usual, she did not understand.

Odd. It was night, and she lay by a campfire, that was all. She lay warm, wrapped in something warm, and she felt very sleepy. . . .

She stood at the narrow mouth of a cave, with stones hitting her from behind. Her people, they were stoning her, they wanted her to go into the darkness under the mountain and face the dragon for them. The stones hurt and she could not understand what they were yelling at her, but her mind leaped like a deer, flew like a winged flint, and she understood that there was something they needed, her people, something they wanted the dragon to give them or give back to them. She sweated with fear but she had to do it, because she, the girl who said "yooks yike," was the only one who could. She went in. . . .

"Water eyes," she murmured. "The dragon had water eyes."

"Go back to sleep," a man's voice grumbled from the darkness beyond the embers of the campfire.

She understood him for a change. But where was the dragon?

She slept.

Her mother crouched on the mountaintop, weeping, weeping, and her mother was a greatness the size of the mountain, her mother's tears ran down over the crags like snowmelt falling in cataracts ever greater until tears filled the world like water in the palm of a god's hand and drove the frosty green mist away. In the face of the water—no, it was her mother's face, eyes red from weeping, eyes like bunchberries. They *were* big red berries awash in tears. The girl flew, she could fly in water, she had winged hands, she flew to the surface and gulped her mother's red berry eyes. They filled her and made her content.

She woke up. The hero old man crouched over the fire, feeding twigs to the embers. The sky glowed all fire colors. It was morning.

"Because I am evil," the girl explained.

Sitting beside her on the lowest crag overlooking the muchwater, the old man eyed her with his shaggy white eyebrows raised. "They gave you those bruises because you are evil?"

"Yes."

"And in what way, pray tell, are you evil?"

"I—there are wrong things in me."

"Such as?" As he questioned her, the hero dotus man pulled out of his pack a stick around which was wrapped the thinnest sinew the girl had ever seen.

"There are oddnesses in my mind and they leap from my mouth. I say wrong things. I said the sun was like a cake."

"Well, so it is, sometimes." He flipped a rock, plucked a grub from under it, and skewered it upon a feathered device at the end of the sinew.

"I said the man they wanted me to mate was like a turd."

The hero dotus laughed and unwound sinew from his stick.

"I said he *was* a turd. That was evil."

"It was rude, perhaps. But perhaps it is true?" The hero dotus tossed the grub like a flying feathered thing to settle on the top of the muchwater. Like a serpent made of cloud wisp the sinew followed.

Yes, it was true. No, it was not true. The girl could not answer.

The hero dotus asked her, "What is your name, little one?"

To name a thing was to say what it was. But perhaps a god was allowed to ask and know. The girl pointed at the wonderwater glimmering midnight sky stone tree colors below.

"Your name is Tarn? Pool? Deepwater?"

Instead of answering—if she could have answered— the girl gasped, for the selfwater roiled and out of it leaped a shining rainbow arc. She saw the red eyes, the maw, the moongleam jaws as it seized upon the feather-bone-grub thing.

The old man shouted and yanked his end of the sinew, pulling the gleaming mystery clear out of the water.

With a scream the girl leaped up, standing rigid. It flapped like a wing, but it was not a wing. It shone like running water, but it was not water. It writhed like a serpent—

"It's just a fish!" the hero dotus yelled at her. "Big one! Dinner!"

He hauled it in. On the rock it thrashed wildly, and behind its eyes red slits opened like wounds, and—and it suffered from being brought out of the wonderwater into the world, the girl saw, standing back, shuddering. But the hero dotus quickly put an end to its suffering with a stone. It lay still.

"I have never seen such huge trout as there are in this tarn," he said.

The girl took two cautious steps forward and crouched by the dead—thought?

"Fish?" she whispered.

"Yes. Trout. Big one."

With one tentative finger she touched its gleaming flank, all the colors of a wet dawn.

"Do not touch the fins. Or the gills. They're sharp."

Fins? Gills? She pulled her finger away.

The old man said, "It's a pity when they flop so. The one you caught didn't struggle. Not at all."

Her mind thrashed like the hooked trout, then leaped free and flew. She whispered, "You gave me a—a one like this to eat?"

"Yes. Why?"

"Because—because it is a thing from out of my mind."

For once he was the one who did not understand. He

raised his cloud-white brows at her, his rain-blue eyes peering.

"When I ate it," she said, "in my mind there was a young god who took me flying. And there was a dragon under the mountain. And—"

"Dreams," the hero dotus said. "It gave you dreams. Sometimes, if you eat heavily before you sleep—"

"Dreams?"

"Yes."

"But I never—I never did dreams before."

Sleep became like the wonderwater—or tarn, as the hero dotus named it. The mountain pool. Sleep was a dark surface under which mysteries shone, a black cave in which shining dragons dwelt, a deep womb in which every night she was reborn.

In the days the hero dotus taught her the names of things. Fish, fins, gills, swim, bait, hook. Mantle, robe, toga. To the hero dotus everything had a name or ought to have, even the mountains—Mount Etna, Mount Atlas, Mount Olympus. The hero dotus told her stories of the gods and stories of a village called Athens, far below the moss-colored mist, where the huts were made of stone. And he wanted to know stories of her village, but she knew none.

"My people do no stories," she explained as they sat by the fire after yet another excellent dinner of cresses and wild onions, seedmeal cake and roast trout. "My people do no dreams either."

"And names?" the hero dotus teased her, for every day he asked her name, and she did not answer. "Do your people do no names either?"

"Just to say girl, boy, man—" She thought of the turd

man. "It was because I gave him a name that they drove me away."

The hero dotus gazed at her, his brow troubled. After a moment he made a long arm and plucked a wildflower from somewhere in the dark. He asked her, "What is this?"

"A flower."

"Yes, but what kind? Do you know?"

She shook her head. Kind? "It looks like a little sun," she said.

He smiled. "It's called Day's Eye. The sun flower."

"Flowers have names?"

"Indeed they do. And so do trees. And fish. And so should you."

The girl sat mute.

The hero dotus asked her, "What are you like, girl?"

And yes, yes, she knew exactly. "The tarn."

"Why?"

She could not quite explain the darkness, the mystery. "Because odd things leap out of me."

He laughed, but not the way the men of her people had sometimes laughed at her; his was a good laugh.

"Your name," she asked, "what does 'dotus' mean?"

"I beg your pardon?"

"Pardon for what?"

"I mean I don't understand. What did you say?"

"Your name is hero because you are. But what does 'dotus' mean?"

He laughed heartily for a considerable time. Then he stopped laughing but shook his head and chuckled. Then he said, "It means I am a hero in my dotage!"

"I, um, I beg your pardon?"

"Very good!" He sobered, smiling. "Dear child, my

name does not matter. It is just a misfortune inflicted upon me by my parents. But you—you are indeed like the tarn, my girl. The most wonderful things leap out of you."

"My people did not think so."

"Your people were mistaken. Beautiful things swim in you, is it not so?"

She nodded yes. "Dreams," she said. It was the most important name she had yet learned from him.

"Would you like me to name you? Shall I call you Dreamfisher, little one?"

"I—I'm not sure."

"But it need not be your only name. Like a flower, you can have many names. Even better, you can name yourself if you like. What would you like to be called?"

She shook her head. She had no idea.

"Will Dreamfisher do for now?"

She nodded.

"Will you go back to Athens with me, Dreamfisher?"

She shook her head. She whispered, "I must go back to my people."

The words jolted him so that he sat up like a rock rat, rigid with shock. "But why? They are cowardly, ignorant—they might kill you!"

"I have to." Dreamfisher thought of the deep pool with shining fish in it, the midnight depths of her own mind into which she dove and flew, the great under-mountain darkness in which a dragon flew, guarding a nameless treasure. She said, "I have to. They need me. No one else can help them."

"How dare you!" snarled the Turd, hefting a stone the size of his head in both hands. Others stood poised to hurl stones almost as large. The dreamfisher girl stood unsurprised, for she had not attempted to conceal her return, toiling upmountain under her heavy packs. Hero dotus had fashioned the packs for her out of the strange not-hide stuff he called cloth, and he had given her a robe of white cloth to wear. He had wanted to protect her more, but she had not let him. She had to do this alone.

Yet she felt his protection like a warm arm around her shoulders, for it clothed her. If it were not for the white robe making them wonder, making them hesitate, they would probably have stoned her to death by now.

Without giving the Turd more than a glance she eased the packs from her back to the ground. The packs also were making them wonder, she knew, and making them hold back their wrath. Standing tall now, with the packs at her feet, she thought of the tarn and the hero dotus to strengthen her voice as she said, "I have returned—"

Someone burst through the crowd and hurtled toward her. Sobbing, her mother lunged to embrace her, arms around her neck, head on her shoulder, crying, "Go, flee now, do not come back. They will kill—"

"Hush." Feeling a campfire warmth in her heart, the dreamfisher patted her mother's back. "Don't cry, brave one." She risked the name because her mother deserved it, putting her body between her daughter and the stones, putting herself in peril. "I have come home to stay." She hoped this was true. "You will see." Gently she pushed her mother aside.

To the others, in her strong voice, she said, "I have returned to you bearing a gift from the gods."

"Blasphemer!" shouted the Turd. "Upstart!"

But at the same moment, some youngster who did not know when to keep his mouth shut cried, "What is it?"

"What is it?" whispered the dreamfisher's mother.

No one else spoke, but the girl saw still, intent faces, hands sagging under the weight of forgotten stones. She said, "It is a gift to all of you from the god of naming."

"Bah! Liar!" The Turd was not to be so easily distracted from his wrath as the others. "Why should we believe—"

The dreamfisher's mother turned on him. "Who but the gods could have garbed her like a white bird?"

"Like an angel," someone else agreed.

She heard a muted babble among the others: Like an omen. Listen to her. Let us hear what she has to say. She may well be a messenger.

From a few hands, stones dropped, thunking to the ground, sending their own wordless message.

The dreamfisher said to the Turd in a quiet, level voice, "It is mostly on your account that this gift was sent. To give you a new and proper name." Without waiting for a reply she crouched, her white robe brushing her bare feet, and began to open the packs. She took her time undoing the knotted fastenings, sensing more than seeing how her people drew nearer, forming a silent circle around her, their hands open now and empty.

When she was ready, she stood and looked around. Yes, the Turd stood there with the others, his face sullen but his hands as empty as theirs.

"This is a gift of names from the gods," the dreamfisher told her people in case they had not understood her the first time; she knew how hard it was to understand sometimes. From the pack she drew something flat and white. "Eat this, sleep this night, and by dawn you will know your name."

"How'?" barked the Turd.

"You will see." She handed him the first slab of dried fish.

The Turd dreamed of a bear and was called Brownbear thereafter. What the bear was doing in his dream, he did not say.

The dreamfisher girl's mother dreamed of a mountain stream and was called Rill.

Others dreamed many dreams of many wonders, and they became Sunwing, Moonbow, Redbuck, Hawkshadow, many others. Some could not choose names from among their dreams and the dreamfisher girl helped them: Leafswim, Skylove, Dayseye.

Her people did not call her Dreamfisher, then or thereafter. Only the hero dotus ever called her that. They called her Wisewoman and brought her gifts and revered her. She lived by herself in a hut a little farther up the mountain and never took a mate, but all the mothers and fathers brought their babies to her to be named. And all the children flocked to her daily, for she loved to play games of naming with them. This stone, what does it look like? That tree? That cloud? This flower? And she loved to listen as they told her their dreams.

THE DREAMS THAT STUFF IS MADE OF
by Josepha Sherman

Josepha Sherman is a fantasy writer and folklorist whose latest novels are *Son of Darkness* and *Star Trek: Vulcan's Heart*, written with Susan Shwartz. Her most recent folklore volume is *Merlin's Kin: World Tale of the Hero Magicians*. Her short fiction has appeared in numerous anthologies, including *Battle Magic, Flights of Fantasy, Black Cats and Broken Mirrors,* and *The Shimmering Door.* She lives in Riverdale, New York.

Now, whenever the Alliance locates a new planet inhabited by sentient beings, it's usual for someone or ones to be sent in to investigate. If the locals are high enough on the technology scale, it's "Welcome to the galactic neighborhood, we don't bite unless that's part of your culture, and what have you got to trade?" But if they're low enough on the technology scale that a true Contact would endanger their culture irreparably, open visits are ruled out, and the planet gets marked, basically, "Do not disturb for a few centuries."

That is, of course, if said planet doesn't lie in a region of space that's claimed by both the Alliance and the Tar'q.

The Tar'q are a strange species, to put it mildly. Not only are they scaled and feathered, which is unusual in any species, they also have a code of ethics that varies without seeming reason from "don't step on that poor insect" to "wipe out that planet because it has no moons."

Exactly. That strange. But the Tar'q aren't stupid: They won't go head-to-head with the whole Alliance, and they have never yet attacked so much as an Alliance Protectorate World. Unfortunately, though, if they even suspect that the Alliance is interested in a planet, the Tar'q just may (if their code of ethics insists on it) act as spoilers. Quite literally. And fatally. As in, "If I can't have this world, no one can."

Equally unfortunately, they already had their suspicions about our interest in this particular world, Ishtasha. How it had happened, I don't know. Maybe one of their scout ships was in the wrong place at the wrong time, or intercepted an incautiously uncoded Alliance message. For the sakes of Ishtasha's inhabitants, we didn't dare give the Tar'q any concrete proof of Alliance curiosity. Yet, for the same sakes, we didn't dare leave them to the Tar'q either. Besides, the Alliance really needed to know if, for instance, Tar'q weapons had already been cached down there.

Surveys from space indicated a Class 4K5 world with some odd variations. It was an oddly homogenous planet, mostly temperate climate but with few real landmarks other than some open water, a couple of ridges, and what looked like unusually wide expanses of steppes. Natural? Or the result of some catastrophic event so long ago the planet had healed? The highest culture seemed to be only about 5.64 on the Technology Scale: essentials like roads and a rather sophisticated network of lighting, but nothing much along the lines of large cities, and certainly nothing along the lines of space exploration. Again, natural? Or some shattered society slowly building its way back from long-ago disaster? There weren't any planetary defenses—and there also weren't any traces of armaments against each other either. A planetary government?

You can only learn so much from even the most detailed of long-range probes. The finest resolution had given a clue as to the inhabitants: humanoid, basically Human-sized. So the rules said: Send in a team of xenologists, preferably from a species that looks the most like the locals. And planetside we went, a team of four Human xenologists, our mission to observe without being observed until we could pass as locals. And then, of course, came the trickiest part: getting the Ishtashans under Alliance protection Just In Case.

We deliberately landed our little craft in an uninhabited meadow of tall bluish grass. The air registered as nicely normal for Humans, the temperature coolish but not unpleasant, and we stepped out onto Ishtasha's surface, secure in the fact that the locals still didn't seem to have any detection devices.

Didn't they? We quickly found ourselves, once we'd gotten out of the craft and couldn't just take off again as just so much "trick of the light," faced with a welcoming committee.

Wonderful. First rule broken right off. No gradual edging into the situation, no chance for disguises.

The Ishtashans turned out to be humanoid, all right, tallish and slender, with short, silvery fur, blue-gray eyes set in long, narrow faces—and with utterly unreadable expressions. There didn't seem to be any sexual dimorphism, no clear division of gender, or any distinguishing marks or ornaments.

At least they didn't seem to be afraid. Their long,

four-fingered hands neatly folded in the sleeves of their flowing gray robes, they bowed like so many reeds in the wind, necklaces of what looked like clay beads faintly rattling together.

One Ishtashan, a touch taller than the rest, asked mildly, "Smoothly dreamed voyage?"

Whatever that meant. The translation coding planted in every xenologist's brain doesn't always work precisely. I tried the usual innocuous, "We're travelers from a foreign land."

But the tall one, face still showing nothing that could be translated as emotion, countered, "Ah, no. You are from the Outside, the Off-World. I have so dreamed it."

Oh, wonderful. Second rule broken. Not only had we been spotted, the locals had deduced that we were from off-world.

From . . . dreams?

Well, some cultures do base their decisions on whatever their collective subconscious conjures up.

Except, this time the subconscious seemed to be working pretty accurately. Or else, more probably, our low-tech friends were pretty good at putting details together and accepting the picture they got.

What now? I, for one, wasn't going to try claiming to be a god; aside from being yet another rule—no impersonating deities—I had a feeling these tranquil folks weren't going to accept that. I felt a little awkward about using an ancient cliché, even if it was true, but I held up my hands to show they were empty and said, "We come in peace."

"We know," the tall one murmured. "That was dreamed as well."

"Oh." At least that made our job a little easier. Warily, I added, "Do you know why we're here?"

The tall one blinked. "To dream, I would believe."

"Ah . . . not exactly," I countered as delicately as I could. I couldn't come out and say, "The Tar'q are thinking of wiping out your whole planet just for the hell of it." "We were curious," I continued, picking my way along. "Once we learned that people lived on this world, we wondered what you were like."

I had a brief flash of worry: What if they, in turn said, "And we want to know more about *you*—namely your high-tech equipment!"

But I was spared that awkwardness by a sudden alarm from our craft. Stevan, monitoring, said tersely, "Tar'q surveillance."

Damnation. Abandoning any attempt at mere curiosity, I said bluntly, "Your world is endangered," and summarized the data about the Tar'q and their spoiler techniques.

All the while I was talking, the Ishtashans showed not the slightest trace of emotion. Whatever body language they used was too subtle for us to read. But when I was finished, the tall one said simply, "Come."

Stevan, of course, stayed with the craft, since we weren't all that trusting. Our tall Ishtashan contact—he? she?—led the way through the gently waving grass to what looked more like a summer camp than a permanent village. Frameworks of wood supported masses of fabric—tents of some elaborate sort, the fabric dyed in soft pastels in intricate spirals. Dream spirals, I guessed.

And then I did a doubletake, as did the rest of the team. "Not wood," Avar whispered.

No, indeed: According to the subtle scan he'd just

made, that was some form of xenosteel. And that fabric was certainly not primitive homespun stuff either.

Summer camp, indeed: I'd guessed right. These weren't primitives, but civilized folks on their equivalent of a weekend in the country. And while I couldn't have given any firm proof, my instincts were telling me that these vacationers were high on the rungs of whatever status ladder the Ishtashans possessed.

A giggle, the first I'd heard on Ishtasha so far, made me start. Aha! Ishtashan children, no mistaking the blunt-nosed little faces, running about and laughing softly. Normal kids, I'd say, for all their relative quiet, healthy and well-fed, which said a lot about the culture.

Though even Tar'q kids were cute. . . .

At any rate, now a xenologist's real work began. In the old days on Humanity's homeworld of Earth, we'd had a narrower scope and been known as anthropologists. Same job, though: listen and observe. Learn. Then explain why you'd come to disturb them. Trouble is, there wasn't much time for any of that, not with Stevan's voice, tinny in my earphone, sending me increasingly urgent updates as to Tar'q progress. . . .

". . . and so," I continued, as I and the Ishtashans sat in a semicircle on soft cushions in the grass, "ordinarily, as I say, we wouldn't have bothered you. Even though you have . . . uh . . . dreamed of space travel and other peoples—"

"We are as we are," the tall one, Ceolaj, said, "but we once were more."

Translation problems again. I said nothing, trying to convey respectful understanding. Ceolaj continued, "Yes. You have already dreamed the answer, you with your mobile expressions. We did once nearly destroy the all. No more will we endanger ourselves—we are one now, and the causes of destruction are buried and lost."

I saw my chance and took it. "The Tar'q won't care. They'll do a total job of destroying the all—but they won't touch a blade of your world's grass if you are proclaimed an Alliance Protectorate World. What this proclamation means is simple: No invasion, no intrusion on Ishtashan ways, merely a notice to all outside, 'This far and no further.' You won't even see another Alliance ship till you're ready to explore space on your own."

"Hurry up, dammit," Stevan's voice buzzed in my ear. "The Tar'q are issuing that damned 'We are about to cleanse this world' speech!"

That bought us a little time: They wouldn't attack till they'd gotten ritual out of their systems.

"Why are you doing this?" Ceolaj's voice was so tranquil he (she?) might have been talking about plucking a handful of grass. "What gain for you?"

"The gain of not seeing your world destroyed! Look, there isn't time to argue, there isn't time to get Alliance ships here, we don't have heavy-duty weapons on our own vessel—but the Tar'q aren't going to believe any of that. What they *will* accept, and they've done it before, is proof of Alliance membership." I had the emergency documents with me. "Please! We can escape, my team and I—but you can't!"

"We will dream of this—"

"There isn't time!"

"—and so will you."

I caught the meaning of it a second too late. Ishtashan bodies closed in on me, Ishtashan hands, alarmingly strong but just as alarmingly gentle, forced my mouth open, forced something sharp-tasting inside, forced me to swallow . . . dimly, I heard the rest of the team shouting in alarm, but I didn't care . . . I was drifting. . . .

And I. . . .

. . . saw strangers . . . Tar'q? Ishtashans? . . . digging, digging, tearing up Ishtasha's soil at the base of a small hill . . . revealing a box . . . no, a coffin, they had despoiled a coffin, and inside it was . . . an Ishtashan . . . an Ishtashan whose eyes flew open—

Alive! They were burying someone alive! I cried out in horror, "No! You can't do this, you're killing him!"

I was awake, lying in Avar's arms. "What the hell just happened?"

"Damned if I know," he said. "You rushed off, yelling something, and started clawing at that little hill, there. Then the Ishtashans let us get you out of the way."

I forced myself to sit up, gritting my teeth against my dizziness, a taste like a dead Tar'q in my mouth, and stared at a storm of activity, Ishtashans rushing, digging, unearthing—

"A weapon!" I sat bolt upright, fighting not to throw up but too frantic to care. "That's what was buried in the coffin—all right, it wasn't a coffin, something left over from a war—"

And I'd . . . dreamed it?

"The Tar'q!" Avar shouted, nearly knocking me over as he sprang to his feet.

There it was, a slim silver needle of a ship, skimming the atmosphere in the first ritual challenge, meaningless since they had to know no one down here had any weapons. . . .

Yes, they did. I struggled to my feet, swaying from whatever drug they'd fed me—and knowing I was lucky it hadn't poisoned me—staring at the ugly machinery that had just been unearthed, the machinery that, for all its long, long sleep, was beginning to hum and glow with power, the machinery that had helped level a whole world into level plains—

"Dammit, no!" I wasn't quite sane yet, but that little thing wasn't going to stop me. "You're not going to use my dream against them!"

"But they are the enemy." That was Ceolaj's tranquil voice.

"They are sentient beings! You're not going to use me to murder them!"

Well, all right, so I really wasn't sane; the fact that the Tar'q were about to murder *them* never occurred to me.

It didn't matter. "You are of true dreaming," Ceolaj said, which seemed to mean honorable, and signaled to the others. With what I could have sworn were sighs of relief, they switched off the machinery and tumbled it back into its grave, hastily covering it up again.

"Now," Ceolaj said, "we sign."

They did, we did, and we hastily transmitted the data up to the Tar'q ship. In the Tar'q way, without so much as an oath or a word of acknowledgment, they zoomed back off into space.

"Gone," Stevan's voice assured me. "All of them."

"You used me," I said to Ceolaj. "You tricked me."

"You dreamed the burial place."

"You knew perfectly well where it was all the time!"

Did the faintest touch of satisfaction edge the calm voice? "But you did dream it."

True enough. Or had there been some mental suggestion in there with the drug? "And what about you? You could have destroyed the Tar'q ship all along."

This time I think that there was an emotion: great weariness. "Our long-ago families fought one war. Fought it very, very well. We do not wish to return to then."

"Neither do we. You are now safe under the Alliance laws. Farewell, Ceolaj," I said with as much dignity as I could muster. "We shall not meet again."

"Except in dreams," he answered calmly.

Right.

No, wrong! I still don't know what happened back there. I only know that I have no intention of letting Ceolaj or any other Ishtashan into my dreams.

But still . . .

I wonder what dreams the Tar'q have.

CONSOLATION PRIZE
by Gary A. Braunbeck

Gary A. Braunbeck is the acclaimed author of the collection *Things Left Behind*, released last year to unanimously excellent reviews and nominated for both the Bram Stoker Award and the International Horror Guild Award for Best Collection. He has written in the fields of horror, science fiction, mystery, suspense, fantasy, and western fiction, with over 120 sales to his credit. His work has most recently appeared in *Legends: Tales from the Eternal Archives, The Best of Cemetery Dance, The Year's Best Fantasy and Horror,* and *Dark Whispers*. He is co-author (along with Steve Perry) of *Time Was: Isaac Asimov's I-Bots*, a science fiction adventure novel being praised for its depth of characterization. His fiction, to quote *Publishers Weekly*, ". . . stirs the mind as it chills the marrow."

> ". . . his raptures were,
> All air, and fire, which made his dreamings clear,
> For that fine madness still he did retain,
> Which rightly should possess a poet's brain."
> —Michael Drayton, *Works* (1753)

The problem is this: when you inadvertently take part in something miraculous—and I'm talking the kind of miraculous that, if you were to describe it to someone in the medical profession, would get you deluxe accommodations in a padded room, complete with a comfy-snug canvas jacket of the wraparound-arms-and-lock-in-the-back variety—there's this overwhelming compulsion to *tell* someone about it, even if they'll write you off as a loon. It itches to get out, pulls and tugs and nags at you, like the sensation you get when you stand somewhere very high up and have that momentary urge to jump just to see if you can fly. You know you probably won't do it, but still there's that nattering little Munchkin voice in your head that keeps urging: Jump off and fly away!

Okay, this thing that I've taken part in, this crazy, scary-as-hell, wondrous *thing*, it wants out. If I don't tell someone about it soon, I'll skid right out of my skin, step up to the edge, do an Icarus and *splat!*

What made me decide to finally put all of this down is that I've started talking to myself—and I don't mean those little under-your-breath gripes that everybody mutters over the course of a day, no; I've begun having entire conversations with myself. This morning, while I was shaving, I said, "It's actually happening, Gene, it's all around you, around *everyone*, all the time, and you can see it!" "Why, yes," I replied to myself, "and an incredible thing it is, too!" Then I cut my chin and bled for a few minutes. Next time, maybe I'll do a Van Gogh and lob off an earlobe, or give myself a nose job if I'm not paying attention.

Therefore—take a running jump and fly, if you know what I mean. . . .

He wasn't so elderly as to be thought ancient, but the shriveled damage to the old man's face was a long time at home. He shuffled through the door a little after one-thirty in the morning, bringing some of the night inside with him—and the night seemed to find itself his welcomed companion; it hung about his shoulders almost exaltedly, soot and ash on the coat of a chimney sweep. He wore a small knitted wool cap pulled down over the tops of his ears, which he removed as the door closed behind him. He stuffed the cap into one of the pockets of the long, tattered blue sailor's coat he wore, took a breath, then stared down at the floor.

The dull buzz of the overhead fluorescent lights seemed to increase in volume, making the depot all the more depressing—and you'd be hard pressed to find a more depressing place than the Cedar Hill Bus Depot at one-forty in the morning.

I watched him look around the empty depot, then dig around in one of his pockets until he found a key. He shambled over to the lockers that cover most of the wall on the depot's east side and inserted the key into #347, opening the door with a loud, grating, high-pitched metallic squeal that made my teeth hurt.

"Not exactly what you were expecting, eh?" he growled.

For a moment I thought he was talking either to himself or to some companion only he could see, but after several moments of silence he repeated the question, this time adding my name to the end of it.

I leaned forward, peering over the counter. "Excuse me?"

He leaned back, his face slowly emerging from behind the locker's door. "Would it have helped if I were wearing, say, long, flowing robes decorated with stars or had ancient charms around my neck or maybe one of those Merlin-wizard caps?"

It took a moment for all this to sink in.

"You're, uh . . . you're the . . ."

"Not the most articulate person, are you?" he snapped, removing a small package from the locker and slamming closed the door. "Listen, I'm tired, I'm hungry, and I'd kill for a cigarette right now, so my social graces are a bit lacking; as far as my manners go, my line of business does not require that I endear myself to people. I suppose that's why I don't get invited to many parties, but we're not here to discuss my dreadful personality problems." He approached the counter. "You asked for a Magus. Here I am. Don't let's get carried away with the mirth and whoopee, it embarrasses me."

"I'm sorry," I said. "It's just that . . . you're not what I was expecting."

"Okay, did I just have a blackout or didn't I say that a minute ago?"

"Sorry."

He pointed to my shirt. "Not quite cold enough yet to be wearing turtleneck sweaters."

"No."

His face softened as he stared at me, perhaps deciding whether or not he thought I was worth the trouble of dealing with; Jenny, my sweet-natured Wiccan friend, told me that he was difficult to deal with, and sometimes he refused to help, even after being paid for his services. "But he's the best there is, for this sort of thing," she'd said, the other members of her coven nodding their heads in enthusiastic agreement.

He placed the package on the counter, then reached over and hooked his index finger into the collar of my sweater, pulling it out and down to expose the finger-thick bruise that encircled my neck.

"I'm surprised you can swallow, let along talk."

"It's a lot better than it was a couple of days ago. I couldn't do either."

"How many times has it happened?"

"Four."

He seemed to make a mental note. "Gets worse every time, does it?"

"Yes. This last time I actually passed out."

He looked into my eyes. "How long since you last slept?"

I shrugged. "Two days, maybe two and a half."

"Is that when it happens?"

"The first three times, yes, but this last time it hit me right in the middle of the day."

He let go of my collar, thought about something, then offered his hand. "Okay, I'll see what I can do for you."

I shook his hand.

His entire body became rigid and he blanched, jerking his hand from mine. "Okay, I *knew* there was something Jenny wasn't telling me." He squeezed the bridge of his nose and sighed. "You smoke?"

"No—but there's an unopened pack right here." I took it from under the counter and handed it to him. "Someone left it here last night and never came back for it."

"Oooh, lucky me." He got his smoke started, then sat down in one of the off-white plastic seats that are scattered throughout the depot. "I'm not gonna yell, so you might as well come over here and join me. And bring the package, will you?"

I grabbed it and joined him.

"Whose dream is it?" he asked.

"My dad's."

"You two not get along, is that why he dreams about—"

"—no, no, it's not that at all. Well, maybe a little— I'm not exactly the kind of son he wanted."

"Did you hear that? The sound of my heart breaking.

Spare me the sob-story details. What do you want me to do?"

"I want you to steal the dream from him—or at least fix it so he won't have it anymore."

He glared at me. "Do you have any idea how dangerous that can be—not just to the dreamer but to the universe as a conceptual whole?"

I shook my head, feeling more and more diminished.

He looked at the clock on the wall. "Let me explain something to you; if—and that's a mighty big 'if'—*if* I decide to do what you ask, it has to be done sometime between now and dawn—that's when all dreams are busy being dreamed and are vulnerable to manipulation, theft, destruction, whatever. We have here perhaps a four-hour window of opportunity. Don't worry about whether or not I like you, or think you're an imbecile, or would want you marrying my sister. Just tell me what you know I need to hear."

My hands were shaking and my throat was dry. I dug some change out of my pocket and got a can of soda from one of the vending machines. A couple of good, deep gulps helped me to find my voice.

I stared down at the dirty tile floor and said, "Before I was three minutes old, I killed two people—my mother and my twin brother. I came out first, and my brother . . . his neck got tangled up in the umbilical cord and it strangled him. I guess they tried reviving him, but it did no good. Mom, she'd developed this heart problem shortly before finding out that she was pregnant with us and it didn't tell anyone, not even my dad. Dad, he . . . he worries like hell over every little thing. I suppose Mom thought it would mean so much to him, having two sons, and she didn't want to ruin it for him by having him worry that—"

"—you're getting into sob-story territory again. Pretend you're Jack Webb: Just the facts."

I took another swallow of soda. "Fine. My mom and my brother both died and I think that Dad always blamed me for it a little, even though he didn't want to and knew it was unreasonable. He's never been cruel or anything like that to me, but there have been times when he's been talking about a football game or baseball or something like that when he suddenly stops and looks at me and then . . . then he doesn't say much. I was never interested in sports or woodworking, I didn't take Shop in high school. I did theater, sang in the choir, read a lot books, and liked movies. And I could see it in his eyes sometimes, you know— *Oh, right, you're the* other *one*.

"One of the doctors at the nursing home told me that Dad's a 'successful schizophrenic.' I mean, he started going on me, mentally, about five years ago. I figured it was the onset of Alzheimer's right? That's probably got a lot to do with it, but it's not the only thing. Dad's invented another life for himself in his mind, okay? One where Mom's still alive and he's got a son who likes all the same things he does, who he's got a lot in common with and can have these long, enjoyable conversations that last late into the night, who likes to go fishing and deer hunting and goes half on season tickets during football and basketball season. He used to just live in this world when he was sleeping, you know? But lately he . . . he slips away while awake. And in this other world, this other life, my brother came out first and *I'm* the one who . . ." I shook my head and drained the rest of the can.

"He's been talking about that a lot lately," I continued. "About how Mom and Geoff—that was going to be my brother's name—about how it wasn't fair that they died. I'm pretty sure that Dad loves me, but most of the time it's like . . . it's like he envisioned this great, happy family for himself, with daughters-in-law and lots of grandchildren and being surrounded by everyone during the holidays . . . but instead he had to settle for the consolation prize—me."

"So you think that when he . . . when he slips into this other world he's created for himself, somewhere in there he relives the moment of your birth but changes the outcome?"

"Yes." I rubbed the bruise around my neck. "I mean, I know it's only natural for someone to imagine a different outcome to something like that, but why is it that he imagines only one of us making it out alive? Why doesn't he dream that *both* Geoff and me survive along with Mom?"

"I don't mean to rub salt in a wound here, pal, but are you sure he loves you?"

"Oh, yeah, I have no doubt that he loves me. I just don't think he ever liked me very much. I think he figures he would have liked Geoff a helluva lot more."

"I'm hearing a lot of 'I think' or 'I guess.' You're basing this on a lot of supposition. For all you know these dreams aren't your father's at all. You could be having the dream yourself and just not remembering it afterward."

I pointed to my neck. "So this could be just a stigmata?"

"There's no 'just' to it—stigmata's nothing to dismiss but, yes, it could very well be. Maybe on some level you've always felt guilty about having survived, not being the type of son you *think* he'd have preferred."

"I have proof I can show you."

"What kind of proof?"

"A copy of a security video from the last nursing home he was in. About six months ago, right after I got off work, I went to see him because it was Father's Day, right? And as I'm walking past the front desk the nurse there looks at me with this surprised expression on her face and says, 'What'd you do, change clothes in your car?' I asked her what the hell she was talking about and she tells me that I'd just left a couple of minutes ago. I get all nervous and panicky and raised three different kinds of holy hell, but eventually they let me take a look at the tape from the security camera that hangs over the entrance to the Alzheimer's unit.

"There I was—or, rather, there Geoff was. He was in better physical condition than me—I guess he's quite the athlete in Dad's dream-world—and he had an air of confidence about him that I never had. He stopped just inside the door and held it open for my mom. Then the two of them went to Dad's room for a Father's Day visit. I've got the tape back at my apartment, we can go there if you want and I'll show it to you."

He stared long and hard into my eyes, then slowly shook his head. "No need. I believe you."

He looked off into the distance, then turned his attention to the package on his lap. He started to open it, thought better about it, muttered, "Not just yet," to himself, then faced me again. "Let's go."

"Where?"

"Where do you think? Jeez, you really aren't the sharpest pencil in the box, are you?"

"I feel so much better now, thank you—and I can't leave. My shift isn't over for another three hours."

"I can see why you wouldn't want to do anything to harm such a glamorous career. Like working here so much that you're willing to risk your life to keep your job?"

"Can I at least call someone to come relieve me? I can tell them it's a personal emergency, that Dad's—"

"—tell 'em whatever you want, just *do it*."

The manager of the depot was not happy with me, but she understood the situation (her own parents both being in nursing homes) and told me to take off, the depot could survive unattended for fifteen minutes until she got there.

Then it was out to my car and on the deserted night roads. My traveling companion said nothing; instead he opened the box and removed what appeared to be an ultra-high-tech pair of binoculars and contented himself with looking at things we passed in the night. Every once in a while I'd hear him mutter something like, "Oh, *there* you are," or, "Lost again, eh?" But he didn't volunteer any information about what he saw, and I didn't much feel like asking.

Before we got to the nursing home, he made me pull into an all-night convenience market where I purchased for him two of the most grotesque-looking frozen hamburgers I'd ever seen, then waited while he microwaved them within an inch of their processed lives. Add to that a bag of nacho-flavored potato chips and a thirty-two ounce Coke and he had himself a meal fit for a stroke victim. He ate in my car and got crumbs everywhere and never once apologized.

As we pulled into the nursing home's parking lot, I

killed the engine and asked him, "If you're a real Magus, then why didn't you just summon up a decent meal for yourself?"

"Parlor tricks? You want me to waste my time and energy on pulling tacos out of a hat or something along those lines? Doing what I do takes a lot out of me, be it something little like making a facial scar disappear or reshaping someone's inner dreamscape. This kind of power has its price, kiddo, so I'm extremely picky about how I choose to employ it. And *don't ever* ask me something like that again, *comprende?*"

"Do you have to be so unpleasant?"

"No, but everyone needs a hobby. Are we done now? Can we go inside and get this over with?"

Now it was my turn to glare at him.

"What?" he asked. "I got something hanging from my lip?"

"Do you have a name?"

"Yes."

Long silence here.

"Mind telling me what it is?"

"You didn't ask for me to tell you my name, you asked if I *had* one. You should learn to be more specific with your inquiries."

"Fine. Would you please, oh please, thank you kindly sir, tell me your name?"

"Well, since you asked so nicely—it's Rael."

I signed in at the nurses' station and was getting ready to offer the pen to Rael when the nurse behind the desk said, "I must be getting tired."

"Why do you say that?"

"I could have sworn there was someone with you."

I started to say something, then Rael whispered,

"Don't . . . just don't. I'll explain later." I looked to make sure he was still there, and he was, very much so, but evidently only I could see him.

The nurse began to turn around to do something, then paused with an, "Oh, so there is someone—" but the rest of it died in her throat when she fully faced me again. "I'm seeing things, I'm telling you."

I made some lame joke, then Rael and I went to my father's room.

He was deep asleep but another him—a younger-looking, vital him—was sitting in a chair talking with someone I couldn't see. It wasn't until I looked away from the dream-him to the figure lying on the bed that I caught sight—albeit peripherally—of two other people in the room.

My mom and Geoff.

As soon as I turned to face them fully, they were gone.

I thought about what the nurse had said, the way she'd reacted.

Rael put a hand on my shoulder. I reached up to touch it just to make sure it was real.

"I have to have a chat with your family," he said to me in a genuinely kind voice. "I want you to go to the vending area for visitors and get yourself some coffee or something. Come back in about ten minutes."

I began to protest, thought better of it, and turned to go. Rael was still very much in my sight as I turned, but when I turned back, full-face, he was gone. Only as I turned once again did I catch a peripheral glance of him, talking with my mom and my brother.

I was glad to leave the room.

I didn't want any of them to see me crying.

I don't remember either buying or drinking the coffee. All I could do was sit there and stare at the tabletop and wonder what the hell Rael was going to do about my father's dream before it killed me.

When he finally came into the room and sat down at the table beside me, he looked genuinely sad. "I can't do it," he said.

"Why?" I hated the pleading I heard in my voice.

"Because it's almost all he's got left, Gene. He's happy there. He loves you, but it's not . . . not enough for him. *You're* not enough, never have been."

"The consolation prize."

"Pretty much. Don't think he doesn't appreciate all you've done for him over the years, but he's not going to be around much longer. He's laying the groundwork for the place he's going Afterward, understand? If I take away the dream or in any way try to alter it, it will destroy that new world completely."

"Then what the hell am I supposed to do? Jesus Christ! If he has that dream a couple times more, it's going to kill me."

"I know."

"Oh, God. . . ."

We sat in silence for several minutes, then Rael tapped my arm. "Remember what I told you earlier? How you need to be more specific in your inquiries?"

"Yeah. . . ?"

"Ask me what you want to know. Be specific."

"Can you do anything to save me?"

"Yes." He handed me the binoculars. "Go over to the window there and look out through these."

I did as he asked.

And was stunned into silence.

Hexagonal heads on classically-sculpted bodies, long gossamer necks, a man made completely of papiermâché dancing on trickles of moonlight, incredible creatures, wondrous, mystifying, miraculous creatures, beings that seemed little more than mathematical equations colliding into one another to assume some kind of physical form, an indescribably beautiful woman who seemed to be composed entirely of prism-glass arms from her neck down, creatures with rose-colored and -shaped heads, a man with a fan-shaped body that unfurled and shook whenever he laughed—

I pulled the binoculars away from my eyes and looked once again into the courtyard.

Empty.

I lifted them to my eyes once again, and there was the dream circus before me.

Rael came up beside me and took the binoculars away. "Do you know what those are?"

". . . not sure . . ."

"Those, my dear Watson, are dreams. Lost ones, forgotten ones, abandoned, broken, incomplete ones, ones that remained in this world after their dreamers had died . . . and none of them, *none of them*, have found a new home yet. They are my family, Gene. Sometimes people come to me and ask to be divested of their dreams because they find them to be too painful." He reached into his pocket and produced a small glass vial that contained some kind of swirling silver substance. "Take this, for instance. This was the dream of a woman who's a housewife. She wanted to be a champion figure skater, but her job, her home, her children, they all came first—and she was happy for them to come first. But, still, there was this nagging dream of glory days that never were and never would be. Dreams like that are fine if they give comfort, but in her case, it only made her mourn for What Might Have Been. She offered it to me of her own free will—that's the only way I can take a dream, if it's freely given."

I looked at the vial. "It's so small."

"This is all that's left of it. She's been destroying bits and pieces on her own over the years, but when it came time to deliver the final blow, she couldn't do it. So she came to me and offered me her dream and I took it. I'll carry it around with me until I find someone who needs a dream like this, then I'll give this to them, just like I'll find a home for all the dreams you see out there.

"But I can't do it alone, Gene. I need some help. Work with me? Help me find homes for all of my family." He hung the binoculars around my neck. "This is how you'll be able to see them; once seen, their images stay inside the lenses so you'll never have to worry about losing track of them."

"How does this . . . how will working with you. . . ."

He silenced me by lifting his hand. "Like me, you'll have to give up some small part of your humanness. You'll become slightly peripheral to the rest of the world—only seen from the corner of the eye most of the time. When you *choose* to, you'll be able to be seen just like a normal, corporeal person . . . but most of the time you'll be peripheral, and since you'll be peripheral, you'll never again be fully a part of this world."

"And since I'll be living on the periphery—"

"—the borderline between dreamworlds and the real one, yes—"

"—then Dad's dream won't affect me at all?"

"No. So, what do you think?"

I looked through the binoculars at the miraculous creatures once again.

There really was no choice.

Things have gotten better since I decided to write all of this down. I don't so much have the desire to tell people about it—that is, during those times that I am fully a part of this world.

Dad passed away about six months ago, in his sleep. He was smiling when I found him.

I like the epitaph that Rael chose for Dad's headstone:

Don't Wake Me Up
I Should Be Dreaming

Whenever I am in the Peripheral, finding homes for Rael's family, I feel more a part of life than I ever did when I walked the world with other people.

Here, I matter.

Here, I have purpose, and contentment, and peace.

Here, I am not a consolation prize.

Time to take a running jump now, and fly away. . . .

A BUTTERFLY DREAMING
by Susan Sizemore

Susan Sizemore read her first vampire novel (Stoker) when she was thirteen, her first fantasy (Tolkien) at fourteen, her first science fiction book (Heinlein) at sixteen, and her first romance (Woodiwiss) at nineteen. She is still happiest when reading or writing in any one of those genres. Actually, she's happiest when mixing those genres. She backed into professional romance publishing by writing a time travel novel, and into writing vampire novels by being the fan of a television show. When not writing, she's either at a movie or walking her dog.

"Y ou honor us, my lady."

"You flatter me." Maggie smiled at Villia as the other woman made room for her on the crowded bench. Maggie had to lean her head close to the other woman's to be heard over the mingled roar from conversations and singing minstrels. "I never thought Chela was going to have that baby. A boy," she added to Villia's curious look. "And healthy."

Villia dipped her head quickly, murmured, "Thank the Dark God."

Maggie hid the urge to smile. She knew very well that her assistant was anything but devout, but the walls seemed to have developed ears lately. Like Villia, she was also aware of the black-robed presence of a good many frowning priests in the hall for the feast. The frown, she assumed, was as much standard issue as the

coarse black clothing worn by the terminally melancholy members of the priesthood. The priests didn't
like the wizards, who also dressed in black, but acces-
sorized with lots of gaudy jewelry. The wizards pretended not to care what the ascetics in coarse wool
thought. In normal times the two groups simply bick-
ered, crows cackling at ravens was how Maggie
thought of them. But these were not normal times, and
the chief priest had the ear of the High King's impres-
sionable young queen. And the queen was very high in
the king's favor since presenting him with twin sons.
So it was good politics on Villia's part to show a sudden interest in religion. Maggie supposed it would be
wise of her to head off to the castle chapel, but she had
too many years of practicing agnosticism in her own
world to change her ways in this one.

   All this plotting and maneuvering was enough to give
a hard-working woman like herself a headache. She'd
done her best to keep her head low and stay well out of
everyone's way as the courts of all ten kingdoms gathered for a great council. As the king's half sister and
personal physician she was entitled to a seat at the high
table on most nights. Fortunately, the gathering of kings
and queens up on the dais on this grand occasion left no
room for such a humble being as herself to have dinner
in their company.

   Once seated next to her chief assistant, the Royal
Physician of Albin nodded cordially to the other people
at the long table just below the royal dais. The feast was
in full swing. Very few people noticed her arrival.
Servers carrying huge amounts of food and drink, and a
succession of entertainers performing in the clear space
around the huge central hearth were far more interesting

to the assemblage than one small woman in a green physician's veil. A war was in the offing, this was everyone's last chance to wine, dine, and make merry. It looked to Maggie as she made her way past fights and frolic and gorging to find Villia, that a good time was definitely being had by all.

Most of her fellow diners at this table were strangers, members of the households of the other nine kings who were at King Tanir's stronghold for the Great Council. She wasn't in any hurry to strike up conversations with any of them. Court gossip was not her forte. Besides, she was hungry. She rubbed her hands together, then gestured at alert servers. Within seconds she had a full trencher of a dish the head cook had prepared just for her. Since she tended their illnesses and delivered their babies and plucked intelligent young peasant women from drudgery to attend her school, she was popular with the castle staff.

"Is that all you're eating, my lady?" Villia asked as Maggie picked up a wooden spoon.

"It's not easy being a vegetarian in the Middle Ages," Maggie answered, and set to as Villia frowned at the comment she comprehended but didn't quite understand.

Villia was one of only two people in this world who knew that Maggie now answered to the name Lady Donli. Donli was King Tanir's sister. The one thing Maggie and Donli had ever shared, not counting the same body, was that they were both physicians. Maggie's specialty was cardio-thoracic surgery, but she'd taken over Donli's more family practice-type services when the king's sister—went away.

Donli doesn't live here anymore, Maggie thought

with a trace of bitterness and a sharp glance for the man responsible for the tangled nightmare of the last several years. At least Maggie was stuck in the body of a younger woman—mind you, a body that gained weight easily and belonged to a family prone to heart disease. Maggie had to work hard to keep her new accommodations healthy, but had to admit being younger and more attractive was the one plus of having been kidnapped into this world.

The echoing great hall was noisy, the room crowded and hazy with smoke from candles, rushlights, and the hearthfire. Almost warm as well, for once, with combined heat from fires and human bodies. Maggie reveled in the temperature. She so missed central heating. The first thing she'd invented upon arrival in this world they called the Dream of Albin was long underwear. No, that was the second thing, she recalled. Heart surgery had been her first contribution to the welfare of the kingdoms, though she thought the underwear the more personally important item.

She ate quietly for a while, listening to lute, pipe, and hand-held drum music that somehow could be heard over the background of voices. She wasn't particularly fond of medieval music—no beat, couldn't dance to it—but you took what you could get in a world that had no concept of the importance of rock and roll. Her thoughts drifted as she picked bits of root vegetables out of the thick sauce that was soaking into the flat round of bread that served as a plate. The delivery had gone well, if longer than expected. No complications expected there. The rest of her caseload was pretty light right now. Good thing, too. She needed to concentrate on preparing to handle casualties in the upcoming war with the Dasan. The invaders were ravaging the south coast of the Ten Kingdoms right now, and the barbarians could literally be at the gates soon. That was the reason King Tanir had called a Great Council. He and the lesser kings had military strategy to prepare. She had to organize the doctors of the land to do their bit for the war cause.

"You're looking worried, my lady," Villia said, bringing Maggie out of her thoughts. "You should relax." Villia pointed toward the center of the hall. "Watch the jugglers."

"I don't do jugglers."

"Wait for the stonesinger, then. You'll enjoy him." Villia's voice was full of enthusiastic anticipation.

"Does he play a lute?"

"Of course."

Maggie grunted disdainfully, but looked up from her plate and tried to get her mind off tomorrow's work. First her gaze found Tanir, a big man seated at the center seat of the high table. He was her constant care and concern, and tonight he was looking pretty good. He was dressed in velvet and ermine, and the tip of the long scar on his chest just showed above the square-cut neck of his tunic. He was a brave and mighty warrior, proud of his scars, but the one she noticed was not the manly memento of a battle. At least not one that the king had won with his mighty sword. The fight had been hers, what would have been a simple bypass under normal circumstances, grafting saphenous veins from Tanir's leg to bridge the occluded heart blood vessel.

She wasn't sure now how she'd managed that first operation under such primitive conditions. At least the knives had been sharp. It had helped that she'd half-believed she was dreaming the whole thing while performing heart surgery in a torchlit castle tower. It didn't hurt that she'd had a wizard to help with little details like sterile fields and blood supply. She'd been changing the way medicine was practiced in this low-tech world ever since. She'd done a few bypasses since she'd trained a proper surgical team and designed adequate equipment and taught them about blood typing and transfusions. The people of Albin learned quickly, though they always grumbled superstitiously for a while before going along with it. They seemed to think that if it couldn't be done with magic it shouldn't be done at all. Thankfully, that attitude was changing a bit. Someone had said something to her recently about how it was a good thing she had invented sterilization, since the wizards were getting too fat and lazy to cast even a simple cleanliness spell these days.

Maggie chuckled to herself at the thought, realizing that thanks to her and the medical school she'd founded, the world wasn't quite as low-tech as it used to be. Technology was as efficient as magic any day. She wondered what the priests would think of that. Then she shuddered, knowing exactly what they'd think. Being burned at the stake might finally get her warm, but only briefly. And ending up as a pile of ashes was not how she wanted to go.

"What I have done is forbidden," was the first thing Stang, the Royal Wizard of Albin told her when she woke from a dream of being stabbed in the heart and dying to find that she'd been stabbed in the heart and died. "It will mean all our lives if the priests of the Dark

God discover that you dwell within the shell of Donli's dreaming, and she in yours."

Chewing thoughtfully on an overcooked piece of carrot, Maggie glanced up to the gallery high up over the royal dais, where the wizards sat in their jewel-infested black robes, reeking of smug superiority and feigned indifference to the affairs of mere men. She didn't much like wizards, though as a surgeon she could identify with their confident arrogance. The difference between members of her profession and the wizards were that surgeons only *thought* they were gods. With wizards it was a bone-deep belief.

Stang had thought nothing of using magic to bring her from her own world to his. He valued her skill, but her wishes meant nothing to him. To be fair, which she hated to be where Stang was concerned, he hadn't planned to murder her. Things had just gotten out of hand on her side of the barrier between realities. He and Donli had hatched the plan to use a forbidden spell to find help when they determined that there was nothing magic or medicine could do to save her ailing brother's life. They decided that King Tanir was too important to the Ten Kingdoms to be allowed to die. So Donli volunteered to switch bodies with a physician in another reality—another Dreaming as they called it—and Stang then performed the dark, secret ceremony to bring a suitable candidate across the barrier of consciousness, switching Donli into Maggie's body and putting Maggie into Donli's. Part of the ceremony was that the two bodies had to be on the point of death as the switch was accomplished. Donli got to take a poison, with Villia standing by to resuscitate her. To get Maggie's body to the point of death, Stang had to first put a spell on someone in Maggie's world that got him to murder her. Maggie had a vague and horrible memory of one of her twin sons holding a sharp kitchen knife.

She shook off the trace of memory with a shudder of horror and switched her attention away from the hated wizard. The nastiest part of the whole thing was that after she'd performed the bypass Stang told her he couldn't send her home. He'd promised her that she and Donli would both be returned to their own bodies, but Maggie's body had died before Stang could perform the reverse spell. So, Donli was dead and Maggie was trapped in Donli's world. And somebody else was raising her sons—one of whom might be serving time for offing Mom.

"Sometimes I think this whole thing is just a bad dream." She sighed, and Villia turned a terrified look on her. "Look," Maggie said to distract the other woman. "Is that your stonesinger?" Villia immediately turned her head toward the center of the hall as an expectant hush fell over the crowd. "That is the stonesinger, right?" Maggie asked, unnerved by the sudden complete silence.

A tall blond man walked with quiet confidence to the round central hearth. He wore a gold brocade tunic and the large stringed instrument he held so lovingly had a gold sheen to it as well. He drew the eye of soldiers, servants, and the kings on their high seats. Maggie noticed the wizards lean forward up in the gallery, perching like an expectant murder of crows. It was rare for them to take time out from trying to impress each other to turn their attention on the entertainer. The guy must be really good, she thought. Then she recalled that a stonesinger wasn't a common minstrel. He was some sort of specialized wizard that built things by singing at them, and he was the only one left. So the wizards were checking out the competition rather than looking to enjoy a show.

Within moments she forgot about the wizards. She was as caught by the charisma the minstrel exuded as everyone else. When he reached the central hearth, the fire backlit him like a stage light. He cradled the beautiful instrument in his long-fingered hands. His expression was still with pure concentration. At first she didn't understand the heat that rushed through her as he bent his head and began to play, caressing the strings like a skilled lover.

After the first flush of heat spread through her she smiled, remembering that while her mind belonged to Maggie, a woman in her late forties who'd enjoyed motherhood but had never had much interest in sex, she was also Donli. Donli was a healthy young woman with all the hormones and urges that came with youth and regular menstrual cycles. This realization left her slightly embarrassed, but no less attracted to the man.

He could play, too. His fingers moved surely and swiftly over the stringed instrument, drawing out melancholy sounds that even she found beautiful. Okay, she wasn't exactly an expert on medieval music, but she figured that if this guy ever got his hands on a Les Paul, he could pull out some killer riffs. And he could sing, sweet and clear and full of emotion. He owned time, for it seemed like hours passed in only a few minutes as he went from song to song and won their hearts. He sang of lost loves and made women weep, sang of battle and got the soldiers roaring to go to war, sang a tale out of myth

of sacrifice and patriotic courage that had everyone
looking to their High King like he was the hero of the
ancient tale. The singer ended with a soft, sad lullaby
that left Maggie longing for the children she'd left behind. And when he took his bows and walked away
while everyone stood and cheered, she found that she
still wanted him. It was lonely, lost Maggie as well as
young and untouched Donli who ached to pull the man
down on her bed.

She took a deep breath, and shook her head, slightly
embarrassed at her reaction. And was glad to see the
same look of unrequited lust on Villia's face when she
glanced at her trusty assistant. "Good," she said with a
hearty sigh. "It isn't just me."

"Warm in here, isn't it?" Villia responded, fanning
herself with her hand.

As they laughed at their response to the stonesinger,
Maggie looked around to see that most of the women,
and a few of the men, were as flushed with excitement
as she was. That was when she saw Colme. The High
Priest of the Dark God was an ascetic fanatic of about
the most depressing religion Maggie'd ever encountered. While wizards spoke of dreaming the world, the
priests talked of nightmares. As far as Maggie could
tell, people here lived their lives with the same
grounded-in-hard-reality prosaic stoicism as in her own
world, but both of the metaphysical camps talked a
good game.

Colme had been preaching that war with the Dasan
was punishment for the magicians upsetting the balance
of the natural order. With all the kings gathered as an
audience Colme was doing quite a bit of rabble-rousing
preaching, with the young queen drinking in every

word. He was a brilliant speaker, and there were mutterings from the populace that maybe he was right. Though she couldn't put her finger on why, watching Colme glaring at the stonesinger's exit with such laser sharp intensity sent a shiver of fear through her. Well, she told herself, the man was a minor wizard. Colme was probably experiencing serious envy for a rival with more ability to move the masses than he had. The stonesinger could move masses by the ton, or so she'd heard. She did know he was the most charismatic entertainer she'd ever listened to—and she'd been to a few live concerts in her time. When Colme's gaze shifted around the room, she ducked her head in hopes of being ignored by him. The priests didn't like technology any more than they liked magic. She'd been avoiding any confrontation with the priests for a long time, and wasn't going to do anything to draw their attention now. She waited a few minutes for the crowd to grow boisterous again, then made her own exit, using the merrymaking as cover.

Going to her room didn't help her get her head off the stonesinger, though. She lay awake for a long time, humming one of the songs he'd played that vaguely reminded her of something from an early Queen album, and wishing she'd asked Villia for more information about the man. Such as the man's name and age, and was he married or seriously involved with anyone—

Oh dear, she thought before she finally drifted off to sleep, *how embarrassing to develop a crush on someone at my age*. . . . Her only consolation was that she couldn't be the only woman who'd been in the hall tonight who went to bed with the same thoughts. For the first time since waking up in Albin she regretted going to bed alone.

The next morning dawned gray and cool, not unusual for the time of year, but not helpful for the sense of melancholy that covered her like cold fog. Ugly weather and bad mood notwithstanding, she dutifully went out for her morning walk. She'd found that no matter how healthily she ate, Donli easily gained weight without lots of exercise. So, rain, shine, or blizzard, she did her laps up on the battlements the first thing every morning. Running was right out for a royal lady in this medieval society, but the guards on the wall didn't look askance at a brisk walking pace.

There were more guards on the wall than usual these days, and both the inner bailey and the open ground that stretched down Castlehill were filled with troop tents and royal pavilions. Smoke from early morning cookfires obscured the town below the castle, the wall that surrounded the town and the deep forest beyond. She saw the black robes of priests moving among groups of soldiers below the wall. The soldiers of each king were distinguished by the colorful tabards with the devices of various kingdoms worn over their chain mail armor. Maggie wondered what the religious and military contingents were doing fraternizing with each other so early in the morning. She told herself she imagined receiving several hostile looks from below as she continued on her way. Or that, perhaps, the outlander soldiers had more faith in village wisewomen than castle-trained physicians. She was used to friendly respect from Tanir's people, but feared that not all the wary looks came from strangers. She adjusted her hood, and told herself she was dreaming, that nothing was wrong. Except for the palpable tension in the air and the nasty feeling of being watched, all seemed quiet and peaceful.

She found herself walking faster, wishing she could run. Not around the walls of the stronghold, but away from the whole impossible world in which she was trapped.

She was halfway through her second circuit of the wall, and panting for breath more from worry than exertion, when she heard the lute music. She didn't want to slow down, but the music struck her like a physical force. It struck at her nerves and her heart, and for a moment she thought she imagined hearing it. Or, more likely, that she'd gone mad. There was nothing else she could do but stop and listen.

She'd reached a part of the wall where several deep window embrasures formed sheltered niches. Benches had been set in the niches, where ladies came to embroider and gossip during the day, and lovers met at night. The musician was hidden in one of the shelters. Maggie held her already short breath as the notes burst like champagne bubbles in her brain. The lively, complex pattern of the tune spilled out into the morning to dissipate her paranoia and make her smile. She finally allowed herself to recognize what was familiar about the song. She'd heard the man play last night, of course she recognized his style no matter what he was playing. Her smile widened into a grin. She stepped forward to get a good look at the player.

The stonesinger continued through the end of the song, his elegant fingers flying through the complex patterns of chords. When he stopped he saw her, and looked puzzled to see the Royal Physician standing in front of him with her hands on her hips. He was courtier enough to quickly hide his surprise and rose gracefully to his feet. "You look as if my simple melody brings you joy, my lady."

"Oh, yes," she answered, taking a step back as he bowed to her. "I've always liked that song." She waited for a deliciously anticipatory moment before she looked him in the eye and added, "Though it's the first time I've ever heard "Little Red Corvette" played on a lute."

He was quite pale when he straightened abruptly, jerking as though he'd gotten an electrical shock. He had a face like a lived-in angel's. She noticed this just before he grabbed her and kissed her. She heard the lute crash noisily onto the stones of the wall, then forgot about everything else but kissing back for a few minutes.

"Well," she said, adjusting her hood, her veil, and the top of her gown after the stonesinger finally let her go, "that was interesting."

"I'm called Gryfyn here," he told her, rushed and breathless. He grasped her shoulders and held her very close. They were quite alone, but he wisely looked carefully around before rushing on. "My real name's Mark. I was an architect, with a band on the side. Next thing I know, boom! I'm here wearing the body of a famous minstrel. Been here for about four years."

She nodded. "Me, too."

"I'd always been a little telekinetic, able to bend spoons and stuff. When they put me into the body of a dying stonesinger the ability blossomed. They taught me the magic that moves stones and I've been singing their fortresses into being, but— Who are you, really?"

"Donli," she answered, remembering the politics of the place, and the feeling of being watched and hated. "Sister to King Tanir."

He had aquamarine eyes that studied her with shrewd intelligence. After a moment he nodded. "I spoke rashly, Lady Donli."

She took a turn to look around. "Fortunately, Master Gryfyn, there are no guards nearby."

He took her arm. "Can we go somewhere private?" He leaned close, put his hands on her shoulders and whispered in her ear. "The priests in my own king's court have been watching me."

It felt nice to have him so close. She put her arms around him, snuggled close and whispered back, "Colme's been watching you. I'm beginning to think they suspect me as well. My room," she added. "We'll go to my room."

He hooked his arm around her waist and they walked close together like lovers to her quarters, getting no comment from the many guards and servants they passed on the way. She did notice a few smiles and shrewd looks, and didn't care a bit that there would be gossip about Lady Donli having a tryst with the stonesinger flying all over the stronghold within minutes. Her attitude made her realize how sick and tired she'd become of hiding everything she was and felt. She wondered if it was the stonesinger's doing, because she felt the walls inside her starting to crumble. She knew it was dangerous, but with someone to share this nightmarish life with at last, she almost didn't care.

"Do you know why they brought you here?" was the first thing Gryfyn said when the door was safely closed behind them.

She nodded. "They needed a surgeon to save the king's life. Stang's magic couldn't help him."

He looked anything but surprised. "Of course it couldn't. The wizards' magic is failing." He saw that his words surprised her, and quickly explained. "I thought it was only the wizard who kidnapped me that was having trouble, but it must be all of them. I'm having more and more difficulty doing what I do. Kol, that's my wizard, he said he brought me here because I have a natural gift, but that the gift won't last forever because, and I quote, my spirit is not truly part of the dreaming." He slammed a fist into his palm. She jumped at the force of the impact, and at the fierce anger in his rich, deep voice. "I think the bastard will use me up, then kidnap somebody else's soul to take my place."

She sat down on the bed and stared up at Gryfyn. He was agitated, talking fast because, like her, he finally had someone to talk to. He was as excited as she was, she knew. She, too, was stunned because she finally had someone to talk to. Suddenly there were possibilities, like the world was opening up before her. She wasn't alone anymore. Having someone from her reality to speak to freed thoughts she'd buried rather than try to express even to herself. All the suspicions that she'd been telling herself were foolish speculation welled up and started to spill out.

"I'd come up with this theory that maybe the wizards, at least Stang, had this plan to steal technology," she told Gryfyn, who nodded understandingly. "I thought that I was an experiment that got started out of necessity because they needed a surgeon. I've suspected from things he said that he was waiting to see how my medical school worked out before he went any further. From what I can tell nothing has changed in this world for thousands of years. It's like they developed to a certain point, then stopped."

"They had magic. They didn't need technology."

She nodded. "I figured that Stang and Villia were the first people to look outside the box—the dream—in a thousand years."

"Maybe they're starting to wake up." He came to sit beside her on the bed. "Do you know that the spellwall the wizards conjured to keep the Dasan out started to fade the instant they finished the spell?"

"They claimed the Dasan wizards had discovered a new form of magic."

"The Dasan don't use magic. There are records on the Dasan going back for thousands of years—epic poems and folksongs and lays. I've studied every reference I could find. The Dasan are your average, good ole rape, pillage, and burn barbarians. The wizards have lied to all of us. About everything."

She didn't question this, but tried hard not to believe it. Trying didn't work. When she gave him a shocked look he took her hand, as much to comfort himself as her, she thought. Contact with another human was certainly welcome. "I thought I was the only person who'd been snatched," he went on. "When I didn't think that I was completely insane and locked in a padded room somewhere."

"Oh, I know that feeling."

He looked at her seriously. "How many other people do you think know the feeling?"

"How many more have been taken?" He nodded, and outrage began to build in Maggie. Somehow, the notion that she wasn't the only one had not occurred to her before. Surgeon's arrogance? She wondered. Or was the thought too awful to contemplate? "They told me that Donli sacrificed herself to bring me here. They told me that my body was dead back home. They told me that what they'd done was a great crime and punishable by death."

"That part's certainly true."

She remembered the priests in the war camp, and the hostile stares this morning. "I think we could be in very big trouble."

"Colme's very popular with the army. Been making speeches about how sin has entered the world with strangers."

That sounded ominous. She'd been so careful, but . . . "I didn't know that he was suspicious about anyone committing the Great Crime."

"The priests have been searching for evidence for some time. Not in Albin, maybe, but in the other kingdoms. They're quite adamant in their belief that sin must be purged with fire or the Dasan will prevail."

Fear gripped her, but also a sense of inevitability that of course this odd and interesting life was certain to end. She looked at Gryfyn. She noticed they were seated on her bed, the place where she had wanted to bring him last night. Inevitability? The logic of a dream? She gestured at the mattress covered in luxurious furs. "You want to have sex?"

A smile played on his lips, though the worry stayed in his eyes. "Hey, I am a musician."

They were still in bed together two days later when

the Dasan attacked the High King's stronghold. She went to tend the wounded, Gryfyn went to sing at the walls to strengthen the fortifications. They didn't meet again until the soldiers came for them and dragged them to the throne room where the queen waited, with Colme standing beside her throne on the dais. Stang and Villia were there as well, and a wizard Maggie didn't recognize. They were flanked by watchful guards.

Maggie exchanged a worried glance with Gryfyn as they were pushed together from opposite sides of the room. She was tired, and covered in other peoples' blood. The stonesinger didn't look much better. She'd heard that he'd been rebuilding walls as fast as the Dasan siege engines had pounded them down. She'd been practicing medicine under primitive conditions, Gryfyn had been facing flying boulders and fire. As she saw the stony looks on the queen's and Colme's faces, she could tell that they weren't exactly grateful for the physician's and stonesinger's hard work and dedication to duty.

"No one's going to be pinning medals on us this afternoon," Gryfyn said quietly as he took her hand.

Colme took a step forward and pointed a finger dramatically at them. "There stand the abominations, your grace. Soul thieves." He spat. It landed at Maggie's feet. "Your presence has brought the invaders to our gates." He swept a hand toward Villia and the wizards. "Your creators have confessed their sins."

The queen gave a disdainful sneer as her gaze swept over Maggie. "I should have known what you were when I allowed you to give my children such ugly, foreign names. I didn't want to believe what Colme accused you of, but how else to explain calling my children such strange names as Alexander and Jonathan? I've had the name records of the Ten Kingdoms searched, but no one else has ever borne such names. For cursing my sons in such a way, I condemn you."

Maggie put her hands on her hips. "Those happen to be my sons' names. They're beautiful names!" Tanir had given her the honor of bestowing birthnames on the princes. How odd that the only reminder she had of her own children had helped seal a trap that would kill her.

Colme threw his hands up joyfully. "She confesses! You will all burn!"

Stang spoke up, arrogantly facing the queen. "Your Grace has no authority to pass judgment. We are the king's servants, madam, not yours."

"Excuse me," Gryfyn added, "But don't we get a chance to defend ourselves? What sort of trial is it without a defense?"

Maggie looked around nervously as the throne room, full of priests and soldiers, became noisy with muttered questions and controversy. She didn't think they were going to be allowed defense attorneys, or even to make their one phone call. There was muttering and debate among the people in the room, but no one asked the prisoners' opinions. The priests favored torture and death. The military men recalled that Maggie tended their wounds, and Gryfyn built their defenses. They favored a trial—then torture and death. No one paid much attention to Stang's argument that the queen and High Priest had no authority.

"My lord husband is fighting against the invaders," the queen finally spoke up. "I rule in my lord's place."

"I do not recall the High King naming you regent, Your Grace," Gryfyn answered. He looked around and smiled sardonically, exuding all his considerable charisma. He pitched his voice at its most persuasive as he went on. "I know the laws of the Ten Kingdoms. We serve kings: the wizards, the physicians, and I. Where is the king to judge us?"

"You are demons!" Colme shouted. "Called forth from hell." He pointed dramatically at Villia and the wizards. "They are the ones who called you! You will all die."

"I was called from my home and my family," Gryfyn answered. "I did not volunteer to become a stonesinger, but I have served well in that capacity. The Lady Donli was given no choice, but she has saved many lives in the king's service."

"You took the true Lady Donli's life," the queen accused. "Drove her soul from her body."

"I did that," Stang said. "At Donli's urging. The Lady Donli chose the dream of another world to save her brother's life. It was a true sacrifice for the greater good."

"Abomination," Colme countered. He didn't have much to say, but he said it with conviction. "They have brought a curse upon the Ten Kingdoms. The demons must be destroyed."

Gryfyn stood tall and handsome in the hall, a figure that drew the eyes of everyone in to him. His voice was deep and mellifluous as he said, "I am not a demon. I am a butterfly."

"A butterfly?" an even deeper voice questioned from the back of the room. "I don't understand, stonesinger."

Everybody turned to stare at Tanir the High King as he moved assuredly through the crowd to the throne dais. He was still in armor, and looked exhausted. Maggie caught a whiff of old blood and sweat as he strode confidently past her. When he reached the throne, he gently pulled the queen to one side for a quiet, intense conversation. When the royal couple took their seats beneath the sky blue canopy, they both looked calmly regal, but the queen's face was white, her lips pressed together in a thin, bloodless line.

Tanir leaned forward in his chair. His gaze traveled around the room, quieting the hysteria with his calm, sure manner. Maggie had long practice in being unobtrusively still, but found it hard not to fidget until the king's calming gaze came briefly to rest on her. Then his attention moved on to Gryfyn. The two men looked assessingly at each other for what seemed like a long time. Then the king spoke at last. "You said something about being a butterfly, master stonesinger. Please explain."

Gryfyn and the king looked squarely at each other for another long moment before Gryfyn began speaking. His trained voice was as penetrating and persuasive as the king's presence, but he also had a natural storyteller's flair in his repertoire. "On our world there was once a wise philosopher who fell asleep in his garden. In his sleep he dreamed he was a butterfly. This dream was so detailed and vivid and *real* that when he awoke in his garden, surrounded by his books and his loved ones, he was not sure if he was a man who dreamed he was a butterfly or if he was a butterfly who was dreaming that he was a man." He paused for a few moments to let his words sink in. "So you see, my lord, dearest queen, priest, wizards, and loyal subjects of the Ten Kingdoms born," he went on, with his hands folded placidly on his flat stomach. "I do not know if I am

Mark Cunningham dreaming I'm the Master Stonesinger Gryfyn or if I am Gryfyn dreaming I am Mark.
Perhaps this whole world exists because I am asleep in
my own bed dreaming that I'm trapped here in a
stranger's body. Perhaps you only exist because my
sleeping mind says you do. Perhaps we are all dreaming
together. Or perhaps Donli is dreaming our existence."
He looked Tanir over slowly and carefully, and the king
straightened in his chair. "Perhaps it is you who is doing
the dreaming that you are High King. Do we all exist
because you want us to, my lord?"

Tanir stroked his jaw. "Perhaps I am dreaming," he
said with a smile. "What man would not want to dream
he was king?" He patted the queen's hand. "Especially
with the vision of such a lovely lady at my side."

"I would not want to be king," Gryfyn replied
promptly. "I am content dreaming I am a stonesinger.
Lady Donli is content to dream that she is your sister
and physician." He gave an elegant bow, and Maggie
followed suit with a deep curtsy. "We are trapped in our
dreams, my lord, but we are content to dream that we
serve you."

The king nodded slowly. "It is true that you have
done us no harm, butterfly dreamer."

"They bring the Dasan!" Colme chimed in loudly. He
pointed accusingly. He was good at that. "They bring a
curse."

"The Dasan were on our shores in my grandfather's
day," Tanir answered. "And two centuries before that.
We fought them back then."

Stang chuckled, stroking the heavy white beard he
cultivated for just such weighty occasions. "Or we

dreamed our warriors and our spells drove the barbarians back."

"Then it was a good dream, my wizard," Tanir answered Stang. "May the dream turn out as happy this time."

"What do you think of the dream—" Colme sneered the word. "That the wizard's magic is fading?"

"And since when do the priests care whether there is magic in the world or not?" Stang retorted. "Besides, magic doesn't disappear, it merely goes dormant every few thousand years. We are at the end of a cycle." He didn't look happy about admitting this, but he was fighting for his life.

"Is that so?" the king asked. "Magic's going away? How interesting. We'll have to have a long talk about why you have not mentioned this cycle to me sooner, Stang." The wizard grimaced, but nodded graciously to his king. "I have been called here to pronounce sentence." Tanir stood. He crossed muscular arms over his wide chest, looking every inch the wise warrior king. "Very well. For the wizards who practiced the forbidden art, I sentence you to three years exile as soon as the war with the Dasan is won." Neither wizard dared to complain. "Villia," the king went on. "You are sentenced to return to your duties among the wounded."

She bowed, threw Maggie a relieved look and hurriedly left the throne room.

The king then turned his attention back to Maggie and Gryfyn. He rubbed his jaw again.

"And what of the butterflies?" Colme asked with a bitter sneer.

"We offer our apologies for the sins we committed against them," Tanir answered.

"We. . . ?" the high priest sputtered. "But . . . "

"They are the ones who had their lives stolen. From what I understand of the matter, the true Donli and Gryfyn agreed to what was done." He gestured. "This lady that I am proud to call sister was brought here against her will, as was our good Master Butterfly. They have earned their places in the courts of the Ten Kingdoms. We can only hope that they will forgive us."

Tanir was looking at her earnestly, so Maggie decided that this was her cue to nod graciously and say, "There is nothing to forgive, my lord."

"I serve you with all my heart, my lord king," Gryfyn added.

Maggie noticed that they were still holding hands, and exchanged a smile with the stonesinger. Maybe they didn't have home, but they had each other. She was actually rather glad the whole thing was finally out in the open. Maybe she could accept this place if it could accept her. She looked back at Tanir. "I have work to get back to, my lord."

"Then I suggest you get back to it, my sister." He gave the soldiers in the room a hard look. "And we have a war to fight."

They cheered the king as he came down from the dais and walked among them. Maggie and Gryfyn followed in Tanir's wake as he shepherded his warriors back outside to face their real enemy. She and the stonesinger lingered on the staircase outside the stronghold door after all the others were gone. The air was smoky with the fires of battle. There was shouting and screaming in the distance. There was a war going on not very far away. She had the dead and dying to face in a few minutes. Gryfyn had to go back into the thick of the fighting. Somehow, she wasn't worried about the outcome of this crisis. It was all a dream, after all, wasn't it? Tanir's dream, maybe. He wouldn't let the dream end with defeat.

She sighed as Gryfyn's arm came around her shoulders. "I don't believe what happened in there."

"That we were put on trial?"

"That we got out of it." He threw back his beautiful head and laughed. Then he looked into her puzzled eyes and said. "Of course, once Tanir got involved, there was no way we weren't going to win."

She didn't understand. "Why?"

He laughed again. "Don't you get it yet? Think about it, sweetheart. Who do you think Tanir used to be back in the real world?"

"You mean—" Slowly the light began to dawn. "He's one of us."

"I saw it in his eyes," Gryfyn answered slowly. "I think Stang must have brought him here to fight the war with the Dasan."

"When?" she wondered. "How? Never mind, I know the answer to that one."

"Are you prepared to ask the High King those questions? I'm not."

"Me, neither," she agreed. "Not right now at any rate."

She contemplated the enormity of it all with a certain cheerfulness as Gryfyn walked with her back toward the storerooms she'd turned into a field hospital. They passed through a quiet kitchen garden that was so far untouched by any sign of war on the way, and their footsteps stirred up a cloud of tiny blue-and-yellow butterflies.

As the delicate creatures fluttered and spun around them, Maggie said with an odd and foolish joy, "Oh, look, it's a family reunion."

"Let's hope they're dreaming happy lives for us," Gryfyn said, and kissed her before they went off to their separate battles.

MARTY PLOTZ'S RULES FOR SUCCESS
by Bruce Holland Rogers

Bruce Holland Rogers is no stranger to anthologies, having appeared in *Feline and Famous*, and *Cat Crimes Takes a Vacation*. When he is not plotting feline felonies, he's writing excellent fantasy stories for such collections as *Enchanted Forests*, *The Fortune Teller*, and *Monster Brigade 3000*. Winner of the numerous Nebula awards, including the 1998 Short Fiction Award for his story in the anthology *Black Cats and Broken Mirrors*, his fiction is at once evocative and unforgettable.

So now that I'm famous, people ask me, "Marty, how did you do it? How did you save the Earth and win the Nobel Prize and all that?" Well, I've been thinking about that myself. How *did* I do it, exactly? As I've looked back, I've noticed how certain things led to success, things that could be made into rules. So here are my tips for getting to be just as rich and famous as me, Marty Plotz.

Rule Number One: Never Quit

I'm not a quitter. That's the thing my stepfather couldn't get, no matter how many times I explained it to him, like after I resigned from the job at the soy processing plant. That night, I mentioned at the dinner table that I would not be moving out and getting my own apartment, after all. Not yet. Later, when I found a suitable job and had the necessary funds. . . .

My stepfather's face got all red and swollen. A real tomato face. "I pulled every string I could pull to get you that job!" he said. "Then you quit before you've worked two whole days?"

"I didn't quit. I resigned."

"You quit the parks job. You quit the gas station job. You quit at Arby's, the gravel pit, the two grocery stores." He counted them off on his fingers. "Ten jobs I can think of without even trying. Four times you started and quit at the community college. Marty, you're almost thirty! You haven't stayed with anything for two weeks! You always quit!"

"I always *resign*," I corrected. "See, quitting is what you do without a reason. A quitter just quits. Me, I make strategic resignations. I leave when I see that a situation is not taking me where I need to go."

My stepfather's face got even redder. The guy needed to learn how to chill. He looked across the table at my mother. "Help me out here, Leslie."

So my mother touched my hand and said, "Marty, where is it that you need to go?"

"See, that's just the thing," I told her. "I'll feel it. I'll know it when the situation is right. It just hasn't been right yet."

"That seems reasonable," my mother said.

"You're coddling him," my stepfather said. "He's a grown man."

"You think I like living at home?" I said. "You think I like mowing the lawn for an allowance at my age? See, I just have to find a job that makes use of my talents."

"Your talents?" my stepfather said. He made a face. "What talents? Name one."

I thought about it and said, "I can nap anywhere."
He grunted. "That's not a talent."
Little did he know.

Rule Number Two: In Hard Times, Do Your Best

I had some hard times after they threw me out of the house. I thought my mother would save me at the last minute, but she just stood there next to my stepfather, tears on her cheeks, and said, "Marty, this is for your own good."

My own good. Right. Like I would have any real opportunities to find myself while living the kind of life they forced me into. I had to pay rent. I had to buy groceries. The pressure! Man, I get a headache just thinking about it! These were really hard times for me.

The really awful thing about my situation was that I had to delay my strategic resignations. When I did finally leave a job, I'd have to look for another one immediately, or else I'd be out on the street. I worked in a Taco Hut for two months, then for nine weeks as a security guard at a hotel. I'd never had to go so long between resignations. It was tough. And, actually, I didn't really officially resign the security guard thing. I was kind of asked to resign when I got caught taking a nap in one of the rooms.

But in every one of those jobs, I did the best I could do. Even though none of these positions made full use of my talents, even though I could see that they weren't taking me where I needed to go, I did my best. When I was napping during that security guard job, for instance, it was so I could be fresh in an emergency. I tried to explain that to my boss, but he refused to see how I was giving everything I had to that job.

That's a hard truth about life. Sometimes you do your best, and you don't get credit for it. That's just the way it is.

Rule Number Three: Be Open to New Experiences

When I took a job as a late-night Laundromat attendant, it was a new experience for me. I had never been a late-night Laundromat attendant before, but I was open to the possibilities.

For one thing, it was a job in which I could experiment with some new ways of sleeping. As I sat by the cash register, I found I could lean way back in my chair and kind of half-doze. Now this doesn't sound like much, but really it is a very specialized kind of napping to be able to do. Not everyone can do it on purpose. With this kind of dozing, I could get some rest and kind of dream some dreams while still being awake enough to sit up and make change if someone needed it.

On this one particular night, I was dreaming of being on a beach, drinking piña coladas and dozing. I often dream of dozing. This is a way of getting some extra rest.

One of my customers was this really cute chick about my age with hair so blonde it was almost white. Sometimes I put her in my dream, in a bikini . . . or out of a bikini. In the dream, I was showing her how she could fly by taking deep breaths and holding them. When I was pretty much awake, I tried to catch her eye a couple times so I could give her The Look, but she was reading *People* magazine, and it was understandably hard to get her attention. Her clothes were in the dryer, so she'd be leaving soon and I would probably miss my chance with her tonight. But there would be a next time. That's the thing with laundry. The customer will be back.

After she left, the only customer I had was a woman who reminded me of my mom, only more worn out. She was washing lots and lots of clothes, like her family had been saving them up all winter, and she had ten of the washers going, with two more heaping laundry baskets full of stuff to go in.

I half-dozed some more, making use of the special opportunities afforded by my job, being open to the experience. And then the aliens grabbed the Laundromat.

Another way to be open to new experiences is by not running away when things get weird, like when aliens abduct you. There I was, leaned back in my chair, half-dreaming myself onto this beach where the cute chick was putting some suntan lotion on my shoulders, and suddenly there was an earthquake. I started to fall out of my beach chair only it wasn't a beach chair at all, and *bam!* I was on the Laundromat floor. The earthquake wasn't on the beach at all. The cute chick was gone and the whole Laundromat was shaking. Just before the lights went out, I saw Laundry Mom grab onto one of the washing machines to keep from falling over. She looked at me, angry, as if whatever was happening could be my fault. Her wash cycles stopped filling. Everything was silent and dark.

Did I run away? No, I did not. I did jump up and go to the doors and kind of check them, but the aliens had sealed them shut and even if I had wanted to run, there was no way I could get those doors open. Then I could see stars out there where the parking lot used to be. A second later the earth, half in sun and half in shadow, went swinging by. After that, a big shadow blotted out my view of the earth and the stars and everything as the aliens guided our Laundromat into their ship. Whatever happened next, I was open to the experience.

It wasn't like I had a choice.

Rule Number Four: Take Charge

In the darkness, Laundry Mom said, "Just what is going on here?"

Well, I was the employee and she was the customer, so I took charge and said, "I don't know."

"I can't see a thing," she said. "Shouldn't there be some emergency lighting that comes on when the power goes off?"

I said, "I don't know."

"What about a flashlight?" she said. "Aren't there some cabinets under the cash register there? Feel around and see if you can find a flashlight."

I decided that the best thing I could do was try to find a flashlight and calm her down, since the darkness bothered her so much. But once I moved away from the doors, I tripped over a laundry cart and got kind of turned around. I groped along, but the first thing I came to was a bank of washing machines, not the counter where the cash register was. Meanwhile, I heard Laundry Mom moving around in the dark. She bumped into a chair.

"Be careful. Don't hurt yourself, ma'am," I said as I crawled around and tried to orient myself.

She didn't say anything, but I heard her moving stuff around. One of the cabinet doors creaked open, and I figured she was over by the cash register. I headed toward the sound. Paper rustled. A dim light snapped on, and I saw Laundry Mom's face for an instant before she pointed the light at me and said, "Come on. Stand up and help me figure out what's going on here."

So I stood up. That's when the lights came back on, and we saw the aliens. Well, we weren't really seeing the aliens, exactly. What we saw were a man and a woman in 1950s clothes. They were shades of gray and had lots of horizontal lines running across them, like old black and white TV pictures. They were smiling. The woman said, a cheery, "Hello! And welcome." And the man said, "Sorry for the little interruption in your routine. We have a favor to ask you, if you don't mind."

"Little interruption?" said Laundry Mom. "I have to plan my weeks down to the minute. . . ."

"You can call me Ward," said the gray man. "And this is June."

June said, "Pleased to meet you."

"We don't actually look like this," said Ward. He was holding an unlit pipe in his hand. "We received some of your broadcast images on our way here and are projecting holographic images that we hope you will find comforting."

Laundry Mom said, "I'm working two jobs to support my kids, which I wouldn't have to do if I ever got even half of the child support I'm owed. When I do laundry, I have to pay a sitter to stay with my kids. . . ."

"Yes, well," said Ward, still smiling. "You see, about thirty thousand years ago. . . ."

"Thirty-two thousand," said June, also smiling.

"To be precise, yes," Ward said. "Thirty-two thousand years ago, there was an explosion at the galactic core, and an intense wave of deadly radiation has been speeding toward your world. Since we're able to travel faster than the speed of light, we've been outracing the radiation, stopping at planets where all life is about to end."

"You haven't heard a word I've said," Laundry Mom told the aliens.

"We're trying to explain the pending demise of life on your planet," said Ward.

I said, "Maybe we should listen to what he says!"

And Laundry Mom said, "Ex*cuse* me," like she didn't really expect to be excused, "but just who do you think you are?"

"We're servants of the Collector, a great hive mind on the far edge of the galaxy," said June.

"That's not what I meant," said Laundry Mom. "I don't really *care* who you are. Look, I left a twelve-year-old in charge of my kids, and in all likelihood she isn't up to the task. For the privilege of leaving my boys in her unsteady hands, I get to pay her an hourly rate that is nearly three fourths of what I make at the better paying of my jobs. I have more than a dozen loads of laundry to do. My kids are out of clean socks. Did I mention that I'm working two jobs? I don't have time for this. You take us back down to earth right now and let me finish my laundry!"

She was waving the flashlight around like a weapon, so I took charge of it and put it away. There are times when you just have to take charge.

Rule Number Five: Be Brave

I figured that since I was the employee of the abducted Laundromat, I was the one who should really be talking to the aliens. So I said, "What about this favor?"

"Just one minute," Laundry Mom said. "I don't think I've made myself clear. I'm not interested in this favor.

I'm interested in getting back down on the ground and getting the water pipes reconnected to this building so I can finish washing and drying my clothes and go home!"

"All we're asking," said June, "is that one of you let us collect some of your memories as a small record of life on your planet. The process is easy and painless. Isn't that right, dear?"

Ward never stopped smiling. "That's right. Just a little gesture on your part—" He pointed his pipestem at me, "—will ensure that some small trace of your species will remain in the memory of the hive mind that sent us. You won't be *completely* obliterated, even though your planet and everyone on it is dead. We'll have a sample of some of your important memories, and we'll have all that broadcast TV and radio that we recorded on our way here."

Laundry Mom said, "Wait a minute. Did you say everyone will be dead?"

"Absolutely," said June with a smile.

"Positively everyone," Ward said with enthusiasm. He pointed his pipe at me again. "But this man's memories will live on!"

I said, "What do I have to do?"

"Oh, it's ever so easy," June said. She seemed really happy that I was cooperating. "It's almost as easy as going to the hairdresser."

When she said that, the doors of the Laundromat opened, and this beauty parlor hair dryer came gliding in under its own power. You know the kind I mean. A chair with this dome thing that comes down over your head.

"I have to sit in *that*?" I said.

"Easy and painless," June promised.

"Won't take but a minute," Ward added.

"Do you mean to tell us," said Laundry Mom, "that every man, woman, and child on the earth, not to mention all the trees and the grass and the birds and the fish in the ocean . . . Everything is going to die?"

If I sat down in that beauty parlor chair and let Ward and June put the dome down over my head, I was going to look like a real dork. Not only that, but Ward and June and Laundry Mom would all *see* me looking like a dork. But I thought about everything that Laundry Mom had said, about how desperate she sounded, and I decided to be brave and do the right thing no matter what the cost.

"I'll do it," I said. I looked at Laundry Mom, who was staring hard at Ward and June. "Don't worry," I told her. "I'll give them what they want, and then they'll take us back and you can finish your washing."

Rule Number Six: Use Your Talents

It may sound like I wasn't at all upset about the end of the world. Actually, I seriously bummed out about it. It meant I'd never find out what kind of career was right for me. But Ward and June hadn't mentioned that there was anything that could be done about the end of the world, so I figured that the main thing was to keep Laundry Mom calm and get us and the Laundromat back to earth. Then I could use my rent money to get pizza delivered and just hang out watching videos until the world ended.

I sat down in the beauty parlor chair, and the dome came down over my head. I felt my hair stand up as the dome started to hum.

But Laundry Mom was more worked up than ever. She said to the aliens, "Billions of innocent people are going to die! There has to be something you can do to save them!"

"It's not our job to save worlds," Ward said.

"Except in special cases," said June. To me she said, "Now relax, sir."

I told her my name was Marty.

"What special cases?" said Laundry Mom.

"Forget that she said that," said Ward. "Your world is in entirely different circumstances."

"They do have a big natural satellite handy," June said.

"June," said Ward, "I'd rather you let me handle this."

"Yes, dear. Now Marty," she said. "The first things I want you to think about are foods."

"What's this about a natural satellite?" demanded Laundry Mom. "Does she mean the moon?"

"She was speaking hypothetically," said Ward.

"We could do it if there were a reason to," June put in.

"Darling," said Ward, "I do wish you'd let me handle this."

"Sorry. Now, Marty. . . ."

"If there's something you can do with the moon to save the earth," Laundry Mom said to Ward, "why don't you get busy and do it!"

"Think about really tasty things you've had to eat," June said, "the best your planet has to offer. Keep in mind that whatever you choose to remember is going to stand for your whole planet in the annals of galactic history."

I thought of chocolate Moon Pies, ones that had been

in the store long enough for the marshmallow centers to get a little stiff and chewy.

"Good," June said. "That's coming through very clearly."

"Unfortunately," Ward told Laundry Mom, "we're on a very tight schedule. There are other planets that are just as much on the verge of destruction, and we want to collect some memories from them, too. We deviate from our schedule only for special planets."

"But Earth is special," Laundry Mom insisted. "Human beings are special. My kids especially. You *have* to save Earth."

"Actually," said Ward, "your evolutionary path is so common that we almost skipped your world altogether."

"Think of something else, now," June said. "Something else that you like to eat."

That was easy. I thought of banana Moon Pies.

"Our world is not ordinary!" Laundry Mom insisted.

"All right," June said pleasantly. "Now think of a *different* food that you like to eat."

So I thought of vanilla Moon Pies. They're not quite as good as the chocolate or banana ones, but they're still good.

"Are you getting this?" June said to Ward.

"Every bland nuance. Pitiful."

"We really *could* have skipped this planet."

"No!" Laundry Mom insisted. "You've got to *save* this planet."

"Marty," June said to me, "Let's try something else. Just think of something else that's pleasant. Not food. Something worthwhile. Something that's the best that your planet has to offer."

That was easy. I thought of *TV Guide*.

Still smiling, June said, "It's a wonder they *want* to go on living."

Laundry Mom glared at me. "What are you remembering?"

"Cable TV," I said. "Screen-in-screen channel previewing."

"Think of great things!" Laundry Mom said. "Think of the Sistine Chapel! Think of Mozart!"

"I don't know how any Mozart goes," I said. "But I know the words to both versions of the *Gilligan's Island* theme song."

"That's quite all right," Ward said, lifting the dome from my head. "We've collected *something*. We don't have a lot of time here."

"I can't believe you can't be bothered to save our planet," Laundry Mom said. "I want to see your supervisor."

"Ma'am, our supervisor is a hundred-thousand light-years away," Ward said.

"We do appreciate your time," June said to Laundry Mom, "and we're sorry that we have inconvenienced you."

Laundry Mom continued to argue with them. While she did, I thought of something else that Earth had to offer, something that was related to my particular talents. I said, "Hey, June. What about sleep?"

But they were paying attention only to Laundry Mom, who was insisting that they at least *call* their supervisor. So I pulled the dome back down over my head, got comfortable, and went for a snooze.

I dreamed I was sitting on the beach, and the cute chick was putting suntan oil on my shoulders. The ocean was a greenish yellow, and I knew it was the Sea of Mountain Dew. I could see Moon Pie islands in the distance, and the sand on the beach where we were sitting was pink. Our island was a strawberry Moon Pie. The world was going to end pretty soon. There was a clock floating on the waves, and when it showed high noon, that would be the end of the world in this time zone. The world would end later, Central and Pacific, I knew, and I wanted to be in another time zone. I took a breath and blew myself up like a balloon, and I floated up higher and higher to where I could see that all of the Moon Pies were really giant jellyfish floating in a sea of stars.

It was just a little slip of a dream, but when I woke up, Ward and June were staring at me wide-eyed. Laundry Mom was looking from them to me and back at them again. She said, "What? What happened?"

Ward said, "What kind of memory was that?"

"That wasn't a memory," I told him. "That was a dream." I stretched and yawned.

"Incredible," said June. "*That* was dreaming?"

"I don't get it," said Laundry Mom. "What did he dream?" She looked at me. "What did you dream, Marty."

"I was on this beach," I started to explain.

Ward said, "We've encountered sleep thoughts on other worlds, but we had no idea that in your species they could be so . . ." He waved his pipe around in little circles, looking for the right word.

"Uncontrolled," said June.

"Irrational," Ward said. "So strange."

"It's very collectable," June said.

"Yes! Yes, I'm sure it is," said Laundry Mom. "Oh,

yes, absolutely! It's one of our greatest accomplishments. Every human being dreams like this!"

"Really?" Ward said.

"You want dreams? You want to collect dreams for the hive mind? Humanity can give you billions and billions of them. Billions! Just as long as there are billions of human beings around to dream them for you."

Rule Number Seven: Hold on to Your Dreams

The rest of the story, everybody knows: How the Laundromat landed at the United Nations building. How Laundry Mom—everybody knows her as Nancy Atchity now, but she'll always be Laundry Mom to me—explained the deal she had made with the aliens. How the aliens smashed up the moon and glued it back together to make a shield to protect the earth when the radiation pulse came through a week later. How everybody on the planet gets to be in a lottery now to see who goes up to Ward and June's space ship and get their dreams collected. I was the only one who got to do it without the lottery, and I didn't dream for the aliens because of luck. It was because of my special talents.

I was famous. I got paid a lot of money to be on TV, which I would have done for free except I didn't tell anyone that. Then that Hollywood guy called me up and asked if I wanted to sell my story for six million dollars. Heck, I'd have done that for free, too! But I took the money. After that, a Nobel Prize guy called me up. He said Nancy was going to get a Nobel Peace Prize. He said that upon reviewing my unique contributions, the Nobel committee wanted to give me a special, one-time prize. He asked if I would accept a special Nobel Prize for Napping, I said, "Yes." And they paid me *even more money!*

But I still hadn't achieved my dream. Not until I had built the house I had always figured I would own someday, after I found the right career and made a lot of money and retired.

And now that's where I live. The very first people who saw it were my mom and my stepfather. The place has thirty rooms, and in every one of them, even in the bathrooms, there's a TV and a comfortable couch. I have thirty subscriptions to *TV Guide,* so no matter what room I'm in, I always know what's on.

I told my stepfather, "This is what comes from having a dream, man. It all comes from strategic resignations and not being a quitter. See? I just had to be in the right place at the right time."

My stepfather's face was white. He was staring at my Nobel Prize medal, which I wear around my neck all the time. I could tell that he just didn't know what to say. But Mom said it for him. She said, "We're so proud of you, Marty. Aren't we proud, dear?"

My stepfather couldn't do anything but nod and go on staring at the Nobel Prize. You can't argue with success, man. You can't argue with the Nobel Prize, *TV Guide* in every room, and a dream come true. You just can't.

SHELTER
by Michelle West

Michelle West is the author of *The Sacred Hunt* duology
and *The Broken Crown, The Uncrowned King,* and *The
Shining Court* published by DAW Books. She reviews
books for the online column *First Contacts*, and less fre-
quently for *The Magazine of Fantasy & Science Fiction*.
Other short fiction by her appears in *Black Cats and Broken
Mirrors, Elf Magic,* and *Olympus*.

> *I dream, therefore I exist.*
> —J. August Strindberg (1849–1912)

> *If a little dreaming is dangerous,*
> *the cure for it is not*
> *to dream less but to dream more,*
> *to dream all the time.*
> —Marcel Proust (1871–1922)

When I saw the little boy's hand in Sergi's, I knew
that it was over. The transition from the wilds of
nightmare to the calm and the safety of the collective
was almost complete.

We were maneuvering our way through, of all things,
an airport. This was the point at which the boy, an eight-
year-old with solemn eyes and a very serious demeanor,
would wake up screaming or crying or clutching the
blankets in the dim lights of the lab's sleep study room.

We would take him at once to his parents, wheeling the bed into the room across the hall, where he could see them.

In the nightmare, though, they were gone. He would turn in the crowd and realize that his hand was attached to nothing, and then he would look from face to face, and then he would start to search for them. The search would grow frenzied and desperate, his heart rate accelerating until sleep could no longer contain him.

We started out by being a familiar presence. We wore the faces of a married couple roughly the same age as his parents, and the same genotype. We approached him and asked if he needed our help, and he shook his head mutely, carried by the nightmare.

Normally, the process should have taken three days. With the boy, it took three weeks, and they were grueling. The nightmares were strong. But persistence was stronger. By being familiar, even in the distorted wilds of nightmare, we were able to win the boy's confidence. By putting all of our reserves into the nightmare understructure, we were able to support the benign and gentle image that we desired him to see, and on the twentieth night of his stay in the sleep study wing of the Jerrend Institute for the Collective Unconscious he slid a shaking hand into Sergi's.

Sergi walked him across the crowded floor to where his parents stood waiting. "Peter Jenkins," he said quietly, just before his parents came into his field of vision, "you're in the airport, but you will never lose your parents in it again if you don't want to. We're here to help you find them."

*   *   *

"Congratulations," I told him, when we'd both woken up and were reading the results of the monitors. "But . . . this is a bit . . . wild. See the A spike?"

He nodded, massaging the back of his neck.

"Don't smoke in here," I said, without looking at him. "The last time you did, it set the sprinklers off and they nearly gave you the boot."

He paid as much attention to the entreaty as he usually did. Fire glowed a moment in reflexively cupped palms; I could see its reflection in the screens. "A spike is high. But the B spike is higher, relative to its norm." He frowned.

"What do you think?"

"I don't know. The boy wasn't in the collective. We'd have seen him; his parents would have found him. But this, and this—they bear the distinctive markings of dream contaminate."

"Not possible. Not in the wild dreaming."

"No. Or it shouldn't be if the Jerrend theorems, as given, hold true. Interesting, though."

Great. "Maybe you can bring it up with Dr. Jerrend." I didn't bother to keep the sarcasm out of my voice.

"Maybe," he said, fiddling absentmindedly with a matchbook, "I will."

That night, freed from the constraints of the boy's dreaming for the first time in three weeks, I joined the collective with almost obscene glee.

I don't know if Sergi even notices its absence, but I do; the edge of the untamed dreaming grates on my nerves with its lack of sense or causality. Raw dreaming is the state that existed before the Jerrend breakthrough gave us something better: the full power of our minds;

the ability to imagine, perceive, conceive of worlds at a speed, and with a depth, that circuitry couldn't keep up with.

Jerrend not only gave us access to the much theorized collective subconscious, but control over it as well. I remember the day that he chose his researchers; the day that he unveiled his formulae in all their eclectic and confusing beauty; the day he came to us in the middle of REM and invited us into the collective—*from* the dreaming. No one speaks of their personal paradigms when they allude to their first encounter with another living intellect in the collective; it's too embarrassing.

Judge for yourself. In my mind's eye, I can see him, winged and limned in fire, his eyes as dark and absolute as the eyes of an archangel. He did not offer so much as command, and I followed without hesitation, although if I had been thinking with my conscious mind I wouldn't have recognized him at all. But it was apt, I think; some part of my hindbrain knew that he would offer us paradise.

You can't imagine what the next few months were like. We approached what he offered with hesitation, but we approached it, building on it as we realized what it could be used for. I don't think we ever reached a limit; I don't think there was one.

It was in the collective, wearing faces and bodies that reflected our truest sense of self, that we were free to express our truths in ways that wouldn't destroy us. We could see others' fears and angers in a way that made us understand that all fear and anger was natural; that it was not, did not have to be, an event in isolation; that it could be something other than emotional viscera. Seen as such, it became less threatening, less all-consuming;

instead of facing it alone, we drew on the strength of our friends, balancing the anger with joy, the fear with courage, the panic with an abiding sense of calm.

In the common, in the collective, we flew. We visited the solar systems of planets that only academics could claim any waking understanding of. We didn't need their waking knowledge; it was the knowledge that they shared with us, in the dreaming, that brought those worlds to life. We could understand why they had their obsessions; we could make them understand our own. We walked in the valleys of the untouched Mesozoic; we watched the great lizards, felt their hunger, fed it a bit with our own. We told our children stories, and the stories were not words on the page; they were moving spectacle, display, something that captured what we felt as children by our parents' sides.

There was a depth to the collective, a quality to it, that had everything to do with communal experience; we were trying to tap that, to use it, to become a part of it.

We were building a history that had nothing to do with time and everything to do with living life.

We wanted it to be safe.

We didn't want to leave anyone behind.

But the dreaming anomalies that we had encountered with Richard Jones were not events in isolation; it became clear to the psychologists on the project that the collective itself was becoming harder and harder for the children to reach. In and of itself, that was tragic, but worse: the quality of the nightmares that drove them not only from the collective, but from sleep as well, lingered well into their waking hours. The patterns of their daytime thoughts were influenced to a far greater degree than we had witnessed in our control groups prior to our awareness of the collective.

Dr. Jerrend came to speak at the Institute three days later.

His arrival had a way of putting the entire efforts of the research institute—with the possible exception of the support staff who actually made life possible—on hold. It's not so much that he held the purse strings—although he did. Even Sergi genuflected—in any practical way his nod of respect and recognition *is* genuflection—when the man who brought us the Amelian sleep cycles, named after the daughter he lost decades ago, enters the institute's impressive doors.

I found him intimidating. I don't find many men intimidating, but while Sergi's intellect occasionally eclipses mine, which has led to an interesting confrontation or two, Jerrend's dwarfs it. I don't mind feeling ugly, or plain, or frumpy, or old; I don't mind feeling out of touch with current style or fashion. But I loathe feeling stupid. Stupidity is a mortal sin, the eighth—or, in my books, the first. And Jerrend makes me feel like I'm going to hell for a long time just by existing.

In ones and twos we gathered in the auditorium.

Jerrend seldom interfered with our work at the Institute; so seldom, in fact, that it was easy to forget just how much of it he owned. We had jobs here, roots, research grants and the possibility of fame and a place in history, and if he chose, he could take those away from us without blinking twice. Or once, really.

"Ladies," he said, all old-fashioned grace, "gentlemen. You've seen the results of the practical use of

Amelian cycles as they pertain to the studies of the volunteers in the Institute. There can be no doubt that use of the dreaming time as a substitute for the vastly more primitive virtual reality has been a far greater success than we . . . please pardon the humor . . . ever dreamed possible."

There was, of course, the expected laughter, but the words were dry enough that the laughter was polite—and short. No one wastes this man's time more than once.

"The children are already learning more, and at a more accelerated rate, than they have at any time in the past; our results are a vast improvement over any results that normal, daytime enrichment programs have ever succeeded in producing. And not only do children learn quickly, but they have the time to play and to learn the social lessons out of which we build a civil society. Their parents, harried in the work day, have the time in the dreaming to spend with their children, building the psychological and emotional bonds that experts believe —and I believe rightly—produce healthy, rational adults.

"By brokering the Amelian cycles into useful, collective experiences, we have managed to solve the time dilemma that many of our volunteers face." He turned away from the lectern that barely contained him.

He had said nothing that we hadn't already known. The silence, as we waited for some enlightenment, stretched. Stretched. Stretched. Fine and thin. And then some poor fool stood up. I recognized him. Jeremy Graham.

"Well?" Professor Jerrend said softly.

"I have a question sir. About the nightmares."

"Yes," he said quietly. "I thought you might."

And I knew, the minute he spoke, that he *had* expected that question. That if he had known who would ask it, he might have skipped the whole lecture entirely and gone straight to its source. Or maybe not.

He said, quietly, "There are some . . . qualities . . . that science cannot precisely measure. What exactly do you mean by question, Mr. Graham?"

Mr. Graham paled beneath freckles that had endured adolescence and followed him into adulthood. "Once we make breakthrough, sir, the dreamers never seem to experience nightmares again; they control their sleeping environment in a way that . . . defies the current meaning of the word subconscious."

"Go on."

"But the children have had trouble adjusting. Especially the ones that we can't walk across. . . ."

"Go on."

But he was silent.

Which left the floor to the only man who actually had the guts to take up the thread of the conversation and face down the demon. It was, after all, his specialty.

"The children that we can't walk across, through the means of the Amelian cycles, seem to get trapped in the nightmares that they're having; they lose the definition that divides waking fear from sleeping terror."

"This is not unusual in young children."

"It is," Sergi said quietly. "A young child holds the fear of nightmare as if it were reality; this is true. But the physical symptoms of that fear—the actual adrenalin levels, the cerebral activity—these do not normally continue in a heightened fashion for the length of time we've observed."

"And your concerns?"

"I'm concerned, sir," he said, with all due respect in his deep, slow voice, "that you were aware of our concern before it was voiced. I'm concerned that you expected this difficulty and did nothing to warn us of it."

"Oh?"

"I'm concerned that you have some indication of the dangers in using the Amelian cycles, in making the dream-state readily and widely available, that you've chosen not to share with us."

Job, Sergi, I thought. But he's no mind reader. He looked across at Dr. Jerrend, dark eyes intent on dark eyes; they were like a mirror for a moment, older and younger versions of the same obsession. But there were shadows in the faces of both men beneath the harsh academic lighting.

"Anything else?"

"No, sir."

"Good." He turned away from the lectern, and then turned back. "You," he said quietly, to Sergi, "and your unfortunate partner, will now be pulled from the main body of the project to assist me with a matter of concern involving the unusual state of nightmares as noted. Thank you for volunteering.

"The rest of you may now return to your groups. Continue with the work you've been doing."

"I don't particularly like you," Jerrend said to Sergi. The two men stood in a room that could have been used as a blue screen in a movie production, it was that empty. If you didn't count me, and obviously they didn't.

"Is that relevant?"

"One never knows," the older man replied. "In the

dreaming, like, dislike, desire or revulsion, exact a price
if one is not aware of them before one enters."

"We're not in the dreaming sir."

"No?" The old man's smile was thin. "We've turned
the dreaming into such a tame place, how could you be
expected to tell the difference?"

Because, I thought, *we'd never dream of you.* Luckily, I knew I wasn't as brilliant as Sergi, and that made
me expendable.

"Let me introduce you both to a young woman who
made her way to the center grounds by climbing over
the fence. She has been in convalescence; she broke her
right arm and her right ankle in the fall, and seemed
oblivious to the damage; enough so that she somehow
walked halfway to the front doors before collapsing.
One of the project children found her."

"Her, sir?"

"Yes." He put his hands behind his back and stiffened, a physical gesture that announced the coming end
of the interview. "I believe that if she can be brought to
the collective, we can . . . help her."

"Help her?"

"Yes. The only thing she would say for three days
was her name. Tiffany. Tiffany. Tiffany. She has an extraordinary voice."

This is an example of Jerrend's dry sense of humor.

Tiffany didn't speak.

And in the quiet isolation wing that we needed four
magnetic cards and eidetic memory to enter—and you
can laugh because you haven't tried those key codes—
there wasn't a lot of sound if we didn't find our own

voices charming. We were still considered part of the
Amelian project, but we weren't part of it; we didn't eat
with our colleagues, we didn't engage in political feuds,
we didn't sleep with them; we might as well have been
in outer space.

Jerrend forced us to focus on Tiffany, and only on
Tiffany. Sergi didn't need to be cut off from reality in
order to do it, but it probably helped me; I found the girl
disturbing. It was almost as if we were the ones shut in
with her, rather than the other way around.

Her lips, when they moved, moved over a hiss of air
as unconstrained by tongue or teeth as the open breeze.
She showed no sign of being an abuse victim, or at least
none of the standard signs. We didn't know her last
name. We didn't know if she was given a middle name.
We didn't know where she was born, although things
had been done that might give us some of that information—fingerprints taken—I can still see her slender fingers dancing over ink pad and paper as if to play at
music, art, or time—dental impressions made. They
were sent away to the appropriate authorities, or so we
were told.

Jerrend gave Tiffany into our care.

And you know, his presence is such that I didn't really stop to ask him how. How was she made a ward?
How could she just be given to the project, like a beautiful and disturbed lab rat?

If not for Tiffany's silence and the oddity of her lop-
ing gait, her awkward, sudden lunges into empty space,
hands curved like trowels or stiff like boards—if, in
fact, she could have been deprived of movement and
made to sit like a quiet child, she would have been
lovely. Her hair was pale. Not white, not quite that, but

not so yellow that it falls into cliché; her skin was
golden with sunlight, with the tan that speaks of play
and health beneath an open sky. But it was so hard to
notice these things. Her clothing was stained with food
and water, with dirt and grass and the occasional display
of incontinence that a child her age should have been
well past; she wouldn't meet your eyes for more than a
minute, and her smile, when it took the corners of her
mouth, was sometimes sharp and sometimes maniacal
and sometimes. . . .

Evil.

She didn't much like us, which was fair; we lay in
wait in the waking world because the waking world was
ours.

Bring her to the collective.

Fair enough. But the trip to the collective is only easy
once you've managed to find her on the fringes of the
wilds, where her dreams and ours—all of ours—over-
lap. We've been trying to find the door and the key to
her dreamworld. Which is bloody hard when she won't
even speak. Sort of like trying to find the individual
dreamworld of a dog or a cat.

I've always been good at laying foundation; at asking
the right questions, at picking up the little details: colors
loved or hated, toys loved or hated, people missed. But
Tiffany didn't *speak,* and her inability to function in the
day to day here and now stumped us both for weeks. We
were left to simple observation, and that yielded nothing
except our own reactions. She was not consistent in
anything that she did.

I was afraid of Tiffany. I wasn't particularly proud of
that fact, and it made the job much, much more complicated. Had we the choice, I'd've deserted the post in an

eyeblink. She knew, of course. Children always know when you're frightened.

Sergi was no fool. We did not discuss Tiffany in great detail, but I believe he was afraid of her as well.

It's just that his fear *for* her was the greater fear. Sergi is patient. Infinitely patient. She bit him, fastening her flat little teeth to the side of his hand. Her lips were red with his blood when he pulled the hand free. She smiled at him, her eyes wide with surprise and delight, her face—for a moment—a child's face.

I took about four steps back before I could stop myself; she turned on me with that smile—and he stepped between us, holding out his hand. I don't know what he was thinking, but he held out his hand and she took it, fastening her ruby lips to the cut she had made.

That day was the first breakthrough.

It was not what we were hoping for.

I found her in the dreaming that night. I found her, but I didn't recognize her at first; I had stumbled off the path.

That's dream-speak. There is no real path, but those of us who have spent enough time with the collective have become adept at carving out spaces in which a concrete sense of rationality holds sway. The nightmares that I'd had since Jerrend chose to lock us away with the mad girl had been spectacular; it was almost as if I'd returned to childhood myself; I would wake up, heart pounding, lungs taking in more air than the body could process, the sting of my nails making crescents in my palms. All the nightmares were strong.

I thought at first—when I woke at the sound of a scream, and realized from the rawness of my throat that it was mine—that this was another such nightmare. I had stumbled off the path into Snow White's forest. The trees grew limbs and fingers long as thigh bones, but the creatures that flew out of nightmare interpretations of willow switches all had Jerrend's face.

They flew at me, howling, voices raised to a pitch it would have been impossible for me to hear in the waking world. Dreams follow their own logic—I saw this at a remove created by waking—and the creatures drove me into the wilderness of a forest unbroken by civilization. There should have been a cottage; I realize that now. Instead, there was a clearing—as if in Nightmare not even a hovel could be erected—and in that clearing, pale as snow but somehow dark as pitch, a very beautiful, very dead young woman. She lay in a coffin, whose lid was made of glass, but her chest did not rise and fall; she looked like ice.

What had she eaten, to end up here, waiting for the kiss of a prince?

Her eyes opened as I approached her.

She smiled, and her lips, red as rubies, dark and shiny and wet, parted.

Vampire. The bats were screaming in voices I could hear, but I was too terrified to force myself to catch the words. It was only after her long teeth had sunk themselves into my throat that I recognized her: Tiffany.

I decided I would let Sergi handle her.

I should add: He was there when I woke. I asked him about it later, and he said that he'd heard me screaming as if I were being murdered. Made sense to me; it took me a quarter of an hour to stop hyperventilating.

But later, I remembered that I'd left him in the lab, in the sleeper bed.

Good news travels quickly. Unfortunately, so does every other kind. Jerrend showed up on our doorstep the next day, face haggard, eyes gleaming with a curiosity that, from the jaundiced eye of a trained psychologist, seemed a bit too bright and shiny.

He said, "I hear that you've managed to make contact with Tiffany."

I glanced at Sergi, who had already turned a moment before to glare at the side of my face. I hadn't spoken to Jerrend; it's clear that Sergi hadn't either. A hundred different replies—all of them career limiting—came to mind. And stayed there.

"Take me to her," he said, with the easy imperiousness of a man who is refused nothing. We did. She was, oddly enough, awake when he entered the room. She stared at him as he entered, and her eyes, like his, were a little bit too bright and shiny.

But neither of them spoke a word.

If he could have pulled us from every other project we were working on in order to concentrate on this one, he would have. Unfortunately for him, he'd already done that; that left the essentials: breathing, eating, and sleeping. I half-expected him to ask us to give at least two of those up. He didn't. Instead he contented himself with sharp and pointed questions, all aimed at Sergi. Sergi had to content himself with slow and careful answers. Neither man looked completely satisfied with the situation, and after watching it for about an hour and a half, I left the room.

Then I turned and walked back in. "Doctor Jerrend?"

Both men turned to look at me, as if unaware of my momentary absence. They probably were.

"There isn't a man who knows more about the collective than you do. No one—not even Sergi, although he's probably the only one who comes close—knows how to map it, how to work with it, how to build on it while maintaining identity, *half* as well as you do. You *built* the collective. You taught us how to reach for the group subconscious, the shared experiences."

I had to pause for breath. I would have been grateful for an interruption, but there wasn't one. His face was as expressionless as a rock.

"I don't understand why you aren't attempting to integrate Tiffany yourself. I don't understand why you brought her to *us*." *Since she's obviously so important to you, you have to circle us like a carrion bird.*

His lips compressed slightly. "No," he said quietly. "You don't."

That ended the argument. He walked out of the room without looking back. Sergi watched him go.

"Meg," he said, when Jerrend's footsteps had ceased to echo in the empty halls. "Do you remember where the name Amelian comes from?"

That afternoon, we talked to Tiffany. Or rather, I did; Sergi, pencil hanging loosely from one hand, sat in a chair with his back to the window. I can see him clearly if I close my eyes: He looks like a silhouette against the bright light. The curtains are not drawn; they remain undrawn; I have to squint to look at him at all. But I know that he doesn't do this for effect; he wants the best view of Tiffany's facial expressions, and the natural light banishes all shadow.

She didn't seem to be aware of Sergi. All of her attention was focused on me; I would swear that she was, on purpose, staring at my neck. As if she could remember my exposed throat and her teeth in it. I've had a lot of dreams in my life, and very few of them feature me as the undead killer.

I smiled back at her, hiding teeth. "Tiffany," I said quietly, holding up a book, "today we're going to read you a story. Would you like that?"

No answer; her shoulders and arms shuddered as she sat up in her bed.

"This is the story of Snow White and the Seven Dwarfs."

Sergi did the run that night. He found nothing. Whatever it was that gave us the glimpse into that wilderness, it wasn't a fairy tale. While Sergi was in the bed, the monitor lights fanning out in a flash of letters and lines above his forehead, I went off to do some research of my own. Sergi's question was entirely rhetorical: everyone knew that Jerrend had named the Amelian cycles after his only child. She had passed away several years ago, and the marriage that had produced her had soon followed. Sometimes a death brings us closer together, and sometimes it erects a wall that nothing living can breach.

Jerrend did not remarry. He wasn't a young man, although he could have fathered children if he desired them. I think I would have pitied any child of his, but I don't know that for a fact; the most severe and repressive of men can be a joy and a delight to their children;

they can show a vulnerability that only those children can touch. I wanted to think that a man who named one of our greatest discoveries in honor of his daughter was such a father.

But I couldn't confirm it. There was no interest in Jerrend or his theories when he was a young man, and therefore no interviews, no print trail to capture and store. There was no mention of his wife, other than a brief note that one had existed.

"Meg?"

It was about four in the morning—if the wall clock is accurate—when Sergi showed up in the doorway.

"Any luck?" It was a purely rhetorical question. The creases in his forehead spoke of frustration, and no success does that to Sergi's face.

But he did me the courtesy of answering. "No."

"Why don't we try Bram Stoker tomorrow instead?"

Silence. I stood up. "Sergi?"

"Have you spoken to anyone outside in the last week or two?"

"Several times."

"Did any of them tell you that there's been a sharp decline in the number of children that we can walk across?"

No.

"Has anyone mentioned that there are children outside of the project's studies that have begun to show increasing 'nocturnal agitation'?"

No.

"What are we trying to do here, Meg?"

I started to tell him it was a coincidence. I might have even meant it. But in the shadows beyond his broad shoulders, I suddenly saw her jet black eyes, her lips red and slick with his blood—or *mine*—and I forgot to breathe.

"There is no failure more profound," he said, into my silence, "than that of a man who fails his child."

"Or woman?"

He shrugged. "We need more information."

I knew, then, what he was asking for. I thought about it for a long time. "Maybe." I closed the notepad that was curling with the weight of my cursive script. "You realize that you could lose everything if he—"

"I'm willing."

Damn him anyway.

Information is a business.

And once it's out there, it's out there, waiting to be found. People imagine they have privacy. In the collective, we know there's no such thing. But in the outside world? People commit all kinds of information to the ether. I have my friends in that world. They're older and more respectable than they used to be, but when I tell them that it's important, they believe me. They sit down at their computers, phone hooked to one ear, fingers on old keys; they don't keep me long.

I called one of them. Actually, I'm lying. I called two of them and made it a friendly contest of skill and speed. What did I ask for? Nothing much. A picture of Amelia Jerrend. Medical records. The date of her birth. The date—and the manner—of her death.

We had a fax machine in the office. Two days after I'd finished my briefing and my dare, it started to hum, and paper began to stack up in the tray. The fax was a color fax; the paper was a heavy bond that tended toward gloss more than I liked. Sergi chose both. The project had the funds for it. Still does.

I didn't get past the first sheet, although I waited, pinching myself the entire time, until the fax told me it was finished. Then I picked up the pieces of cooling paper and I ran to find Sergi.

He was in Tiffany's room.

"Tiffany," he said softly, as I opened the door upon the almost genius and the girl who, in sleep, looked so beautiful. "Tiffany is a name that means epiphany."

"I thought it was furniture."

"Ha ha."

"No, I'm serious."

"It comes from theophany." He paused. Rolled his eyes. "Revelation; usually in the presence of something divine."

I looked at her face for a long minute and then I handed Sergi the papers in my hands. He lifted the one on the top of the stack and carried it to the bedside lamp.

The lamplight was reflected off the face of a girl who bore a striking resemblance to the one in the bed.

It wasn't an exact image. If it was, I think we might have both quit on the spot. But the girl in bed had slightly higher cheekbones, slightly larger eyes; her chin was a little more delicate. They had almost the same hair, though, the same nose, the same complexion.

"Well?"

He put the picture face down on the end table. "What do you think?"

Sergi almost never asked me what I thought. He was so certain of hearing it one way or the other he didn't waste the effort of social nicety. But this was new to both of us. "What do I think?"

"I said that already."

"Ha ha." I was afraid that Tiffany would wake; that she would hear us. "I don't know. If I had to guess—and it's going to sound stupid—I would guess that Dr. Jerrend believes that the collective does house the—the subconscious memories of the whole of mankind, past and present."

He raised a dark brow.

"It's in the theorems," I said, in way of self-defense. "We die at staggered intervals. If it's true that the collective remembers what *has been* dreamed by its living members, then the edges of *those* memories are tainted by the dreaming of earlier, but dead . . . contributors. The only way to cut us off from our history would be to destroy us all at once and start again."

"You think he's trying to find her dreams?"

I looked at the girl on the bed. "I don't know. Yes. No."

"Which?"

"Why don't you answer the question yourself?"

"Because, Meg, I don't know. He lost a child. From the look of the report, she died of blood loss in a car accident. *He* was the driver."

"And the vampire image stems from that."

"I would say that the vampire image stems not from the daughter, but from the father; she—the *fact* of her death—has driven him mercilessly. It has been kind to the rest of us; I don't believe we would have the Amelian cycles if not for that death. But. . . ."

It made no sense.

"Why does he want us to walk Tiffany through the

wild dreaming, then? Why does he want her brought into the collective?"

"I don't know. But *this* girl . . ." He held up the photo. "Is she even real?"

He laughed; the sound was short, harsh. "He has many capabilities. Creating life, except in the usual way, is not one of them."

"Do you think she—" I nodded toward Tiffany.

"I don't know. I don't know if she started out insane, or ended up that way."

"Pardon?"

"I think you asked him the right question. But—I think neither of us understood it at the time."

"Sergi?"

"Why didn't he walk her through to the collective himself? I think . . . he did. I think that whatever part of Amelia's psyche he had found preserved in the collective he brought to the girl."

I didn't want to think of the implications of that. "You can't impress another personality on one that's already there." Flat words. Immutable truth.

"No," he said quietly. There was no conviction at all in the syllable.

"Amelia?" I said, as softly as I could.

Her eyes snapped open.

Sergi whispered the name, and she turned, unblinking, to stare at his face. Then she began to scream.

We had so little time.

Sergi played with drugs like an old pro. No surprises there. The common wisdom in the project is that you can't force the dreamer—not to dream. Waking is different.

Well, so much for common wisdom.

This time, Tiffany made no attempt to bite Sergi. Her eyes were round and dark, so dark I thought his damn drugs had entirely distended the pupil. No.

"Amelia," he said, holding her hand in a tight grip as he pierced her lower arm with his needle.

She stared out at him, her expression shifting and twisting until it perfectly captured the sharp-eyed malice I'd come to dread. "She's not here."

I lost my breath for a moment. Her voice was unlike any voice I had heard before—while awake. In sleep, in the collective, there were voices that had this timbre, this power. Sergi didn't even blink.

"I know," he replied calmly, swabbing the needle's exit point with disinfectant and taping that swab in place.

"Then why are you calling her?"

"You won't answer to any other name."

"Yes I *will!*"

"No, you won't."

"I WILL!"

"Tiffany?" He said it softly.

Rumplestiltskin, I thought. Her eyes lost focus. Bright and shining until the lids closed, she stared at me as if I were a long way in the distance.

Sergi held up two more needles. He handed one to me; kept the other for his own use. No time. We made it to the beds; fitted ourselves with the cathodes and bands that the computers used to monitor our systems. Closed eyes.

"Sergi?"

"Here." He was dressed in the robes of a Wizard;

stars, moons, pentacles in bright yellow against a fabric of night sky. I would have laughed, but it suited him. "Is this the forest?"

"Yes." It was. Trees rose like specters to either side of where we were standing. I don't remember if they were there before he asked; the dreaming is mutable.

"And she was in it?"

"Yes. But—"

The bats came flying out of the darkness, trailing it like smoke, like exhaust. Sergi took a step forward, and I followed him into sudden night. Sunlight was forsaken here. All light was, although we could still see clearly. That's the logic of the dreaming. The wind spoke in a ghost voice, a symphony of torment relieved of words.

I found the bats terrifying. The trees pressed in on me, the ghosts screamed and shrieked. Sergi touched my hand.

"Pull yourself together," he said, his voice a grim series of connected syllables. "She needs you."

As food, I thought. But he was right. With effort, I could force myself into a state of calm. Great effort. But Sergi's respect is something I obviously desire; I forced myself to be calm.

The forest grew silent. We wandered through it looking for footpaths. And looking. And looking.

Then, rueful, I turned back to him. "Let's do things my way, all right?"

I let the fear back in.

We found her corpse almost instantly; came upon it not, as we had hoped, by accident or fairy-tale design, but by following the trail of my growing dread until I could not take another step. And just as the fear grew strong enough to paralyze, the coffin appeared.

In it, she lay, her hands clasped loosely beneath her breasts, a garland of red, red roses around her neck, a single stem, headless, in between her palms. Her hair incongruously pale now, her lids closed and edged in gossamer lash.

For just a moment, I could see the blue gown, the hospital bed, the headboard that sat between mattress and monitor, where her body lay in the waking world.

Then her eyes snapped open, her heavy, bruised lips spreading in a smile that revealed all her teeth. My heart stopped beating. She rose.

And Sergi said, "Amelia."

But I lifted a hand. "No. Look at her. She *isn't* Amelia."

He frowned. Not the type of man who enjoys being corrected, and certainly not in front of children. "But—"

"She *is* Tiffany. Sort of. If that was ever her name. But—" I lifted a hand as Tiffany approached me. "We were wrong. Jerrend didn't make her what she is; it's not Jerrend's fear or psyche that's chosen the form of this dreamworld. It's Amelia's."

"She's dead."

"Yes. But it doesn't matter. He's not going to let her rest."

The vampire laughed, her voice too deep, too full. "You don't belong here, you know."

"No, we don't. You don't either."

"I'm *dead*." Teeth bared, she looked like a Stoker Vampire. Like a child's fear. "And the dead have to live forever."

"Tiffany," I said, "If that's your name—we need your help."

"I'm going to kill you slowly," she replied, licking her lips.

"We need to meet the one who made you."

She rose. Her feet hovered above the forest floor. I'd forgotten to feed her. I looked at her face, and I could see, in the evil of it, the accusation of failure. Ours. For just a minute I met Sergi's gaze, but in some ways, in the end, her gaze was easier to hold. He felt what I felt: fear, not only of failure, but of responsibility. Had we created her? Had we, inadvertently, destroyed her? Would all of the children become, in the end, as she had become?

No.

I held out my wrist and she took it, coming as a frightened child comes for a parent's hand. I only flinched a bit when her teeth found the vein—or the artery—in my wrist. In my other hand: Sergi's hand. His grip was steadying, hers, wild. Slowly, because I trusted him, and because—on a level that she could never be aware of, *so did she*—he led us both from the willows.

And before we emerged into daylight, I said, "Sergi, we have to find a different way." My skin was white, now. White and pale as hers.

"What?"

"We can't go with her to the collective."

"But we—"

Her teeth were still attached to my wrist, but her eyes were on my face as I turned to meet her gaze. Something there . . . something. . . .

"She wasn't crazy," I said at last. "Before he found her. Before he chose her. She wasn't insane."

Sergi's lips are a thin, thin line. "This is the land of nightmare, Meg."

"But in the wild-dreaming, there are two nightmares that shouldn't have existed at all. We don't know enough. We . . . the other children can hear it, I think."

"Hear what?"

"Amelia. She'll devour them whole. She'll take their places, use their bodies, live the absolute lie—and *no one will ever miss them.*"

"Meg—I think you should turn back."

It took me a moment to realize that he meant *wake up.* "I can't. You're a better chemist than a psychologist."

He sat down on a large rock.

"It's not Tiffany that has to come to the collective."

"He wanted—"

"He's not sane. He feels responsible for his daughter's death, and for all we know, he was. He's willing to—" the ground shuddered beneath my feet.

"To kill? And we're going to accuse him of that? With what evidence?"

The vampire's eyes were luminescent. So were her cheeks. "No," I told him gently. "We're not going to accuse him." I bent and touched the girl's face; her chin had disappeared below the line of my arm. "I'm one of you, you know."

She would not detach herself from my wrist, so her words were muffled. "Not unless you bite me."

I understand the rules of childhood and fear. I bit her.

The risks are huge.

I didn't know it then, and I barely understand it now. But I bit her, and I let the wild dreaming define *me.* I was used to the collective. I could become one with the communal mind, should I so choose; I could allow it to inform me. The first time it happened, I was overwhelmed by the multitude of voices contained within a fellowship of similar emotion.

I should have been prepared.

But the dreaming swallowed us whole. I held on to Sergi. It was the only smart thing I remembered to do.

We traveled down a tunnel whose walls were like a long, long canvas across which was painted—in perfect, vibrant colors—every nightmare that I'd ever had. It started with the most recent, and then burrowed, crawling back toward time. She no longer clung to my wrist with her teeth; it wasn't necessary. I, too, had done the forbidden. We were bound and made monstrous by that act of consent.

"This is where the undead live," she told me quietly.

"And will I live here as well?"

She nodded.

"Do you know who I am?"

"No."

"Do you know who you are?"

For just a minute, cheek dimpled on the left side, eyes dipped to ground. She was like a child. A shy girl. She said, "Rana."

Sergi's grip on my hand was, pardon the pun, a death grip. I didn't ask him what he was seeing. What I was seeing was difficult enough. But I found that the sound of a young girl's name was not eclipsed by the humiliation of public nudity, by the nightmare sounds of growling and screaming and threats, or even by the terror of abandonment.

*   *   *

She was waiting for us: Sergi, to my left, Rana, to my right, and between them, me, research specialist with delusions of grandeur.

I had seen a single picture of her, and it did not do her justice; the dream world had made the flat, old photograph seem pathetic and almost obscenely inappropriate. There was power in the presence of the young woman who waited, arms crossed, in the blood-red light cast by stained glass. The window depicted something red and dark, but only its core was lit. It rose from the floor to the heights, where shadows pooled.

She was dressed in white, bridal white. Above her pale hair, a tiara rested, and from it fell the translucent plumes of tulle veil.

She looked at Rana, at me; Sergi seemed beneath her notice. "Why are you here?"

"I made her," Rana said softly, her voice a plea. "I made her. I thought—"

"Amelia," I said quietly. "Rana made me, as you made Rana. Can I not take her place?"

Amelia's laughter was hollow. Terrible. "Did you think it would be that simple?"

"What is not that simple, Amelia?" Sergi stepped forward. His robes whirled, and although they contained the moons and the stars that had seemed so ridiculous to my adult mind, when they moved, they suggested the depths of the cosmos, and all the knowledge it had ever contained.

"Do you think," she said coldly, "that I made myself? You're a wizard, you know what *can* be done."

"Yes," he said softly, "I do."

"I am very tired," the regal white creature in darkness said.

"I know. And he knows it as well, although he is afraid."

"Of me?"

"Of you."

Her smile was very cruel. "And this?"

"A way of preserving you against death."

She laughed and laughed and laughed. Rana shrank away, behind me. "Preserving me *against* death? The old fool. All I am *is* death, and dead. There is nothing else for me here."

"But he has promised you life."

"Yes."

"And—"

"And he always told me what would happen to me if I made promises I couldn't keep."

Sergi bowed; for a moment I saw him as she saw him; old and proud and infinitely wise. "The girl?"

"I cannot release her, any more than I can be released. But I cannot live within her. I have tried; there is no space for me. If she were gone—"

"No. Come, Amelia. It is time."

"Time?"

"Your father has sent us to escort you in safety from the dreaming to the collective that he built in your name. There is life there, but I must warn you, there is no hunting."

"My father sent you?"

"Indeed."

She was quiet. Something about her was twisted and broken, but in this light, I could only see the pain she felt and not the pain she had caused. "I'm sorry," she said quietly. "But I can only be what I was made to be." She held out a hand to him.

And Sergi, foolish Sergi, Sergi who could be wrapped around a willful child's finger, stayed his ground. After a moment, the hand fell. "I do not judge you," he told her. "The collective will not judge you. There will not be one man, or one woman, who has not felt some of what you feel; perhaps, with the help of the collective you might become more than you are."

She frowned. "And you believe that?"

He did not answer directly. "You are not compelled to obey."

"You do not know my father well."

"No. Indeed none of us do."

She turned her face to the window; the red light added a blush to her skin that robbed it of the semblance of death. She would have been beautiful, in life. Without turning to look at Sergi, she simply said, "I will come with you, then."

He waited until she began to walk toward the grand set of doors that appeared in the wall as the shadows slowly parted. Then he followed. I watched from a safe distance; Rana watched from behind me. It was as if the aspect of the deathless had been leeched away from both of us with each step Amelia took. "What will happen to me?" Rana said softly.

"You? If I'm not mistaken, you'll wake up."

"Where?"

"I don't know." I started to follow, and after a moment, hesitant, the girl did the same.

A walk from nightmare to the collective is not always a literal walk. Sometimes it involves the instant transubstantiation of matter as one dreamscape dissolves into another like peaks in a wave; sometimes it involves an unfolding, a peeling away of layers, as if nightmare itself is mere onion skin. It depends upon the person in question.

And neither Sergi nor I understood fully what this young woman was.

Sergi chose to walk. She chose to follow. Beneath their feet the ground changed from stone to earth, from earth to wood, from wood to earth again.

"Amelia," I said, and she paused. "Do you remember what happened?"

"I don't know. But I've had no memory of waking for a very long time now."

Does time pass? Does time pass for someone who can't possibly be real? I wish I had asked her. I didn't. Her teeth were glinting, the only light in the darkness. She stepped through the doors at Sergi's behest, and then, beyond them, through the gates of the castle and the towers from which she might have ruled the landscape.

I wanted to ask Sergi what he was doing, but I knew. After all, I had refused to let him take Rana through to the collective. Jerrend is so terribly bright.

Why aren't you doing it?

Because if he is not a man with a conscience, he is at least a man with human weakness: Better to let two people commit murder and believe that they have healed the ill than to commit murder oneself. What was left of Rana in Rana, what was left of Amelia in Rana, was nightmare, and only nightmare, and I think he hoped that in the transition she might be left behind and what was left of his daughter might finally emerge, unencumbered by that previous life.

I wonder if Sergi understood what would happen to

Amelia. I almost warned him . . . but there's nothing about the dreamscape that he doesn't know as well as I do.

The collective is the best place in which to face a nightmare and dispel it. Sergi knows that better than anyone.

Amelia stumbled, once. Twice. She reached for his hand. He stepped back, which I thought wise. But as she struggled against the weight of the earth, he chose to take a risk; his large hand engulfed her small one as he pulled her to her feet. She seemed slimmer somehow.

I had seen this before. I had seen this before dozens of times; that hand, and a small hand tucked into the folds it made when it closed.

"Is it day?" she asked softly.

"Not yet, Amelia, not yet, but soon." In the distance, the ground shifted. The dry packed dirt gave way to damp grass, night vegetation. There were flowers, wild and small, closed against the night. I knew how we would arrive at the collective; the signs of dawn, at Sergi's expert suggestion, were everywhere.

At my side, the younger girl hung back. She hissed quietly and I knew that in her present condition she would not reach the collective. "Rana," I told her gently. "Can you wait here?"

"For you?"

"For us."

"For how long?"

"It won't be long. The trees here will protect you from sunlight." I stressed this clearly, reinforcing her belief with the strength of my own. Then I turned quickly and followed Sergi and his young charge.

As so often happens when we bring a new person into the collective, a parent was there to meet us. And in the collective, she had only one: Doctor Jerrend. He was, I thought, dressed for a weekend; casual attire that was neither too frumpy nor too crisp or stylish. His hands were behind his back. His expression was . . . unbearable.

I had never really liked Jerrend.

But I pitied him in that instant, and my memory holds on to it long after the fact has receded. He looked down the slope with such incredible hope, with such fierce, terrible desire, with a slowly growing joy . . . all of it, exposed to us. Sergi looked away. An act of kindness. I wish I could have done the same.

But I watched as the expression crumbled; as the intellect that had built the collective saw who was following Sergi, and where she was following him to.

He strode forward, the steps a one-two one-two jerk of motion that resembled a spasm, not a walk. "AMELIA! NO!"

Sergi dropped her hand as the larger man collided with him, driving them both back. Jerrend drew strength from the collective, grew in size, ferocity; his face filled the landscape until it was the only thing we could see from one side of the horizon to the other.

But Sergi drew strength as well, a different strength. He did not gain size or weight or obvious power, but the blows of the older man, the frenzied attack, became ineffectual. "Oscar Jerrend," he said quietly. "We are in the heart of the collective. What you see before you is your nightmare made real. But we're here to help you face it, if you desire our help.

"We're here to help you let it go."

The collective stirred as he spoke the words that we

had all spoken at one time or another. They could not help but feel Jerrend's pain.

The slender young woman who was what he believed remained of his daughter stepped forward; gestured; lifted her hands up, palm exposed, in supplication. Jerrend was suddenly dwarfed by something sweet and terrible: Her desire.

"Daddy?" she said softly, and she held out her arms, and in rage and terror, he became the size of a merely mortal father as he swept her up into his own. She held him quietly. And I heard it then: Her voice, in the collective, high and terribly sweet. She was singing a lullaby.

Oscar Jerrend began to weep.

"But I saw her," the young girl says. "I saw her burn up in the sunlight."

I hold her hand. "Yes, Rana, I know."

"I can't go out into daylight. I have to be in before dawn. You know what I am."

"I do. And I know that it's safe here."

"You *can't* know—"

"I do. Remember? You bit me. I drank your blood. We're the same, you and I." I'm the only one who can bring her across; she was the most hurt, the most injured, by all of the pain and the loss. But it's not easy.

I look up across the bridge as the mist parts; that's her paradigm, mist and shadow, and burning at it like fire, the beautiful heat of the sun. I hold out a hand. She takes it. And then I look across the bridge, where my partner for this very special young woman is. Her grip on my hand tightens, and he stares at her, not smiling, not frowning, a forlorn man.

"Rana Tarrent," he says, holding out a hand, "You're

here in the heart of the collective, and if you can walk past one tired old man, you will never have this nightmare again." It's not quite the phrase we use when we bring the children through the chrysalis of nightmare, but it's a start, and because he's Oscar Jerrend, and not Meg, not Sergi, she feels his regret and the love that drove him near-mad and the sorrow that he has denied in a frenzy for half his adult life. And she is a child, but she has a child's pity; what I have begun, she continues, her arms reaching out a moment to comfort not a nightmare, but a tired, fragile man.

It's a start.

KATE ELLIOT

CROWN OF STARS

"An entirely captivating affair"—*Publishers Weekly*

☐ **KING'S DRAGON**   UE2771—$6.99
In a world where bloody conflicts rage and sorcery holds sway both human
and other-than-human forces vie for supremacy. In this land, Alain, a
young man seeking the destiny promised him by the Lady of Battles, and
Liath, a young woman gifted with a power that can alter history, are about
to be swept up in a world-shaking conflict for the survival of humanity.

☐ **PRINCE OF DOGS**   UE2816—$6.99
Return to the intertwined destinies of: Alain, raised in humble surroundings
but now a Count's Heir; Liath, who struggles with the secrets of her past
while evading those who seek the treasure she conceals; Sanglant, believed dead, but only held captive in the cathedral of Gent, and Fifth Son,
who now builds an army to do his father's—or his own—bidding in a world
at war!

☐ **THE BURNING STONE**   UE2813—$24.95
Liath and Sanglant, made outcasts by their love, are forced to choose
their own path—lured by the equally strong claims of politics, forbidden
knowledge, and family, even as Alain is torn apart by the demands of
love, honor, and duty.

Prices slightly higher in Canada   **DAW: 211**

Payable in U.S. funds only. No cash/COD accepted. Postage & handling: U.S./CAN. $2.75 for one
book, $1.00 for each additional, not to exceed $6.75; Int'l $5.00 for one book, $1.00 each additional.
We accept Visa, Amex, MC ($10.00 min.), checks ($15.00 fee for returned checks) and money
orders. Call 800-788-6262 or 201-933-9292, fax 201-896-8569; refer to ad #211.

Penguin Putnam Inc.   **Bill my:** ☐Visa ☐MasterCard ☐Amex_____(expires)
P.O. Box 12289, Dept. B   Card#_____
Newark, NJ 07101-5289
Please allow 4-6 weeks for delivery.   Signature_____
Foreign and Canadian delivery 6-8 weeks.

Bill to:

Name_____

Address_____City_____

State/ZIP_____

Daytime Phone #_____

Ship to:

Name_____ Book Total $_____

Address_____ Applicable Sales Tax $_____

City_____ Postage & Handling $_____

State/Zip_____ Total Amount Due $_____

This offer subject to change without notice.

Tanya Huff

- ☐ **NO QUARTER**   UE2698—$5.99
- ☐ **FIFTH QUARTER**   UE2651—$5.99
- ☐ **SING THE FOUR QUARTERS**   UE2628—$5.99
- ☐ **THE QUARTERED SEA**   UE2839—$6.99

He Sang water more powerfully than any other bard—but could even Benedikt Sing a ship beyond the known world?

- ☐ **GATE OF DARKNESS, CIRCLE OF LIGHT**   UE2386—$4.50
- ☐ **THE FIRE'S STONE**   UE2445—$5.99
- ☐ **SUMMON THE KEEPER**   UE2784—$5.99

VICTORY NELSON, INVESTIGATOR:
Otherworldly Crimes A Specialty

- ☐ **BLOOD PRICE: Book 1**   UE2471—$5.99
- ☐ **BLOOD TRAIL: Book 2**   UE2502—$5.99
- ☐ **BLOOD LINES: Book 3**   UE2530—$5.99
- ☐ **BLOOD PACT: Book 4**   UE2582—$5.99
- ☐ **BLOOD DEBT: Book 5**   UE2739—$5.99

Prices slightly higher in Canada   **DAW: 150**

Payable in U.S. funds only. No cash/COD accepted. Postage & handling: U.S./CAN. $2.75 for one book, $1.00 for each additional, not to exceed $6.75; Int'l $5.00 for one book, $1.00 each additional. We accept Visa, Amex, MC ($10.00 min.), checks ($15.00 fee for returned checks) and money orders. Call 800-788-6262 or 201-933-9292, fax 201-896-8569; refer to ad #150.

Penguin Putnam Inc.   Bill my: ☐Visa ☐MasterCard ☐Amex_____ (expires)
P.O. Box 12289, Dept. B   Card#_____
Newark, NJ 07101-5289

Please allow 4-6 weeks for delivery.   Signature_____
Foreign and Canadian delivery 6-8 weeks.

Bill to:

Name_____

Address_____City_____

State/ZIP_____

Daytime Phone #_____

Ship to:

Name_____ Book Total $_____

Address_____ Applicable Sales Tax $_____

City_____ Postage & Handling $_____

State/Zip_____ Total Amount Due $_____

This offer subject to change without notice.

Don't Miss These Exciting DAW Anthologies

SWORD AND SORCERESS
Marion Zimmer Bradley, editor
☐ Book XVI   UE2843—$5.99

OTHER ORIGINAL ANTHOLOGIES
Mercedes Lackey, editor
☐ SWORD OF ICE: And Other Tales of Valdemar   UE2720—$6.99

Martin H. Greenberg & Brian Thompsen, editors
☐ THE REEL STUFF   UE2817—$5.99
☐ MOB MAGIC   UE2821—$5.99

Martin H. Greenberg, editor
☐ MY FAVORITE SCIENCE FICTION STORY   UE2830—$6.99

Denise Little, editor
☐ ALIEN PETS   UE2822—$5.99
☐ A DANGEROUS MAGIC   UE2825—$6.99
☐ TWICE UPON A TIME   UE2835—$6.99

Nancy Springer, editor
☐ PROM NITE   UE2840—$6.99

Prices slightly higher in Canada   **DAW:105**

Payable in U.S. funds only. No cash/COD accepted. Postage & handling: U.S./CAN. $2.75 for one book, $1.00 for each additional, not to exceed $6.75; Int'l $5.00 for one book, $1.00 each additional. We accept Visa, Amex, MC ($10.00 min.), checks ($15.00 fee for returned checks) and money orders. Call 800-788-6262 or 201-933-9292, fax 201-896-8569; refer to ad #120.

Penguin Putnam Inc.   **Bill my:** ☐Visa ☐MasterCard ☐Amex_____ (expires)
P.O. Box 12289, Dept. B   Card#_____
Newark, NJ 07101-5289

Please allow 4-6 weeks for delivery.   Signature_____
Foreign and Canadian delivery 6-8 weeks.

Bill to:

Name_____

Address_____ City_____

State/ZIP_____

Daytime Phone #_____

Ship to:

Name_____ Book Total $_____

Address_____ Applicable Sales Tax $_____

City_____ Postage & Handling $_____

State/Zip_____ Total Amount Due $_____

This offer subject to change without notice.

THEY'RE COMING TO GET YOU. . . .
ANTHOLOGIES FOR NERVOUS TIMES

☐ **FIRST CONTACT**   UE2757—$5.99
Martin H. Greenberg and Larry Segriff, editors

In the tradition of the hit television show "The X-Files" comes a fascinating collection of original stories by some of the premier writers of the genre, such as Jody Lynn Nye, Kristine Kathryn Rusch, and Jack Haldeman.

☐ **THE UFO FILES**   UE2772—$5.99
Martin H. Greenberg, editor

Explore close encounters of a thrilling kind in these stories by Gregory Benford, Ed Gorman, Peter Crowther, Alan Dean Foster, and Kristine Kathryn Rusch.

☐ **THE CONSPIRACY FILES**   UE2797—$5.99
Martin H. Greenberg and Scott Urban, editors

We all know that we never hear the whole truth behind the headlines—let Douglas Clegg, Tom Monteleone, Ed Gorman, Norman Partridge and Yvonne Navarro unmask the conspirators and their plots—if the government lets them. . . .

☐ **BLACK CATS AND BROKEN MIRRORS**   UE2788—$5.99
Martin H. Greenberg and John Helfers, editors

From the consequences of dark felines crossing your path to the results of carlessly smashed mirrors, authors such as Jane Yolen, Michelle West, Charles de Lint, Nancy Springer and Esther Friesner dare to answer the question, "What happens if some of those long-treasured superstitions are actually true?"

Prices slightly higher in Canada.   **DAW 215X**

Buy them at your local bookstore or use this convenient coupon for ordering.

PENGUIN USA   P.O. Box 999—Dep. #17109, Bergenfield, New Jersey 07621

Please send me the DAW BOOKS I have checked above, for which I am enclosing
$_____ (please add $2.00 to cover postage and handling). Send check or money order (no cash or C.O.D.'s) or charge by Mastercard or VISA (with a $15.00 minimum). Prices and numbers are subject to change without notice.

Card #_____ Exp. Date _____
Signature_____
Name_____
Address_____
City _____ State _____ Zip Code _____

For faster service when ordering by credit card call **1-800-253-6476**

Allow a minimum of 4-6 weeks for delivery. This offer is subject to change without notice.